Conspiracy of Lies

Richard S. Rachlin

Sawtooth Press —Sun Valley, Idaho
Paperback ISBN: 979-8-9890031-0-5
eBook ISBN: 979-8-9890031-1-2
Hardcover ISBN: 979-8-9890031-2-9
Library of Congress Control Number: 2023916301
Title: *Conspiracy of Lies*
Author: Richard S. Rachlin
Digital distribution | 2023
Paperback | 2023

This is a work of fiction. The characters, names, incidents, places, and dialogue are products of the author's imagination, and are not to be construed as real.

Dedication

For

Mom, Dad and Andrew

With love, always and forever.

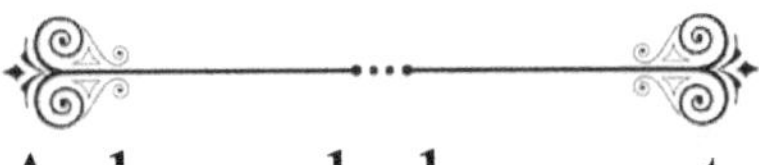

Acknowledgements

First and foremost, I would like to thank my daughters, Julie, and Fatima, for their abiding love, support, and encouragement in making this book a reality. It was more important to me than they could have imagined. In the early stages of my writing, I was set on the right course by Malena Watrous, an exceptional novelist, and the Creative Writing Coordinator at Stanford University. Thank you, Malena. Much of the inspiration in writing the courtroom scenes was gained from Albert Krieger, who I consider the sine qua non of trial lawyers who deserve our respect and admiration. Em Hughes, Senior Editor of New Book Authors, was enormously helpful though her hard work, dedication, and never-ending professionalism, far beyond the call of duty. And last, I am forever indebted to Aki Takahashi for her kindness, devotion, and cheering me on when the light at the end of the tunnel was not always so near and bright.

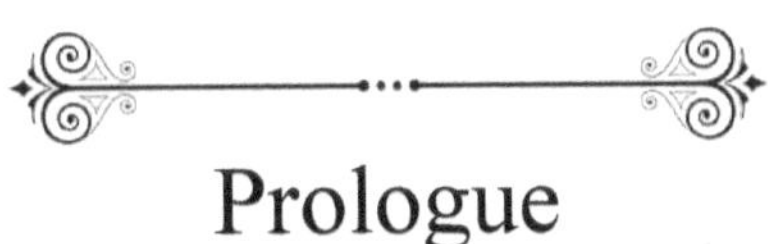

Prologue

October, 2004

The old man scratched the gray stubble of his three-day growth and fixed his gaze on the autumn sun as it began its descent behind the housing projects to the west. He shivered from the cool breeze unusual for this time of year; angry at himself for leaving behind his worn cotton suede jacket, a hand-me-down from his grandfather, a fisherman like himself. He hooked his last live shrimp to his line and shuffled to the edge of the river bank. Twenty minutes more, then he'd gather his gear and catch the Overtown bus home. He knew better than to be here alone after dark.

As the last traces of daylight all but disappeared, the old man's line grew taut. Instinctively, he began to reel, but whatever was out there just wouldn't budge. He bent on one knee over the neck of the river and tried his best to steer the shadowy object toward him. His pulse raced as thoughts carried him back to more than twenty years ago and the days of Miami's cocaine cowboys when it was not uncommon for fishermen to scoop up 'square groupers', or wrapped bales of marijuana tossed overboard from speed boats smuggling their loads in from the Bahamas.

Grudgingly, he cut his line and hurried down the river bank for a better look at his bounty. Inching closer, he froze in horror. "Dear Mother of God," he cried. Aided by a strong current, the partially decomposed body of a brown-skin man drifted toward him, his dark eyes fixed open in a grotesque stare, his throat slashed from ear to ear.

PART 1

Chapter One

Five Years Later

In the dead of night, Jake Dalton shot up in bed. Was it another nightmare about Drew? He glanced at Elena, his wife, lying beside him, asleep. Still half-awake he reached over to shut off his alarm but then realized the loud ringing came from his cell phone.

Within minutes, he drove like a bat out of hell through the rain-soaked streets of South Miami, swerving to avoid hitting a parked UPS truck before skidding to a stop in front of the ER. The usually bright sign for Miami Children's Hospital was dark. His Saab's radio blared that the worst of the tropical storm was about to hit. In the passenger seat, Elena had already flung off her seat belt, her body twisted halfway out the open door. In the back, Nicole, their four-year-old daughter, sat strapped in her car seat, squeezing the life out of her stuffed bunny.

"Elena, wait," Jake shouted over the fierce winds.

"I got to find Drew," Elena yelled back. "Get Nikki."

Jake parked, and shielding Nicole from the deluge, sprinted past the security guard and caught up with Elena inside. Together, they rushed to a gray-haired woman sitting behind the Information desk. At three in the morning, the hospital was eerily quiet.

"Drew Dalton," Jake pleaded. "Where can we find him?"

"Are you a relative?" The woman asked, her tone robotic.

"Yes, yes," Jake snapped, "he's our son." Jake swiped the rain from his face with his hand.

The woman opened the spiral-ringed notebook in front of her and slid her finger slowly down the page, line by line. "You say Dalton?"

Jake nodded. "Yes, right. For God's sake, can't you go any faster?"

Finally, she looked up. "He's been transferred to neurology, intensive care unit, third floor."

"Neurology?" Jake repeated the word, not believing his ears. He looked back at Elena, her face frozen in fear. He scooped Nicole in his arms and tore for the elevators, her damp hair whipping across his face. Inside, he gripped Elena's hand. "It's my damn fault. We never should have left him."

As the elevator doors opened to the third floor, he handed Nicole to Elena and raced for the nurses' station. The overhead florescent lights flickered as successive bolts of lightning flashed outside the window.

"Drew Dalton," he asked a young nurse. "Please, where is he?"

She pointed over his shoulder down the hall to a slender woman with flecks of gray in her short black hair, a stethoscope hung between the lapels of her white lab coat. "There's Dr. Goya leaving the ICU now."

Thank God, Jake thought. Not another intern.

"Dr. Goya?" he called, stepping briskly toward the woman, with Elena and Nicole right behind.

"You must be Drew's parents." She lowered her clipboard, her shimmering brown eyes exuding an air of confidence.

Jake struggled to find the words. "Is he okay? Can we see him?"

Goya's gaze shifted to Elena. "*Senora.*" The doctor pulled open the sliding glass door and stepped aside for them to enter. "We've given your boy medication to help him sleep."

Elena pushed a strand of her hair out of her eye and nodded her approval.

Jake knelt in front of his daughter. "Sweetie, we're going to see your brother now. He's sleeping, so we have to be *very* quiet." Jake pressed his forefinger against his lips.

Taking Nicole's hand, Jake followed Elena into the dimly-lit room and gasped. Drew, wires attached to his pale, six-year-old body, lay in a raised bed. His wavy chestnut-colored hair combed straight back, not at all how Drew liked it. Jake gazed at his son, trying to ignore the IV bag hanging from a metal pole near his head. Nearby, a sleek black monitor beeped, registering his son's heart rate and rhythm, a sound Jake clung to for comfort.

Jake studied the neurologist. She seemed at ease as though she'd been in these situations a hundred times before. "What in God's name happened?" he asked. "We were here just a few hours ago and everything was fine. In fact, Dr. Witkin told us that Drew would be coming home tomorrow."

Goya motioned Jake and Elena to follow her to the far corner of the room and spoke softly. "Your son's platelet count fell unexpectedly, to alarming levels, and his bone marrow isn't producing as much as we'd like to see. It could be from a viral infection. With acute ITP, one can never be sure."

ITP. Idiopathic Thrombocytopenic Purpura. Jake had spent the past year researching the rare blood disorder and still couldn't pronounce the damn thing.

Elena leaned toward the neurologist. "How far did it drop?"

"To forty thousand. But there's no indication that bleeding has spread to his brain."

Elena's body swayed backward. She grasped Jake's arm for support.

"We're doing what we can to control it," Goya hastened to add. "I want to start him right away on a new drug, Eltrombopag. Clinical trials have been quite impressive. It's designed to stimulate platelet production, but it's expensive and I doubt insurance will cover it."

"Do it," Jake said. "I don't care what it costs."

Drew murmured in his sleep. "Daddy," he moaned before going quiet.

Jake stepped close to the bed, trying to appear calm. "Hey, big guy," he said, his voice barely above a whisper. He caressed his son's cheek. "Everything's going to be ok. I promise."

Elena bent and kissed Drew's brow. "Daddy and I are here, *carino*. We love you."

Drew's eyelids fluttered, his breathing slow and steady.

"Let's step outside so he can rest." Dr. Goya ushered the family into the hall. "I promise to notify you the minute more results are in. Until then there's nothing more to do but wait." She offered a tight smile and walked away.

After she left, Elena nudged Jake. "The hospital called again about the bill."

He frowned. "I don't doubt it." He took Elena's hand and placed it in his. "You can fold that little problem up and file it in the forget about it department. It'll be taken care of the minute I finish this trial."

"Oh, really?" Elena made no effort to conceal her skepticism.

"I mean it." Jake put his arm around her shoulder. "The case is a sure winner, way better than the others. Not even close. In fact, it's just about to go to the jury and when they come back with the verdict, believe me, all of our bills will be paid, and then some."

Elena eyes narrowed. "I wish I had a nickel for every time I'd heard that."

"No, no, I mean it. A game changer. I swear."

She pulled away. "Oh, Jake. Please. Don't do this, don't let me get my hopes up. Not again."

"I'll bet the farm on this one. The jury loves my client. I mean *loves*. You should see the way they look at her. They're ready to sock it to the insurance company like you won't believe. Our lives are about to be turned around for good. You'll see."

Elena softened. She reached over and kissed him tenderly on the lips. "You know, baby. Nobody in this world is rooting for you to be a winner as much as I am."

Chapter Two

Flying dangerously low at two thousand feet, Tommy Tifton stiffened in his seat in the cockpit, cursing the moment he'd ever boarded this God-forsaken turbo prop. Served him right; Jessie had begged him not to go, and Jessie was always right. He glanced to his left at Butch, ex-military like himself, sitting behind the wheel, feverishly working the controls of the Cessna Conquest. Just outside Tommy's window lightning flashed, barely missing the trailing edge of the wing. Fierce turbulence tossed the Cessna around like a toy as blackened skies thundered all around. Frozen in his seat, Tommy tried to swallow, gagged, but didn't puke. At least, not yet.

Tommy looked over and checked the fuel gauge. The needle had moved to amber. The Cessna was flying on fumes. "I smell fuel!" he yelled, veins in his neck pulsating like a jackhammer. He'd faced death in the first Gulf War, but not like this.

"The fuel hose bracket must have shaken loose," Butch said, half-turning toward him, his hazel, cat-like eyes devoid of all expression. "Gotta land this sucker, now." He lowered the nose of the aircraft and descended to twelve hundred feet. "Forget Key Largo, we'll never make it."

Tommy stared into the moonless night, trying to see if they were still over water. "Lights at two o'clock," he shouted, "gotta be Miami," though sheets of rain made it impossible to be sure. "We gonna make it?" Tommy asked, barely recognizing his own voice.

Butch pushed the yoke forward, and let out a nervous laugh. "No fuckin' idea."

The engine coughed, choked, seeking, craving whatever fuel that remained. Without warning the turboprop dove and banked hard to the left, driving Tommy face-first into his side window. His nose gushed blood. Images of flying reconnaissance over the Iraqi wasteland flooded his mind. Beads of sweat rolled down his face. One thing was sure: he would not be burned alive.

Tommy tore off his seat belt and scrambed for the passenger door. Dark thoughts consumed him. He patted his trousers' pockets. His meds, where the fuck were they?

Butch yelled over his shoulder. "Where the hell you going?"

Tommy kneeled and pulled on the passenger door handle. It wouldn't budge. The turboprop continued to dive, its high-pitched whine setting off horrific memories of when he and his unit fought to stay alive aboard the Apache chopper while it spiraled out of control seconds after being struck by an RPG. Then, moments before crashing, all Tommy could hear were the screams of his buddies, ablaze; a sound he never thought humanly possible.

"An airfield!" Butch shouted. "Hold tight. I'm taking her down."

Tommy turned to the distant voice in the cockpit and struggled to regain his bearings. No longer was he fighting to stay alive in the desert. Using the cabin walls of the Cessna for balance, he crab walked his way back into his seat.

Butch flashed the aircraft's lights and glared at Tommy. "What the hell is wrong with you, man?" Without waiting for an answer, he grabbed the mike and switched to the emergency frequency. "Mayday, Mayday, this is Conquest one niner four Romeo Delta. Three miles to the east, requesting permission to land on any runway with vectors for final. Negative ATIS, over."

No response.

"Tower," Butch repeated, "do you read? We have an emergency. Out of fuel. Requesting permission to land. Now. Anywhere!"

"Conquest one niner four Romeo Delta, this is Opa Locka Tower. We have you in sight. Stand by. Debris on most runways," a monotone voice answered back.

Tommy grabbed Butch's shoulder. "What you waiting for? Get this fucker down. Now."

"Forget it. I'm not flying in there blind."

Several moments passed before the tower spoke again. "One niner four Romeo Delta, cleared to land straight in runway two seven left. Winds are fifty knots gusting to sixty out of one eighty. Land at your own risk. Repeat, land at your own risk."

"About freakin' time." Tommy gripped the sides of his seat and braced for impact.

"Just about there," Butch shouted. He glanced over at Tommy, his shoulders pressed against the back of his seat. "Hang tight, ol' man, maybe it's not our time to die after all."

The Cessna continued to shake as winds slammed into her side at ninety degrees. Moments later a jarring bounce of the landing wheels signaled that the plane had touched down.

Butch worked the controls and put in full rudder, attempting to keep the plane from cart wheeling off the runway.

Too numb to react, Tommy stared wide-eyed out the windshield, expecting the Cessna to flip at any moment. A violent shudder, a piercing screech from the tires, the smell of burnt rubber filled his nostrils. Tommy shut his eyes, accepting his end.

An eternity seemed to pass before the aircraft rolled to a stop. Tommy loosened his grip on his seat and stared at his blanched hands. "We made it!" He cried and slapped Butch on the back of his head. "Man, you did it. You fuckin' did it."

"You bet your sweet ass I did," Butch said through a laugh as he shut down the engine. He pointed at the front of Tommy's shirt. "Dude, you're all covered in blood. What's the matter? Can't handle a bumpy ride?"

"That was some kind of fun," Tommy deadpanned. "Let's do it again." He pressed the bridge of his nose and winced. Probably broken. Over his shoulder he spotted the lights of a Citation II rolling down an adjacent runway. The turbojet continued to taxi past them, then abruptly crossed in front of the Cessna and turned to face them. Two fire trucks raced up and parked on the tarmac, fifty yards away.

Tommy gestured toward the Citation. "Those guys are coming at us, with guns," he shouted. Fumes filled the cockpit. Tommy knew that any gunfire would instantly cause the Cessna to erupt into flames. "Out. Now!"

He flung off his seatbelt, kicked open the passenger door, only to face a pot-bellied man in a uniform rain jacket, aiming a single-barreled shotgun at his head. The agent had the face of a bulldog, collapsed inward with drooping jowls, his steely eyes gleaming in triumph.

"U.S. Customs. Off the plane!" Bulldog barked, pressing his finger on the trigger.

"Whatcha think I'm aiming to do?" Tommy yelled right back

"That's right, you heard me," he continued to shout, waving the shotgun. "Get out! Slow, real slow. Put your hands where I can see them."

Tommy ignored the command. "Put that gun down, you moron. Can't you smell the fumes?"

Two more agents ran to the front of the Cessna, weapons drawn.

Bulldog waved at his men. "Away from the plane! There might be a leak."

Ferocious winds lashed Tommy's face as he stumbled down the stairs onto the tarmac, Butch close behind. The Customs agent motioned them toward the fire trucks. "That's far enough. Turn around, keep your hands up."

"What's this about?" With his sleeve, Tommy wiped the rain from his eyes and peered at the shotgun. "I told you not to point that thing at me."

"You guys are in a shitload of trouble," Bulldog scoffed.

"What the hell you talking about?"

"Like you don't know. I'd hate to be in your shoes when the Colombians find out you ditched their load."

"What Colombians?" Tommy matched the stare of the agent.

"Don't feed me that crap. I've been chasing you boys for over an hour."

"You've been chasing somebody else," Butch shouted back.

Tommy glanced at the blue and white lights flashing atop two black sedans blockading the runway. One lacked any visible marking, the other read Miami-Dade County Sheriff.

"On the ground," Bulldog ordered. "Hands behind you."

Tommy didn't move. He'd had his fill of taking orders. "*You* get down. We're in the middle of a fuckin' monsoon, or haven't you noticed." Driving rain stung his face, causing Tommy to lose his balance.

The agent pressed the shotgun against Tommy's ribs. "Did I forget to say please?"

Shivering, Tommy gradually knelt and put his hands behind his back while he was being handcuffed. Buddies in his Special Forces unit had executed Iraqi Republican Guards in just this manner. His thoughts turned to Jessie; knew she'd be up all night worrying about him.

Hours seemed to pass before Bulldog grabbed Tommy under his arm and helped him to his feet and removed his handcuffs. The agent turned to his men, who had just returned from ripping up the Cessna looking for contraband, but finding it empty. "Bring the other one."

Butch moved alongside Tommy, rubbing his wrists where the cuffs had been.

"I know what you boys are up to," Bulldog said, pitching their IDs, keys, and the few dollars back to them, "and as soon as I can prove it, you'll see my pretty face again. For now, we'll hang on to the plane."

"I keep telling you," Tommy protested, "you're making—"

Bulldog waved him off. "Forget it. I'm been doing this a long time. It was *you* I was chasing. When we find the drugs, I'll return 'em, right up your ass. In the meantime, I suggest you get yourself one of those high-powered lawyers. You're gonna need 'em." He spat. "Now, consider yourself lucky and get outta here before I change my mind."

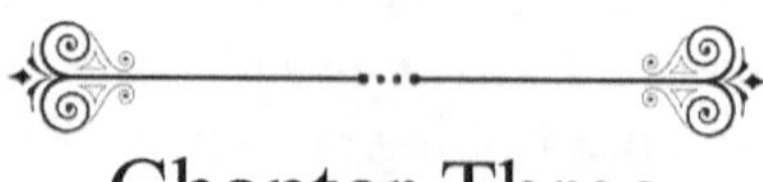

Chapter Three

Days later, Jake stood before the Miami jury, confident his closing argument had hit its mark. From their body language and nods, the jurors were with him, no doubt whatsoever; his first big score since going out on his own now only hours away. His heart felt it was about to leap out of his chest.

Jake thanked the jurors one last time before turning away, vaguely aware of the creak of the old courtroom's wooden floors beneath his feet. He smiled at his client, Carmen Moreno, a kind and plainly dressed housekeeper, as he returned to sit beside her at the plaintiff's table.

Clearly, the case had taken its toll. After all, Jake had agreed to take the case, as is normal in personal injury matters, on a contingency basis, that is, he receives a percentage of the verdict or settlement as his fee (normally, and in this case, a third) and is only then reimbursed for his expenses. If he loses, he ends up with zero and has to eat all costs in the case, such as filing fees, experts, and depositions.

While the judge gave her final instructions to the jury, Jake's thoughts drifted back to his son sleeping soundly in the back seat as Jake drove him home from the hospital, fighting off yet another bleeding episode. This one rocked Jake to the core, and tested his faith like never before.

The judge pushed up the sleeves of her black robe and leaned over her raised bench. The lines that fanned from the corners of her eyes seemed much deeper than at the start of trial a week ago. "Counsel will be notified when the jury has reached a verdict. Until then we stand in recess." She tapped her gavel and left before anyone could rise.

The jurors hastily collected their belongings and began to file out, but not before two of them glanced back at Jake with wide smiles. Jake leaned close to Carmen. "We couldn't have asked for a better jury."

Carmen remained quiet; her lips tightly pressed together. Her gaze left Jake for the heavy-set defense lawyer swaggering toward them. Jake and Carmen stood to greet him.

"Terrific job, kid, you tried one helluva case, but my money still says that jury's not giving you anything near what you're asking." The sixty-something lawyer smoothed back his thinning hair and smirked. "However, you'll be glad to hear I've got authority for one final offer. And I do mean final."

Jake held his tongue, refusing to take the bait. He'd long ago grown tired of the smug sonofabitch, who for the past three years had toyed with him by failing to make one serious offer to settle Carmen's case. But that's what well-heeled insurance companies do.

"I've convinced my claims manager to increase the pot to seventy-five grand, payable in ten days," he continued. "Consider it a gift for...what, a couple of herniated discs." He pointed to the antique clock on the courtroom's rear wall where the last of the spectators were leaving. "You've got one hour to decide. Otherwise, we'll tie your gal up on appeal for years."

"Nice try," Jake shot back while giving Carmen a reassuring nod. Since passing the Bar five years before, he'd never felt so right about a jury. They were ready to slam this guy, but good. "Now, here's what I think," Jake said, his eyes locked on his opponent, "from day one all we've gotten from you were ridiculous offers, nowhere near what the case is worth. I know you've got a job to do, I understand that, but let's get real. We'll accept five hundred thousand dollars plus costs, not a nickel less. Otherwise, let the jury decide. That's *our* final offer."

Carmen tugged on Jake's sleeve. He sensed something was wrong. "I'd like a few words with my client."

"Sure, kid, take as long as you need. I'm in no hurry."

Jake led Carmen to a row of empty benches on the far side of the room so they could talk in private. But before he could say a word, she blurted out, "Take the money."

Jake stepped back, not believing what he heard. "Carmen, I've gone over this a million times, it's what these people do. It's a game they play. Don't fall for their trap. I know this has been hard on you, but the lawyer's talk about an appeal is nothing more than a scare tactic. They do it all the time. It's trial practice 101."

She looked down and stayed silent.

"You've seen the jury," he continued. "They love you, *love* your case. You saw what I did to their so-called expert on the witness stand. I destroyed him. The jury practically laughed him out of court. The defense has no case. They know it. They think waving a pittance of what your case is worth will get you to cave. Hang in there just a little while longer. I'll get you the justice you deserve. I promise."

The petite Carmen stood with shoulders slouched less than a foot from him, her entire body racked with tension. He's never seen her like this before. "Maybe yes, maybe no," she finally answered. "The lawyer says I have my money now, money I really need. If they, as you say, appeal, when do I see my money?"

Jake knew the financial strain they were both under, but he wasn't going to lie. "Technically, anywhere between one to two years." He winced at seeing her body deflate like a punctured balloon. "But they won't," he quickly added. "With the cost of an appeal bond and thousands more in attorneys' fees, it'll never happen."

"But he says I get my money in ten days, no? And you get paid, too? Verdad?"

Jake nodded. "But nothing near what we'd get from the jury. Trust me. I know what I'm talking about. Have I ever lied to you?"

Carmen shook her head. "No, you very honest man."

"Then wait a little while longer. Shouldn't be more than a couple of hours or so. Let's hear from the jury. Then decide. You have nothing to lose. It's a win, win. You saw the jury. Do you think in a million years they're going to give you nothing?" He didn't wait for an answer. "Of course not. They know the kind of truthful person you are, see that your injuries are real and the pain you must live with every day for the rest of your life."

She bowed her head and fidgeted with the top button of her dress. "Maybe so, but I told you before, I no trust your courts, your government. I'm scared, señor Jake. I want it over."

"Scared? Carmen, there's nothing to be scared of. Nobody's going to hurt you. This is America, not Guatemala. You deserve justice for what you've been through. My costs alone are over twenty thousand. I never would have laid out all that money or turned down other cases to work on yours if I wasn't sure of a tremendous verdict. You've—"

She placed her hand on his arm and looked at him with a pained expression, seemingly trying to find the right words in English. "As you say, jury gives me what I want, I never see it. Like Gustavo, my baby brother. Si, he did bad things, sell drugs. I begged him no, but he young, go to jail. Your government say we help. You give us big fish you go home to la familia. Gustavo says ok, I tell. Big mistake." She took her index finger and moved it across her throat in a cutting fashion. "Dios Mio." She crossed herself. "Stupid boy. They throw him in river like garbage. Police, drug dealers, everybody malo, muy malo." She glanced around the courtroom as if someone might be listening. "I say too much." Carmen must have seen the look of disbelief on Jake's face and wagged her finger at him. "You in danger, too. I pray for you and your family."

"Your brother was murdered? When? Carmen, this is crazy."

As though not hearing a word he said, she rose on her toes and gave him a hug, then stepped back. "Please señor, Jake. Tell lawyer I take money. I need money. My children need money."

Jake stood stunned, a potential half million-dollar verdict vanishing before his eyes, together with his fee, which he had already set aside to pay off Drew's bills. He refused to let this happen. "Tell you what, I'll—"

She waved her arms at him. "Enough! Please. I no sleep, I no eat. No mas."

Jake clenched his fists. There was no use arguing further. He eyed the insurance lawyer across the courtroom, who appeared to gloat, watching him argue with Carmen. "Okay, I'll tell the lawyer. It'll make his day."

"I sorry, senor Jake, I—"

"My secretary will call when the papers are ready for you to sign." He bristled, then turned on his heel and approached the insurance lawyer, standing alone in the well of the courtroom.

"I've been authorized to accept your offer," Jake said, refusing to look at the man.

"Whoa, son, I certainly didn't expect that."

Jake lifted his head until his eyes met those of the insurance lawyer. "You and me both."

"Well, between us guys I tried to get the carrier to kick in another twenty, but they wouldn't budge. Anywho, glad it's over. Don't let it get you down kid, there'll be more. I've seen plenty in my day and you got what it takes. You're closing argument really had me worried. I nearly wetted my pants." He laughed and patted Jake on the back. "I'll let the judge know we've settled. Expect a check in ten days."

Jake massaged the muscles at the back of his neck. He knew the lawyer was still talking but Jake could no longer hear a word. Instead, he grabbed his briefcase and tore from the courtroom.

Reeling from Carmen's meltdown, Jake wandered aimlessly into the hall. He had nowhere to go. He glanced up at the words engraved above the courtroom's double doors: JUSTICE FOR ALL. "Such a load of crap," he muttered before making his way through the throng of people, refusing to stop as he passed several lawyers he knew, and entered the men's room. He leaned over the sink, splashed cold water repeatedly over his face. His head was about to explode. He felt like throwing up. What would he say to Elena?

Four years ago, Jake knew the risk he was taking by leaving his secure, hundred and forty thousand dollar a year position as a first-year associate at Baker & Stein, LLC, one of Miami's most prestigious law firms. Then, Elena was making good money designing interiors for luxury homes, Drew was a toddler, in good health, and his daughter, Nicole was not yet born. Life couldn't get any sweeter. But within a year, helping off-shore conglomerates pocket millions by exploiting tax loopholes continued to gnaw at him. He needed meaning, a purpose in his life. Jake briefly considered legal aid or joining the federal public defender's office, heeding his dad's advice to help those truly in need, but he knew that kind of work would never generate nearly enough money to provide the kind of lifestyle Elena had been accustomed to growing up. He finally settled on personal injury law, thinking it'd be the perfect fit: make a decent living while protecting the vulnerable from being ripped off by preying insurance companies. But now, deep in debt and his law practice on life support, Jake felt foolish to have taken the plunge.

A slap on his back hurled him out of his thoughts. "Bummer, Boss. Judge's bailiff just told me the news." Lenny Bataglia, Jake's investigator, offered his usual easy smile.

"Not now, L.B. I'm in no mood for one of your pep talks." Jake tossed the used paper towel into the wastebasket and looked around to see if they were alone. "I tried to do right by her but it didn't matter. Not one damn bit. Carrying on about her dead brother, some two-bit drug dealer getting his throat slit and dumped in the river.

What the hell does that got to do with me or the case? And after promising up and down she'd never settle until I gave he the ok, she turns around and does just that. Fuck! Can you believe this shit? Jake powered on his cell and grimaced at Elena's text asking about the case. "Jesus, I'm so screwed."

"Whatcha talking about?"

He showed the text to Lenny. "I'll never be able to explain this to her. She already has one foot out the door."

Lenny violently shook his head. "Get the fuck outta here. That woman dies for you, everybody knows that." Lenny unbuttoned his jacket and yanked off his tie, his brown pony tail swaying behind his massive shoulders. With a short thick neck on a body weighing over two hundred and seventy pounds, he looked more the part of a 16th century samurai and completely out of sorts in a coat and tie. "Just tell her Carmen buckled. Shit happens."

"Gee thanks, I feel so much better now."

Lenny ignored the sarcasm.

"Aw, come on," Lenny urged, trying his best to put on a brave face. "You'll get it back on the next one."

"There ain't going to be a next one," Jake shot back and pivoted to leave.

Lenny grabbed his arm and turned him back around. "What the hell does that mean?"

"You heard me. I've had it with personal injury crap. To coin your favorite word, *finito*. Nothing but fool's gold. Don't know why I couldn't see it sooner."

Lenny's eyes flashed open. He looked like he'd seen a ghost.

"Don't have a coronary," Jake added, "I'm not about to drive off a cliff, at least, not yet."

Jake flung open the men's room door and marched toward the elevators with Lenny right behind, trying to keep up.

"Boss, like I've been telling ya, forget this contingency bullshit. It's time to give crim law a shot. There's serious coin in that." Lenny's eyes lit up. "And think of all the Benjamins stacked thicker than a salami sandwich handed over for just the retainer. Who wouldn't love that? And about Elena, let me talk to her. I know how she feels about criminal law. But I've got clients, cash paying clients, ready for me to give the word, and once Elena sees your success, forget about it."

Jake mulled over his options, dismissing out of hand Lenny's suggestion. How could he ever convince Elena to give him the green light to defend criminals, knowing what she went through in her native Colombia.

Lenny wrapped his arm around Jake's shoulder as they approached the elevators. "Come on, Boss, I hate to see you like this. Let's swing by O'Malley's, I'm buying. You'll feel better after a couple of drinks. You game?"

Jake punched the button for the elevator to take him down, even further down than he already was. "Another time, Len. I need to check on Drew."

Jake's mind whirled as he waited for the doors to open. The thought of taking up criminal law was never ever considered before. Yet, he knew other lawyers far less able who were making a killing doing just that. He stepped into the elevator and turned to face Lenny as the doors began to close. "LB, you could be right. What I got to lose? One thing's for sure, my life can't get any worse."

Chapter Four

Jake trudged down the courthouse steps, trying to erase from his mind the possibility of Elena leaving him. If he were completely honest with himself, he wouldn't be shocked, and certainly no different than what had happened to his dad when Jake was just a boy. After years of struggling to make ends meet, Jake's mother finally had had enough and walked out for a more successful man, and in her words, "to give me the life I'd always dreamed of." Was Elena at that point now?

As he was about to cross Flagler Street toward his car, a familiar voice called, "Hey, Dalton." Jake half-turned and eyed Samuel Pendleton, one of his poker buddies, a ridiculously rich real estate lawyer, running toward him.

"I tried you at your office but your secretary said I'd probably find you here. Still waiting on that verdict, eh?" Sam teased.

A steady drizzle began to fall. "I'm surprised to see you downtown," Jake said, skirting the question. "Thought you avoided court like the plague."

Sam unbuttoned his cashmere jacket, apparently unfazed if it got stained from the rain. "You're right. You couldn't catch me dead in a courtroom, but my dad just snapped up another hotel in foreclosure. I came to record the deed." He glanced down at his watch. "Hope I'm not too late."

Jake nodded absentmindedly. "I'd like to hear more," he lied, "but I'm trying to get home, spend more time with the kids."

"Yeah, Marilyn told me the news. How's that boy of yours doing?"

"Better, much better, thanks."

"Man, that *is* good news. What a horror show you guys must have been through."

Jake pivoted to leave.

"Hey, I almost forgot," Sam said, grabbing Jake's arm. "Got a call from a client this morning, really pissed. He wants a kick-ass litigator to get his property back. Says it's all a big mistake and is willing to pay bookoo bucks for someone to handle it. I thought of you."

Jake moved closer. "Seriously?" In the years they had known each other, Sam had never sent him a case.

"I never joke about business." Just then Sam's cell phone rang. He shook his head as he read the caller ID. "Speak of the devil. My ol' man's already on my ass about the deed."

"Let it go to voicemail," Jake urged, trying not to sound desperate. "I'd like to hear more about the case."

Sam covered his cell with his hand and smiled at Jake. "Never bite the hand that feeds you. I'll fill you in at poker."

"Come on, Sam. At least, give me an idea what it's about."

Sam nodded. "Last week my guy's Cessna got seized by Customs."

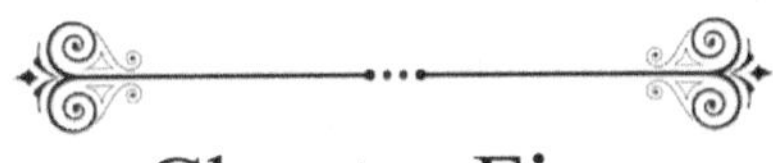

Chapter Five

Isora Gonzales, Jake's secretary, ambled into his office just as he had finished leaving a message for Drew's doctor. Iso, as Jake liked to call her, had been only an infant when her parents escaped by boat in the middle of the night from Castro's Cuba and brought her with them to Miami. Since the day Jake went out on his own, she had been not only his secretary but his most loyal fan. They both knew he'd be lost without her.

Jake slid his feet off his desk as she approached. "What's up?"

"A Samuel Pendleton is holding on line one. Says it's important."

"Yes!" Jake pumped his fist into the air.

"Is that a smile I see on that sad puss of yours? It's only taken you forever to get over that case." Iso turned before Jake could say a word and left, closing the door behind her.

Jake punched the flashing button and cradled the phone against his ear and spoke. "Well, you must be feeling pretty good after last night. Never in my life have I seen a guy pull so many cards out of his ass. Glad I could contribute to the cause."

"Yeah," Sam said with a chuckle. "Think I broke my own record. What was the damage on your end?"

"Two grand."

Sam let out a whistle.

"Yeah, between poker and Jai Alai, I've been getting slammed this year."

"Then maybe I can help turn the tide."

Jake sat up in his chair. "The Cessna?"

"Bingo. The owner's Red Armstrong, but the title's held by one of his corporations. He's a rich redneck from the Redlands. Don't you love the sound of that?"

"Sam, I don't have time for this."

"No, no, I mean it. Hell, I know you're a busy man." Sam's sarcasm cut through the phone.

Jake was tempted to hang up, but didn't.

"Anyway," Sam continued, "The guy owns a ton of acreage near Homestead and is smart as they come. He once did a stint with naval intelligence and now has a degree in environmental engineering, whatever the hell that means."

"Go on." Jake raised his pen and pressed it against the cleft in his chin, envisioning what it would take to recover the plane.

"A while back Red took up flying and bought this sweet turboprop. Gotta be worth two, three mil, easy. Anyway, he had to leave town to check on an investment and was dumb enough to lend it to a former Navy buddy. You can guess the rest."

"I'm all ears."

"Remember that bad-ass storm last week?"

"Uh, huh." Jake flashed back to racing in it to get to Drew.

"Well, that's the night our boy got popped. Apparently, Feds thought he was a druggie. He's not. Got him mixed up with another plane. They finally realized the error of their ways and let 'em go, but held on to the plane."

"Who's them?"

"The pilot—Navy boy—and a passenger."

Jake scribbled a note. "Where's the plane now?"

"Homestead Air Force Base."

"You got a copy of the flight plan?"

"That's the problem. The pilot fucked up, didn't file one, but that's not my guy's fault. Red wants his plane back, like yesterday. He's willing to pay big time."

"You say the guys were released but the plane was not? Strange, don't you think? And why's Red footing the bill? Should be on the pilot, he's the one who fucked up."

"Evidently, Butch—I just remembered the guy's name—is tapped out and Red has no time to wait. He needs his plane to check out investments all around the country."

"Sam, I'm not looking to talk myself out of a fee, but if this Butch was running drugs, and the government can prove your guy's plane was involved, there's not a snowball's chance of getting it back. He'd be throwing good money after bad."

"I've already covered that with him. Red's insists Butch is clean as a whistle. That's where you come in. Now, you in or out? If you're too busy, there're others I could—"

"No, no, I'm in. How well do you know this Red? What I'm asking—"

"I've represented him for years. The dude's a bit eccentric, but totally on the up and up." Sam's annoyance came through the phone. "I gotta take this call. I already told Red you'll need twenty grand up front, otherwise he'll think you're some rank amateur. And Jake, don't fuck this baby up. A lot's riding on it."

Jake eased down the phone and leaned back in his swivel chair. Sam's last comment struck him as odd. Did he go out on a limb to get Jake the case? He gazed at the picture of Elena and his kids, smiling back at him from the corner of his desk, then stood and moved to the expansive window with the million-dollar view overlooking the sparkling blue waters of Biscayne Bay; a view he could hardly afford now.

Still, something about the call didn't sit right. Customs wasn't in the business of snatching planes for no good reason, and why would Sam send him a client after all these years? Had Elena freaked over the tsunami of bills and called Sam's wife Marilyn, her best friend since grade school, to have Sam throw him a bone? Whatever the reason, the call couldn't have come at a better time.

He walked back to his desk and pressed the intercom. "Iso, we need to open a new file. The name's Red Armstrong. He'll be calling for an appointment, and when he does give him whatever time he wants." Jake opened the antique pocket watch his dad had given him to commemorate the opening of his law practice and saw it was almost five. "And Iso, ask Lenny to meet me at O'Malley's, but make sure he knows I've only got time for a quick one. And tell him," Jake caught himself smiling, "at long last the eagle is coming home. He'll understand."

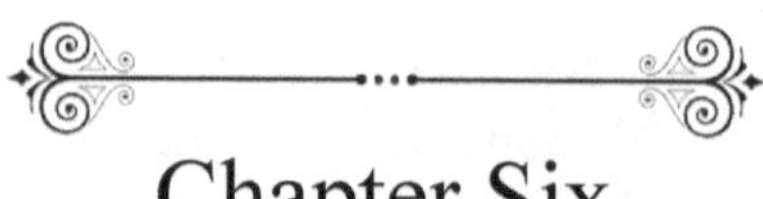

Chapter Six

After four straight days of nothing but rain, the afternoon sun finally peaked through white cirrus clouds as Jake rode his '97 pearl white Harley Davidson through the checkerboard streets of downtown, reveling in the throaty rumble of its dual pipes pounding like a Led Zeppelin classic in his ears. Lenny's instincts were dead on, as usual; criminal law was the way to go. There was no stopping Jake now.

Veering south onto the I-95 ramp, Jake cruised by the luxury high-rise condos lining Brickell Avenue before passing the open secret of Coconut Grove's homeless begging for spare change and rummaging through half-filled cans of garbage. To avoid rush hour traffic, Jake pulled off U.S 1 at Lejeune Avenue and made a beeline for his favorite flower shop in South Miami. He knew fresh roses would be just the thing in the likelihood that Elena and already heard from Marilyn about the beating he took at poker last night.

As he entered the shop, Jake spotted the special: a dozen yellow roses for $34.99. He turned to the noise of loud shuffling behind him. Several bikers sauntered in wearing faded jeans, wide buckled-belts, and heavy boots. The diminutive, gray-haired saleswoman fidgeted behind the counter as if she feared being robbed.

Jake handed her the roses, then reached into his pocket and realized his cash was gone. He cursed himself once more for the beat down he took and pulled out his credit card, passing it to the woman. He glanced over his shoulder. A huge black biker, at six-foot-four a couple of inches taller than Jake, smiled back at him. The biker must have weighed a good two hundred and thirty pounds of solid muscle and on a massive bicep displayed a bright red, white and blue tattoo that read <u>Vets For Peace</u>. Behind him stood several of his buddies, trying their best to act inconspicuous.

Jake turned back to the saleswoman; her brow completely furrowed. She spoke to him through clenched teeth. "I'm sorry, sir, but your charge didn't go through."

"That's impossible," Jake said, feeling the humiliation course through his veins. He'd recently charged the usual meds for Drew, but that couldn't have maxed out his limit.

"I tried twice but both times it came back declined. Master Charge instructed that I cut-up your card," she said in a voice louder than necessary.

Jake glanced over at the roses; no way would he leave without them. "You must be new. Is Kevin here? The owner. I've been coming here for years, and I'm sure he'd let me have till the morning to pay the thirty-five dollars."

She vigorously shook her head. "He's on vacation. And it's $34.99 plus tax."

"Hey, dude. Maybe I could lend a hand," said the smiling biker at his back. His thick beard framed large friendly eyes.

Jake pivoted toward him. "Thanks, but I got it covered," he answered, mostly out of pride.

"No disrespect, but I've been getting a kick watching you go back and forth with the little lady," he said, gesturing to the saleswoman. "Is that your Fat Boy outside?"

Jake nodded.

"Killer paint job. '97, right?"

"You got a good eye."

"I should. I work on 'em all day. Got a small shop, Diesel's Hogs, across from Dadeland Mall. I'm Diesel."

"Jake Dalton." He shook the outstretched hand.

"For the Mrs.?" Diesel shifted his gaze to the roses on the counter.

Jake eked out a smile. "Trying to dig my way out of the doghouse."

Diesel laughed hard, a bellowing sound that seemed to shake the shop. "Dude, we all been there." His buddies chuckled in agreement. Diesel reached into his pocket, pulled out two twenties and tossed them on the counter. He peered at the saleswoman. "This should take care of the roses, and a fat tip for the State of Florida."

"I...I don't know what to say." Jake couldn't believe a total stranger would do this. "Give me your address so I can mail you a check."

"Forget it. Just tell your friends to stop by my shop when they need honest work."

"I got a better idea." Jake pulled his business card from his wallet and handed it to Diesel.

"If you ever find yourself in a jam, I'll take care of it. Gratis. It's the least I could do." Without looking at the saleswoman, Jake grabbed the roses off the counter and tucked them under his arm to leave.

Diesel studied the card. "I'll be a sonofabitch," he said, holding it toward his buddies. "'Board Certified Civil Trial Lawyer.'" Hey guys, can you believe this? A flat-broke ambulance chaser buying flowers for his babe, on a hog no less." He gave Jake a broad smile and slapped him on the shoulder. "You're alright, counselor. Don't run into many of your kind around town. Hope to be seein' ya again."

Forty minutes later, Jake pulled into the driveway of his Kendall home and gazed at his hard-earned accomplishment with a deep sense of pride. Granted, it was only a modest ranch style three-bedroom house, set back on a narrow lot between Australian pines, and a far cry from the digs that Elena grew up in, but still, not bad for the son of a dry-clean deliveryman.

After shutting off the Harley's engine, Jake walked to the mailbox, roses in hand. Sandwiched between medical bills and junk mail was a letter from Drew's pediatrician. He nervously ripped open the envelop. Inside was a hand-written note stapled to a document:

Dear Elena and Jake,

I'm enclosing a report from Dr. Perelman, a renowned hematologist. Drew's thrombocytopenia remains serious and his prognosis guarded. As expected, more tests are needed. I know this has been a difficult time for you, but I'm hopeful we'll find a lasting treatment soon. Please feel free to call with any questions.

Warm regards,
Harvey Witkin, M.D.

With the report on his mind, Jake unlocked the front door and called, "Elena?" No answer. "Elena." The house was strangely quiet. He invariably looked forward to her captivating smile and those sparkling brown eyes that had him sputtering like a nerdy teenager the moment he laid eyes on her seven years ago.

Elena had been sitting alone at a corner booth reading an architectural design magazine in an upscale New Haven café where he waited on tables. She always took the same booth and ordered the same amaretto cheesecake and double espresso, while drawing amazing sketches of interior home furnishings on a row of paper napkins. Instantly, Jake knew she was the one, and as fortune would have it, the two began sharing a studio apartment three months later. He was in his second year of law school and she in pursuit of a master's degree in design. Elena's fiery passion, both in and out of bed, was something he had never experienced before.

Jake entered the foyer, tossed his keys into the Navaho pottery bowl, and started for the kitchen, hoping to surprise Elena with the roses and his plans to make dinner. Before he could take two steps, Drew exploded from his bedroom with outstretched arms.

"Dad-dy!"

A huge grin spread across Jake's face as he put down the flowers and knelt to hug his boy. "Hey, little man. Whassup?"

Drew threw himself into Jake's arms, toppling him backwards onto the Mexican tile. "I can't believe how strong you are," Jake said through a laugh, squeezing his son tight for a few precious moments. "I might just call the Dolphins first thing tomorrow and tell 'em to watch out, 'cause in a few years they'll be lookin' at the next Dan Marino."

Drew giggled and flexed his bicep. "You got that right," he said, his deep-blue eyes flashing with excitement. "Are we getting Terminator tonight?"

"Absolutely," Jake said, lowering his voice. "But let's keep it a secret. You, me and Nicole will go there right after dinner," reminding Jake to ask Elena for her credit card.

"Nikki's not here. Granny took her for pizza."

"Really? Why didn't you go, too?"

"I wanted to be with you."

Jake smiled. "And I'm thrilled you're here. But to be fair, we have to wait for Nikki to get back before we go."

Drew nodded his agreement.

With the hematologist report fresh on his mind, he studied Drew's neck and arms for signs of any fresh bruising, grateful that his son didn't know how sick he really was. Satisfied there were none, he rose to his feet. "Then prepare yourself for one of my award-winning dinners. Time to wash up."

Drew stood to leave and glanced back at his dad. "Mommy's really mad at you."

"Thanks for the heads up," Jake said, and tried to shrug off the warning with a wave.

Jake walked through the entertainment room stacked with Disney DVDs, and into the dated kitchen where Elena stood leaning against the counter, her arms folded tight across her chest. She stared back at him in steely silence. At five-foot-five, with generous lips, a prominent nose—which she hated—and dark brown hair falling effortlessly over her shoulders, she didn't look anywhere near her thirty years. She complained privately of carrying a few extra pounds, but to him she was perfect.

"Hey hon, sorry I'm late. I've got news you're not going to believe." Jake moved to kiss her.

Elena waved him off. "Let me guess. Your poker pals voted to take up a collection for the money you blew last night."

Jake ignored the dig. "Bad news travels fast."

She frowned.

He placed the mail on the counter and stroked the back of her shoulder with his hand. "I'm sorry. I totally screwed up. I get it. It won't happen again."

"Oh, spare me that broken record. I've heard it too many times to count."

He started to protest.

"Two thousand dollars! Have you lost your mind? We don't have that kind of money. What were you thinking?" Her eyes burned into him. "And there's more."

Jake's stomach churned. He stood with trepidation for the other shoe to drop.

"There's something that's been on my mind for quite some time, and I haven't had the nerve to bring it up before. But after last night, I've decided. Enough is enough. I'm done."

A shiver shot through his entire body. Was she ending the marriage? He envisioned being strapped into the electric chair waiting for the switch to be pulled. He held his breath, afraid to ask the next question. "What do you mean?"

"Your gambling, it has to stop. It makes me sick to my stomach. First, it was Monday night football, betting fifty, a hundred dollars at a time. I said OK, let the man have his fun. But then came horse racing, two, three times a week, stumbling through the front door with your head stuck in the paper to see if you'd won. Next jai alai. Now throwing away money we don't have on some pathetic poker game. I can't take any more. I just can't." She leaned toward him and put her mouth against his ear. "Can you hear me?"

Jake nodded. "Loud and clear. But last night was crazy, once in a lifetime. Even the guys thought my luck was the worst they've ever seen. It won't happen again. I'm sorry, I truly am."

Elena stayed silent; an ominous sign Jake never wanted to see. He'd much preferred getting it between the eyes, like any warm-blooded Colombiana had every right to do, instead of having her simmer for days on end. He made sure to choose his next words very carefully.

"Okay, okay. You're a hundred percent right. Forget football, jai alai and betting at the track. No more, I swear. But poker's different. You know that. Hanging with the guys is my way of blowing off steam. I think that's more than fair."

Elena's eyes softened. "Only if you promise to get help. I'm dead serious, and I won't take no for an answer. Can't you see what it's doing to our marriage? Isn't that important to you?"

"Of course, it is. You know that. You're everything to me." He breathed deep, trying to contain his emotions. "Alright, I'll make some calls tomorrow, first thing. Guess I may have a problem. Now let me get rid of my jacket and get to work. I'm about to cook you up one of my famous dinners."

Elena's eyes opened wide. "Dinner? You really are trying to score points?"

"Baby, you have no idea." Jake reached over and gave her a soft kiss on her brow. "And to top it off, I even brought you a surprise."

Elena wagged her finger at him. "You're crazy if you think offering me a bribe will do any good, senor." Her lips opened to a smile. She moved away and opened the refrigerator, then looked back at him with a pained expression. "Better be fish, 'cause tuna's the only thing defrosted."

"No problema, I'll sear it," he said, relieved he was able to change the subject.

He gently nudged her aside and grabbed the tuna, fresh asparagus, ginger, scallions, and soy sauce. He raised the fish to his nose, making sure it hadn't turned bad. "Got another report from Dr. Witkin." Jake filled the steamer with water, dropped fresh asparagus into it, then grabbed a frying pan and placed it on the gas stove. After coating the pan with olive oil, he carefully placed the filet, making sure the fire was just right.

Elena sighed.

"He'll need more tests," Jake added.

"Good God! Hasn't he been through enough?"

"Please keep it down." Jake looked behind him to see if Drew might have heard. "I know, baby, but we can't let on we're worried. Now let me give you some good news."

Elena stayed silent.

"Just this morning I was really depressed, bummed over Carmen settling the case out from under me, getting smoked at poker, and there you were, rightfully angry at the mess we're in."

"And?"

"Sam calls, wants to send me a case. A big one. Could be the break we've been waiting for." He eyed the asparagus and tuna, making sure the heat wasn't too high.

"Sam? You've *got* to be kidding. Of all people, Sam. I don't trust him. Never have."

Jake lifted two martini glasses from the cabinet and placed them on the counter. "I know how you feel about him, but now is not the time to turn down cases, even criminal ones." He braced for her explosion and didn't have to wait long.

"Criminal?" Elena's voiced shot up several octaves. "Are you out of your mind? This conversation is going downhill and fast. And why does that loser, all of a sudden, want to help *you*? He never has before. Boy, do I smell a rat."

"Look, I'm trying to get some bills paid, okay? I know the past year hasn't been easy on you, but it hasn't been a walk in the park for me either. You think for a minute I want to spend my time with criminals? Give me a break. But I've got to make things work. Personal injury was a bust. There, I said it. Happy? I rolled the dice and got craps. What do you want from me?"

"I thought you'd never ask," she snapped right back.

He couldn't mistake the look in her eyes. "No, not that. I'd rather be waterboarded than help wealthy assholes shelter their precious millions. I tried that for a year and considered throwing myself in front of a train."

"A steady paycheck would look awfully good around here. I'm not like you, Jake, getting my jollies living on the edge. Give me boring any day of the week."

Jake loosened his tie. He didn't see it that way. Ever since he was a boy, he strived to be special, stand out in the crowd, the thought of being ordinary was so repugnant to him. If that meant taking risks, so be it.

He flipped the fillet and added sliced scallions and soy sauce, making sure there was enough oil in the pan. He half-filled the cocktail shaker with ice, then poured dry vermouth and vodka into it, trying his best to ignore the tense silence between them.

"Honey," he finally spoke, "listen to me. Please. We're live smack in the middle of the fraud capital of the world. I'd be crazy not to take a shot at criminal law. Look around. On our block alone there's probably a half-dozen homes under water, facing foreclosure. That's all you ever read, mortgage brokers and bankers getting indicted for fraud. It's smack dab in my wheelhouse. A couple of nice retainers and presto, our bills are gone." He'd even be able to return the funds he withdrew from the kids' college fund before Elena ever found out. "I thought," he continued, "when Sam phoned that maybe you'd said something to Marilyn about our… predicament."

"All I said was that things have been pretty rough lately. Surprise, surprise. Phone calls from the hospital and threatening letters from creditors. I even mentioned that when Drew gets better, I'd go back to work."

"No argument there, the money you brought in made all the difference in the world. Thank you for that." Jake caressed her back. "I have a suggestion. Let me try criminal law for a year, just one year. If that doesn't pan out, I'll walk the plank and send out my resume." He raised his hand, extending three fingers. "Scout's honor. But I doubt it'll ever happen. Lenny's already lining up clients—"

"Mafia! Are you high?"

Jake wagged his head. "We're not talking the Sopranos. It's just that Lenny used to hang with those guys growing up in New Jersey. As a matter of fact, Lenny thought Sam's call was a good omen."

"More like a curse. There's something…I can't put my finger on it." Elena grabbed the cocktail shaker from his hands and angrily shook it. "I'll never understand why Marilyn ever married him."

Jake rubbed his thumb and forefinger together. "Um, let me guess."

"No way. Marilyn's not like that. Besides, she has her own money."

"Well, it's good of Sam to help out. He represents only the *crème de la crème*." Jake decided not to mention the twenty-thousand-dollar fee until he had it in hand.

He slid the martini glasses over to her, then turned down the stove. "Pour the drinks, I'll be right back." Jake ran to retrieve the roses in the foyer and carried them back to the kitchen, hiding them behind his back with one hand. The telephone rang and he reached to get it.

Elena grabbed his arm. "Don't! Let it go to voice mail. It's probably--"

"Screw 'em." The ringing seemed to grow louder. He put his arm around her while she nestled her head against his shoulder. "I know it's been hell. But I promise we'll get through this. Criminal law is no big deal, especially the white-collar kind."

"Protecting the dregs of Miami isn't why I helped you through Yale."

Jake handed her the flowers.

Her eyes welled up as she looked down at the yellow roses, then back at him. She reached over and kissed him. "They're beautiful. I won't ask how much."

"I never imagined I could love someone as much as I love you," he said. "I want so much to provide for you and the kids. Please don't give up on me."

Jake thought back to the day after his sixth birthday when his mother waved goodbye through the open window of a red Cadillac as her rich boyfriend drove her away from him to Dallas to give her a taste of the good life.

"But I can't help but worry," she said, caressing his cheek. "You don't know what it's like to live in fear. And I pray to God our children never do." Elena bit her lip. "Being driven to school by a bodyguard, my parents warning of Pablo Escobar and his *sicarios* and how they snatched innocent people off the streets, never to be heard from again. And the lucky ones who were heard from, their family would get severed fingers and ears in the mail to prove they were still alive."

"Honey, that kind of crap doesn't happen here."

"Oh, Jake, if only that were so." She brushed back a strand of his hair. "All right, do your clean collar, white collar or whatever you call it, if you must. Only promise you'll stay away from the violent criminals, the killers, rapists, drug dealers. That I could never take. Is that asking too much?"

"Of course not." He squeezed her tight, feeling her warmth against his body. "Believe me, the last thing I'd ever do is put you or the kids in danger."

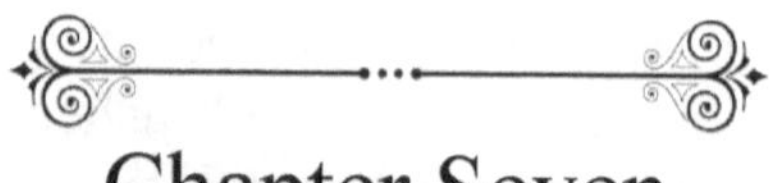

Chapter Seven

Just before dawn, Tommy bolted upright in bed as he fought off horrific memories of the war. The banging on his front door grew more violent, shaking the paper-thin walls of his Coconut Grove condo.

He gently shook Jessie and whispered. "Baby, wake up."

Jessie's eyes flew open and she started to speak.

He shook his head and pressed his finger against her lips and mouthed, "No sound." He rolled on his side and slid open the top drawer of the nightstand for his 9mm. The Beretta was gone!

Jessie sprang out of bed and raced to the closet; her nude body partially revealed by the moonlight streaming through the bedroom blinds. She threw back her long hair while snapping off the safety of her handgun.

"Jess," he hissed, "give me that."

The knocking grew louder. "U.S. Marshals! Open up! We have an arrest warrant for Thomas Tifton. Open the door or we'll break it down!"

Tommy froze. What were the feds doing here in the middle of the night? Only two weeks ago Customs had released him, told him he was free to go. He wasn't running from nobody.

He peered through the back window. The full moon illuminated three uniformed men crouched on the patio, guns drawn. He flashed back to being on patrol in Iraq and motioned to Jessie, raising three fingers.

Jessie reacted as if she could read his mind. She threw on her robe and raced to the front door, pressing her eye against the peep hole. She spun around and flashed two fingers.

Tommy slumped against the wall. Three out back, two in front. Too damn many.

He signaled for her to flip on the lights while he tugged on his jeans. "Jess, make sure they're who they say they are."

She nodded. "Wait. I need a minute to put something on," Jessie hollered through the door, buying time. "Awright, I'm just about there." She slid off the chain lock and cracked open the door while Tommy looked on from the bedroom.

Two uniformed marshals stormed in, pushing her aside. One, tall with a thick neck and dense physique, held in his raised hand a dark grey Glock. The second, much shorter, round-faced with a scarred complexion, aimed a shotgun at Jessie's chest and gawked at her.

"What the hell you lookin' at?" Jessie screamed, cinching her robe tight around her waist.

The tall deputy, apparently in charge, bellowed, "U.S. Marshals. Is Thomas Tifton with you?"

"What do you want with my Tommy?"

Shirtless, Tommy shuffled barefoot toward the two men, his hands raised above his head. He had stuffed Jessie's handgun under the mattress. "What the hell is this about, banging down my door in the middle of the night?"

The tall marshal moved straight for Tommy and shoved him against the wall. "Hands up. Higher!" He barked as he patted Tommy down.

"Leave my husband alone!" Jessie screamed at the two. "He's a war hero, damn you." She ran to Tommy, her eyes flaring.

"You Tifton?" the shorter marshal asked.

Tommy clenched his jaw and nodded. His special forces training had taught him to survive, no matter the odds. He fought to keep his temper in check, knew that if he didn't, anything could happen. "What do you want?" he spit out.

In a panic Jessie turned on her heel and moved toward the bedroom.

The shorter deputy grabbed her by the arm. "Where you think you're going?"

Instinctively, Tommy moved to protect her, then eyed the Glock pointed at his head and thought better of it.

The deputy slowly released his grip on Jessie's arm in an apparent effort to de-escalate the situation. He spoke in a calm voice. "Let me clear the room, then you can change into something. We don't want to use more force than necessary, just want to make sure everyone stays safe. Understood?"

Jessie slowly nodded as her breathing quieted.

"Tifton, you're under arrest for trafficking in narcotics. Hold out your hands," the lead marshal ordered. He then pulled the metal handcuffs off his belt and snapped them tight around Tommy's wrists.

Tommy stood numb and stared down in defeat as he listened to his Miranda rights being read. This shouldn't be happening, not in front of Jessie. Moments later, as though in a dream, he felt the tall marshal pull him by the arm out the front door into a waiting SUV.

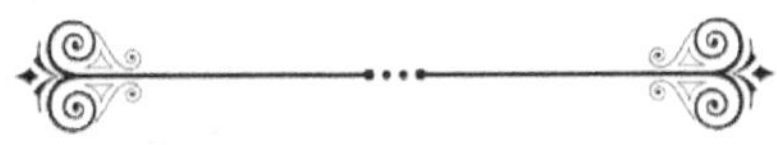

Chapter Eight

Isora ran up to Jake the moment he opened the front door of his office. "Whoa, this gotta be important," he said.

"Could be. While you were in court Mr. Pendleton called. He said it was urgent and asked that you see a Tommy Tifton, right away. I checked your calendar and agreed to three o'clock. Hope you don't mind."

"What's it about?"

"Apparently, Mr. Tifton was arrested over the weekend. Mr. Pendleton sounded rushed and didn't go into details except to say the case involved drugs and was in federal court."

"He stressed it was urgent?"

"Twice."

Urgent meant a nice fee. Sam's timing couldn't be better. "Fantastic." Jake moved into his inner office and checked his calendar, then looked back at Isora. "Why's my meeting with Red Armstrong crossed out?"

"When Mr. Pendleton called, he said that your appointment with Mr. Armstrong had to be postponed because Mr. Armstrong was called away on business. He'll call to reschedule when he gets back in town."

"Get me Pendleton on the phone. I need to find out what's going on."

Isora shook her head. "He was about to board a plane to Atlanta when he called. Said he'd try you tonight."

Two calls from Pendleton in the same week where in all the years they had known each other he'd never before called Jake about business. This was more than just strange.

"Okay. Then ask Lenny to make himself available. I don't like meeting a client alone, especially in a criminal matter."

Isora again shook her head. "He's in Ft. Meyers, interviewing witnesses on the Handsel matter. Maybe we should move the meeting to the morning. Lenny's driving back tonight and I know he'd want to be there."

Jake thought it over. He'd definitely prefer to have Lenny present but he couldn't take the chance of Tifton slipping away, only to be snarfed up by some other lawyer hungry for a case.

"No, keep it at three o'clock. In the meantime, call the U.S. Attorney's office and find out if Tifton has any connection to a Cessna aircraft seized a couple weeks ago by Customs."

Isora nodded and left.

Jake slumped in his chair. If it was so damn urgent, why hadn't Sam called beforehand to bring him up to speed? He tried Sam's cell and got voicemail.

Precisely at three o'clock, Isora escorted two men and a woman into Jake's office.

"Hi, I'm Tommy Tifton," said a lanky, middle-aged man first through the door. He stood eye level to Jake as he approached with an outstretched hand. Jake thought he detected deep scarring on the back of Tifton's neck just above his shirt collar, but couldn't be sure. Tifton's gray eyes were set deep above a long, slender nose and high cheek bones. A sun-burned, burly man and a red-haired, twenty-something woman followed close behind.

"How y'all doing? I'm Jake Dalton," he said, grasping Tommy's hand. Jake's accent came off stronger than he'd intended.

"This is my brother, Dave," Tommy said, half-turning to his right. "I wouldn't be here if he hadn't bailed my butt out of jail." He gestured to the much younger woman. "And my wife, Jessie."

Jake shook Dave's hand and smiled at Jessie. He directed them to the chairs aligned in front of his desk, then returned to his seat, while checking out the potential client.

Tommy wore a navy blazer, pressed white shirt and charcoal gray slacks. He appeared relaxed, self-assured, and clean-cut. Maybe too clean-cut, Jake thought. His brother, Dave was shorter and built like a fire hydrant. He was dressed casual in a flowery Aloha shirt, khakis and sandals. Tommy's wife, Jessie, wore a lavender skirt and tight-fitting white top. She had sky blue eyes and offered an easy smile. She appeared half her husband's age.

Deep South was stamped all over these folks, and Jake would know, he had cousins from southwest Louisiana who carried themselves in just this way.

Jake reached for a legal pad to begin the meeting. "Where you from, Mr. Tifton?"

"Everyone calls me Tommy," he said in a soft voice. "I'm from Beizley. Bet you never heard of it." He chuckled. "It's a one-horse hick town deep in the panhandle, miles and miles from here, in every way imaginable."

"Well, I was born here myself. In fact, I remember as a boy always calling the town Miamah," Jake said, trying his best to connect with the client. "Family on my mom's side is from New Orleans, but I guess by now I've lost whatever accent I once had."

"No, you still got some left." Tommy's paper-thin lips opened into a broad smile, showing a few chipped teeth that were badly in need of a dentist.

Jessie rose from her chair and wandered to the window overlooking Biscayne Bay. "Mighty nice office you got here, Mr. Dalton," she said, admiring neighboring skyscrapers and the island of Key Biscayne in the distance. "How high up are we again?"

"Thirty-nine floors."

She spun around; her eyes gleaming. "Would you believe, just last month for my twenty-first birthday Tommy carried me to a restaurant with such a pretty view —"

"Jessie," Tommy snapped, his hand clutched the arm of his chair with a vise-like grip. "Get over here and sit yourself down. We're here on business."

Jessie sprang away from the window, practically sprinting to her chair. Nervous or scared, Jake couldn't tell which.

Tommy looked back at Jake. "Please pay my wife no mind. She's young and comes across a bit ditsy, but means no harm. To tell the truth, she's even sharper than she is pretty, but just a tad inexperienced in the ways of the world, if you know what I mean."

"Aw, honey, don't say that. What's the man gonna think?"

Jessie flashed what seemed to be a seductive look at Jake. *Was she flirting with me?* he wondered.

"Tommy wasn't like that before the war," Jessie added, "you know temper and all. At least, that's what he tells me."

"Which war is that?"

"Desert Storm, Army Special Forces." Tommy hesitated, "but that was back a ways."

"He don't like to talk about it none," Jessie chimed in. "In fact, he's ain't for talkin' period. And Lord that's a good thing, 'cause I do plenty for the both of us." She laughed at herself. "Where was I? Oh, yeah, right," she said, reminding herself. "Tommy got hurt something awful when his helicopter got blown to smithereens by a rocket propelled grenade. Burnt like bad toast, lost half his belly. Wound up with a Bronze Star and Purple Heart, then crapped on by a government who couldn't give a damn."

A genuine war hero. Crapped on? Jake was intrigued.

Tommy squirmed in his chair. "Please don't get her started."

"That's right, don't get me going cause there's no tellin' when I'll stop." She smiled at Tommy before continuing. "The federal government's been cheatin' Tommy out of what's rightfully his for over twenty years. That's all. VA won't give him the meds he needs 'cause they could give a flying…you know what. My Tommy gets headaches, can't concentrate, always so damn depressed, and my lord, he's bone tired all the time. The Army says the Gulf War syndrome don't exist, but I know better." She tapped her temple several times with her finger. "I researched it on the internet. No different than Vietnam when the government fibbed through their teeth and swore there was no such thing as Agent Orange. But we all know what a big fat lie that was."

Tommy was right. Behind her folksiness Jessie was nobody's fool.

"And to prove the Army wrong," Jesse added, "Tommy picked himself up and went back to college, got himself a degree in military history. Damn near stays up half the night reading those fat books. Reckon it helps his PTSD."

Post-traumatic stress disorder. Jake recalled how his dad, even years after returning from his second tour in Vietnam, would sit alone for days in his favorite chair and hardly speak a word.

Jake pivoted to the buzzing sound of his intercom. Isora wouldn't interrupt unless it was important. "Excuse me." He raised the phone to his ear. "Yes."

"Mr. Dalton, you need to hear this. It's about Mr. Tifton. I just got a call back from a summer intern in the U.S. Attorney's office. Boy, can she talk. I told her you might be representing Mr. Tifton and asked whether there was anything she could tell us about the case."

"And?" Jake studied Tommy in his chair, meticulously picking lint off his blazer.

"Last week a grand jury filed charges against him and a Mr. Dearing for smuggling cocaine. They're still looking for Mr. Dearing, who they say is a fugitive. And the plane—the one you asked about—was involved."

"How much are we talking about?"

"I think she said two thousand pounds. Did I get that right? That seems like a lot of cocaine."

If Isora had heard right, Tifton was caught in a major bust. "Who's handling the case?"

"Apparently, one of their top prosecutors. A Crawford Richter. The intern said he does only drug cases. They seem really sure of themselves, Mr. Dalton."

"Maybe too sure." Jake loved going up against a guy convinced his case was invincible. "Thanks, Iso."

Jake ended the call and realized he was getting into something far bigger than he ever imagined. He wished Lenny were here.

"Tommy," Jake began, 'before we get into your case, I need go over some ground rules. I read about your arrest in the Herald and didn't know if there were others."

"First and last. Never even seen a lawyer before coming to you."

"Well, for starters, I want you to know that whatever you tell me today is strictly confidential, protected by the attorney-client privilege. It applies whether or not I take your case. I tell you this because it's important that you be completely truthful with me."

"Understood. You go ahead and ask anything you want. I've got nothing to hide."

"That's right," Jessie butted in. "Tommy's done nothin' wrong."

"So, to maintain the privilege I have to ask your brother to leave." Jake glanced over at Dave. "Nothing personal."

"Not a problem," Dave said, rising from his chair.

"Wait," Tommy said, motioning toward his brother. "Dave was with me the night they said we were flying in drugs."

Jake shifted his gaze to Dave. "You were together?"

"Damn straight," Tommy interrupted, his voice rising. "Dave and I were in Cozumel at a fishing tournament."

"That's all well and good, but I'm afraid juries won't buy an alibi on the word of a brother alone. You'll need more, a lot more."

"But there were others, it wasn't just me and Tommy," Dave said.

"Okay, if I decide to take the case, I'll have my investigator meet with you at a later date. In the meantime, I need you to dig up any evidence that backs up what you're sayin', like receipts, ticket stubs, photos, anything. That's critical." Jake flicked a glance at Tommy to make sure he was listening,

"I'm on it." Dave put his hand on Tommy's shoulder. "Looks like it's a go. When y'all are done here, meet me at the coffee shop across the street." He turned and left.

Jake continued. "I'd prefer that Jessie leave too, but as your wife there's a limited privilege between the two of you, and—"

"Jess stays. She knows I'm innocent and can help me prove it."

For the next thirty minutes, Tommy recounted being arrested and taken from his home in the early morning hours, spending the weekend at the federal correctional facility and appearing before the U.S. Magistrate where the charges of cocaine trafficking were read to him. The magistrate set a cash bond of one million dollars.

Jake looked up from taking notes. "Where'd you come up with a million dollars cash?"

Tommy sighed. "That was some doing. I've been working at Florida Electric since '92. My first and only job since I left the Army and clawed my way up to fleet manager." Tommy's eyes lit up with pride. "My retirement got to over a hundred grand, but I had to cash that in."

"That'll make you in your forties?" Jake asked, trying not to act surprised. Tommy's receding hairline and his gangly appearance made him appear years older. If he ran drugs, it did him no favor.

"I'll be forty-four in October."

"Don't rush it, honey," Jessie said, chuckling.

"The rest came from Dave. He took out a loan and put up his charter boat business as collateral." Tommy clucked his tongue. "I should have put my money with him years ago. Mr. Pendleton takes care of Dave's investments. That's how I got to you."

Jake sat back in his chair. Maybe these folks were the real deal. "And the pilot?"

"That's Butch, a sometimes drinking buddy. Use to fly jets for the Navy."

"How'd you two meet?"

"Checkered Flag. It's a sports bar in Daytona. We're both dig NASCAR, and before long started trading war stories. He flew sorties in the Second Gulf War. You already know about me."

"Tell me about your flight home when you were stopped by Customs."

"We left Cozumel around zero hundred, maybe a bit later."

Jake thought of his dad and how he'd talk in military time even years after his stint in the Army.

"Midnight? Why not wait till morning?"

"Had to get back to work, plus there was a nasty storm heading our way."

"Go on."

"When we first took off there was a little weather, no big deal. But once we got over the Florida Straits, it felt like the hand of God reached down and shook our plane." Tommy squeezed his eyes shut as though reliving that night. "The winds were crazy, threw us way off course."

"Talk about your nose, honey," Jessie urged. "Gave him just awful memories of the war."

Tommy pressed the bridge of his nose. "Flattened it against the window from the turbulence. Started gushing blood like a stuck pig. I was sitting in the cockpit, right side, then out of nowhere this other plane shows up." He raised his hands in the air like two planes in flight. "Found out later it was Customs. Our electronics went down and we were flying on fumes." Tommy's eyes turned vacant. "Thought for sure we were gonna eat it."

Tommy went on to describe the encounter with the Customs agents after landing.

"Who owns the plane?" Jake pressed.

"Not mine...belongs to a fella named Red. He loaned it to Butch for the weekend. They evidently were buds from their Navy days. Butch used to fly fighter jets, like the F-14 Tomcat. Man, could he rip. He whipped through that storm like a knife through butter."

Jake made a note to have Lenny check out whether any of the cartels flew in drugs from Cozumel. "What were you doing in Mexico?"

"We planned to go fishing, part of an annual tournament. They have the best big-game on this planet. I'm talkin' blue marlin, sailfish."

"This is Thursday?"

Tommy nodded.

"So, you, your brother and Butch fished all day Friday, is that what you're saying?"

"They did, I couldn't. Got Montezuma's revenge from something the night before."

"What'd you do then?"

"I wasn't going to sit around and stare at the walls so I checked out the ruins at *Chichén Itzá*. I dig everything there is to know about the Mayans. You been there?"

"Once," Jake answered. "Did you get a chance to climb to the top?"

"Nope, it's roped off. Besides, I was feeling like crap, so I cut the day short. Damn stupid of me to go in the first place."

Jake knew tourists were prohibited from going to the top but had wanted to test Tommy's story. "How'd you get to the ruins?"

"I hopped a ferry to Playa Del Carmen around 0800, then caught a cab to *Chichen Itza*. Got back to Dave's around 1600, feeling like I was about to die."

"Anyone see you at the ruins, or better yet, do you have anything to prove you were there? Anything at all?"

Tommy tilted his head toward Jessie. "I'm sure folks saw me, but I've no idea who they'd be. I'll check to see if I kept anything, but knowing me, I probably just chucked 'em."

Jake remained silent. He didn't know what to think. Tifton was either telling the truth or damn good at lying. He never once evaded a question. Maybe the guy was getting a raw deal. Lenny would know.

"What'd you do once you got back to Cozumel late Friday?"

"Dave cooked up dinner but there was no way I could keep food down, had maybe a cup of corn soup and tortillas."

"Other than Dave and Butch, anybody else see you there?"

"Yeah, this guy who organized the tournament and his wife. My brother had them over for dinner. First time I ever met 'em."

Jake sat up in his chair. The alibi was looking up. "You know their names, where I can find them?"

"His is Mendoza Diego, or the other way around. I always get my Spanish names mixed up. I don't remember hers. But they've been in Cozumel forever."

"What time was this?"

"Roughly, 2100. A few hours later they saved Dave the trouble and gave us a lift to the airfield on their way home."

"Not Cozumel International?"

Tifton wagged his head. "That's Butch for you. Cheap as the day is long, uses smaller airfields to skimp on fees."

"Other than this Mexican couple, anyone else see you takeoff?"

"Doubt it. The airfield's uncontrolled."

Jake must have given him a puzzled look.

"Nobody manning the tower full-time. To tell you the truth, I didn't even know it existed. Found out later the Navy built it during World War II to fend off German U-boats."

Tifton did like his history.

"And Butch, where's he?"

"He skipped town."

Jake saw Tommy's eyes dart back and forth. "Why would he do that if he's innocent?"

Tommy rubbed his cheek. "I know it looks bad."

Jessie reached over and tugged on Tommy's arm. "I told you he wouldn't believe us."

Tommy shot her a sideways glance. "He didn't say that."

"Look, folks," Jake intervened. "I'm not here to judge your guilt or innocence. A jury will do that. Just be straight with me."

Tommy locked eyes on Jake. "If you ask me, he musta done some things in the past. I didn't know Butch all that well."

"Why didn't you take off with him?"

"'Cause I done nothing wrong. If I'd been running drugs, you can bet your sweet ass I'd be gone in a New York minute."

Tommy had a point. "You think Butch's been running drugs before."

"Yep, but not with me. I figured that out the moment I boarded the plane. Seats were all stripped out." Tommy turned to Jessie. "The two of us want to start a family."

Jake didn't know what to make of it. He knew the chances of selling Tommy's story to a federal jury would be like climbing Mt. Everest in the dead of winter, especially where odds of an acquittal are at best five percent. But Jake couldn't ignore the money, a fee that would pay all his bills and give him the luxury of not worrying about future medical treatment for Drew, and the kind of case that would rocket his career. Jake was starting to believe in Tommy's innocence, because he wanted to, needed to.

He rose from behind his desk and buttoned his suit jacket. "Tommy, I think I can help, and I'd be pleased to represent you."

Tommy and Jessie looked at each other and smiled.

"My fee will be one hundred thousand dollars plus expenses."

Tommy froze. "That's serious money."

"It's a serious case. And before I can start, I'll need an initial retainer of fifty thousand, a cost deposit of ten thousand and the second fifty in thirty days. If there's a plea bargain, then—"

Tommy waved his arms, cutting him off. "You mean say I'm guilty? No frickin' way, I'll never do that. Just watch me prove otherwise."

"Okay then, let's roll up our sleeves and get to work."

"I don't care how bad it looks, there ain't gonna be no deal. I'm not going to admit to something I didn't do. Period. We'll find a way somehow to come up with what you need."

Jessie leaned toward Jake; fear filled her eyes. "What's Tommy lookin' at if he loses?"

"If found guilty on all charges, thirty years in a federal penitentiary."

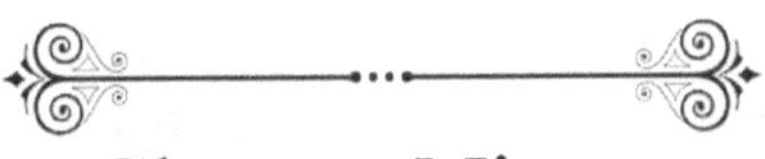

Chapter Nine

With a bounce in her step, Isora strode into Jake's office, waving a FedEx packet in the air. "This will make your day." She handed him an envelope, already sliced open.

Jake looked inside. A business card with the name "Dave Tifton, Charter Boat Captain" was paper-clipped to a pair of cashier's checks, one for fifty-thousand-dollars and a second for ten thousand, with a note that another fifty thousand dollars would arrive by the end of the month. Zeroes seemed to smile up at him; his biggest retainer yet. He couldn't wait to tell Elena over a romantic dinner or better yet, on a weekend getaway at the Pier House in Key West.

"Looks like I'm Tifton's guy," Jake said as he sprung from his chair and gave Isora a high five. "Go ahead and enter our appearance and find out who our judge is. And while you at it, pull the file and ask Lenny to swing by. He doesn't know it, but he's on his way to Mexico." Jake snapped his fingers above his head as though dancing to the beat of a Mariachi band.

"You already have it." Isora gestured to the corner of his desk where a brown accordion folder sat. On top was a typed memo listing the names and known addresses of potential witnesses.

"You're amazing. What would I do without you?"

Isora chuckled. "I often wonder that myself."

As she was leaving, Jake called out, "Iso, before you go, do me a favor. If by chance you speak to Elena, Mum's the word about Tifton. She's got this thing about drug cases."

Isora hesitated. "You sure you want to go down that road?"

"For now. I'll tell her when the time is right."

Rays of sunlight streamed through Jake's office as he leaned back in his leather chair and plopped his size twelves on top of his desk, shaking his head in amazement at the size of his new retainer.

Lenny skipped into Jake's office, his smile from ear to ear. "Just heard the news. Ya see, that's what I'm talkin' about. That check will pay some bills, eh?"

"LB, I haven't seen you move like that since the time we closed that Greek restaurant with you and the belly dancer dancing out of your minds on the bar. But then alcohol was involved."

Lenny bent over at the waist and joined Jake in raucous laughter.

Jake swung his feet off his desk. "One thing's for sure, there's no underestimating the effect money has on the human spirit. Look at me. I felt like I made a hole in one from a thousand yards. Crazy, just crazy. But not a peep to Elena. She'll go ballistic if she ever finds out it's from a drug case."

Lenny stopped smiling. "I don't know. You sure that's the right call?"

"Jesus, you sound like Isora. Don't sweat it, I'll handle Elena. Besides, you think for a second, I'd pass up a hundred grand. No thank you. My daddy raised no fool."

Jake stood and paced behind his desk, feeling a rush of adrenalin like the time he had the dice in his hands for over an hour in Paradise Island's biggest casino, fellow gamblers pounding the table and chanting his name over and over again like he was a returning war hero.

"I don't know why I haven't done this before. Damn! Can you believe it? Pretty soon I'll be able to pay you a decent wage," Jake added with a laugh.

"Boss, I'd work for you for free," Lenny said, laughing right along. "But my landlady wouldn't go for it." He slumped into one of the armchairs across from Jake, his infectious smile bringing to mind the time the two of them had first met.

Only days after striking out on his own, Jake had been sitting at the bar in O'Malley's, checking to see if his horse had won in the fourth race at Hialeah. Half-way into Happy Hour, Lenny sauntered up, called out a Jake Daniels and ginger to one of bartenders, then slid onto the empty stool next to him.

"Whatcha drinking?" Lenny pointed to Jake's glass in front of him.

"Grey Goose on the rocks."

"Oh, I thought it might be club soda." Lenny grabbed a napkin in front of him and meticulously wiped drops of water from the surface of the bar. "There was a time I tried to stop."

Jake smiled. He instantly liked this guy, opening himself up to a total stranger. "I got one better. My wife, who I love to death, is constantly on my case about my betting on the ponies." Jake gestured to the race results in his lap. "She probably has a point but there's no way I can live without the action; it makes me feel so damn alive."

The conversation then expanded---Lenny talking nonstop---and within an hour and two rounds later Jake learned that Lenny had been a state court bailiff for fifteen years but currently on medical leave, collecting disability benefits. Six months before he had been shot and almost killed saving his judge from an assassination attempt. At the time, Jake was looking for an investigator who was okay with long hours and modest pay, and Lenny, at forty-seven, bored with watching spaghetti westerns at home, was seeking to boost his income. In spite of the age difference of nearly twenty years, they both knew the match was perfect.

The next day, Lenny, who had witnessed hundreds of trials as a bailiff, and had done some investigated work on the side, started work. He brought to the practice a street-wise savvy Jake sorely lacked, gained from growing up in a rough Italian neighborhood in Jersey City. Over the past four years, the two had grown close, like brothers each never had.

Jake pulled the calendar from the top of the credenza behind his desk, looking for open dates to inspect the Cessna. "While you were in Ft. Meyers, I had a great meeting with the client. Tifton was a passenger on that turboprop seized by Customs a couple of weeks back. The guy's an honest to God war hero, but you'd never know it. Really low key, down to earth, doesn't say much, suffers from PTSD. The jury will eat him up. Wait 'til you meet him."

Lenny shifted in his chair. "Sorry I couldn't be there."

"Couldn't wait. I might have lost him to another member of the Bar if I had."

"Like blood in the water," Lenny said with a chuckle. "Did Tifton tell you why the plane was snatched?"

"Not a hundred percent sure. Supposedly, they crossed the ADIZ without a flight plan, but you and I know there's gotta be more."

Lenny sighed. "There always is."

"Anyway," Jake continued, ignoring the quip, "his brother and a Mexican couple will swear he was with them in Cozumel at the time. That's where you come in. I need you to check out their story. If you're satisfied, we go with the alibi. It's the kind of case that can put us on the map. The guy just posted a million-dollar bond. Cash."

Lenny let out a soft whistle. "That's a lot of coin for a Florida Electric guy to come up with like that."

"I see you read the file. Yeah, it raised a red flag with me, too. His brother runs a charter boat business and apparently had the bucks to bail him out. Tifton swears he's innocent."

Lenny let loose a booming laugh that filled the room. "Shit, man. They all do."

Jake tried to suppress a smile. He had grown to appreciate Lenny's cynicism.

"What does the owner say about his plane being held by the feds? Can't be none too happy."

Jake shrugged. "Don't know. Red was scheduled to see me about it, but once Tifton was charged, I told him to hold off. The Cessna's now evidence in a criminal prosecution, and no judge would ever release it until the trial is over."

"Red?" Lenny snickered. "Perfect name for a druggie. Feels like I'm watching 'Scarface' all over again."

Jake chuckled. His PI loved any film or book that glamorized Miami's cocaine wars in the eighties. "A poker buddy who referred me the case says the guy's a hundred percent legit; a rich rancher in the business of buying large tracts of land. But I need to be sure."

Lines of concern spread across Lenny's face. "You know, Boss, Tifton wouldn't be the first ex-military type to run drugs. And if he's runnin' for the cartel, it's sure as shit not the kind of case to cut your teeth on. These Mexicans don't fuck around. And once you stick your nose in federal court, there's no getting out."

"Don't want to," Jake shot back, immediately regretting his retort. "Come on, L.B., loosen up. I wasn't born yesterday, and I sure as hell don't plan to take the guy's word for it. But we've just scored our biggest fee yet. Enjoy the moment. And even if he's bullshitting us, the guy still deserves the best defense we can give him."

"I get that."

"Let's say Tifton was running drugs, do you think he'd be dumb enough to say he was coming from *Mexico* when he could have picked a million other places?"

"Who's prosecuting?" Lenny asked, changing the subject.

"Some guy named Richter."

"I've heard of him, and he's not to be taken lightly." Lenny leaned back and sighed. "Just what you need on your first rodeo."

"Well, my money's on our war hero. You'll think different once you meet him. He's got a chest full of medals for jumping back into a burning chopper trying to save two of his buddies. I couldn't have asked for a better client."

"Impressive," Lenny agreed. "If he can convince me, he'll have no trouble with a jury."

"And who knows, you might even start believing in your fellow man again." Jake stole a glance at the jagged, two-inch scar running down Lenny's cheek, left by a sniper's bullet meant for his state court judge.

Jake went on to share with Lenny the details of Tifton's alibi. "How's your Spanish?"

"My Italian's better."

"Then, you'd better brush up. You're on your way to Cozumel to meet señor Diego Mendoza and his wife. Tifton's brother Dave will be there, too. Do what you do best, poke holes in the alibi. Without it there's not much of a defense. In the meantime, as they say in the military, watch your six. I hear Mexico is not for the faint of heart."

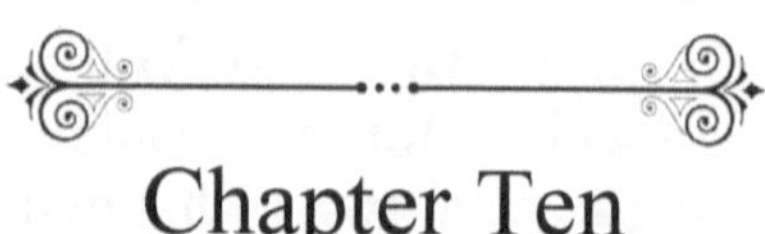

Chapter Ten

The minute Lenny cleared Customs at Cancun International and stepped outside into the sweltering heat he was struck by the overwhelming feeling of a war zone. Mexican *federales* dressed in fatigues with MP5 submachine guns and FX-05 Xiuhcoatl assault rifles were everywhere: in the streets, back alleys and on rooftops. Lenny had brushed up on Mexico's longstanding war against the cartels but he was not prepared for this.

He threw the daypack over his shoulder and ambled through the dusty streets trying to get a feel for this strange land. Scores of street vendors hawking red clay pots and cheap silver trinkets, some even brushing up against him to show off their wares, wouldn't leave him alone. He tried to avoid the posse of street kids in tattered clothing covered with grit and grime, their sad eyes pleading for loose change, but he couldn't do it. After doling out over forty bucks, Lenny elbowed his way through the crowds and hopped into the nearest taxi marked for Playa Del Carmen, a former fishing village sixty-five kilometers to the south. He was on his way to meet with Dave Tifton, Diego Mendoza and his wife, Gabriela to see if Tifton's alibi was the real deal. Lenny, a lifelong skeptic, had his doubts but he was hoping to be proved wrong.

After hitting every pothole known to exist in the state of Quintana Roo, the taxi arrived at the dock for a ferry to take him to Cozumel an hour later. Lenny handed the driver a fifty-dollar bill and hurried from the cab, making sure to grab his Nikon D3 in case Jack needed photographic evidence for trial. A line of natives and tourists calling attention to themselves in their flowery shirts had already formed to buy tickets. Lenny shaded his eyes from the morning sun and checked his watch: 8:56.

With an hour to kill before the next ferry, and with a recent snapshot of Tommy Tifton, Lenny spent the next forty-five minutes trying to find anyone—merchants, cabbies, bus drivers, bartenders,

—that might have remembered seeing Tifton the month before. Nothing. Not even a 'maybe.'

Once he arrived on the island of Cozumel, Lenny walked the pedestrian mall, its shops crammed with traditional *sombreros, guayaberas* and stitched leather cowboy boots, until he found *Café Loco,* where it had been agreed he would meet the three witnesses. The café, with paddle fans rotating above every table, reminded him of his high school days in Jersey City, when he and his buddies would skip algebra and make a beeline for Angelo's where they would sit, shoot the breeze and sip espressos, no different than his grandparents had done in *vecchia madrepatria,* the old country.

Lenny spotted his witnesses seated around a table in the far corner, seemingly in deep conversation. From his charter boat website, Lenny recognized the stocky, deeply tanned man with salt and pepper hair as Dave Tifton, and promptly approached their table.

Dave Tifton half rose from his chair and spoke first. "You must be Lenny." He stuck out his weathered hand.

Lenny shook it. "I won't ask how you knew."

Dave sat back down and beckoned Lenny to do the same. "Jake told me to look for a barrel-chested, pony-tailed Italian who could just as easily pass for a samurai."

Lenny nodded and caught the smiles from the handsome couple seated to his right. The man, evidently Diego Mendoza, had intense brown eyes set in a round, sun-drenched face. His bushy moustache perfectly matched his thick black hair, combed straight back, not a strand out of place. The woman beside him, presumably Mendoza's wife, appeared considerably younger. She looked classically Mexican—dark piercing eyes, a soft, smooth face and glistening black hair that flowed down her back.

Dave gestured to the couple. "Let me introduce you to—"

"Señora y señor Mendoza. Mucho gusto," Lenny said, trying out his Spanish.

Diego Mendozas grinned. *"Igualmente. Cómo estás?"*

Lenny held up his hands. "That's all I got. Took me a week to nail that."

Diego chuckled, then stood and shook Lenny's hand. "No *problema.* My wife, Gabriela and I speak English fluently. In fact, we met years ago—"

"Not so many, Diego," the señora chimed in with a smile that brightened the room.

Already, Mexico was beginning to look better, Lenny thought.

"*Sí, amorcita*," Diego answered back. "At the University of Miami, I studied international business and my lovely Gabriela, barely eighteen, majored in driving men crazy. To this day I have no idea why she chose me, but I thank the blessed Mary that she did." He took his wife's hand and gently brought it to his lips.

Gabriela laughed. "Diego, you're making me blush."

"Sit, please," Diego said, offering Lenny the empty chair. "Señor Dave mentioned you wouldn't have time to join us for lunch, but please, you must try the cappuccino. They tell me it's the best in all the Yucatan."

Lenny settled in his seat and pulled out his notepad. "One cup. I still got a full day ahead. I'd like to talk to each of you separately about Tommy's time in Cozumel." Lenny glanced down at his notes. "The weekend of June nineteenth." He placed his cassette recorder on the table. "Who wants to go first?"

Diego pulled out the chair for his wife to stand. "As you Americans say, 'blood is thicker than water.' Please start with *señor* Dave. My wife and I will be outside enjoying a cigarette." Then from inside his jacket he lifted papers stapled together and gave them to Lenny. "*Señor* Dave will want to discuss these with you." Diego took his wife's arm and led her from the café.

A pretty waitress, dressed in a low-cut pink blouse and pleated purple skirt, came and took their order. As soon as the *señorita* left, Lenny moved his chair closer to Dave and started recording. After announcing the date, time and name of the witness, he began.

"When did you and Tommy first make plans to fish in Cozumel?"

Dave shifted in his chair. "'Bout two weeks before. Guess you already know I own a condo here. I finally talked Tommy into getting some time off. He likes to fish, mostly fresh water but I told him he ain't lived till he's hooked a blue marlin in Caribbean waters. He and his fishin' buddy, Butch said they were a go so I signed 'em up."

"When did they get here?"

"Thursday, the eighteenth. Matter of fact I checked my calendar before you got here to make sure." Dave pointed to the papers in Lenny's hand. "It's a list of those who participated in the tournament.

If you go to the last page there's an official seal from the Cozumel Board of Tourism."

Lenny flipped to the last page and saw the blue-inked notarized stamp and raised seal.

"Diego is president of the board, so he was able to get that for us," Dave added. "You wouldn't know it but he comes from a long line of wealthy cattle ranchers, going back more than a hundred years."

Lenny studied the paper, dated, June 19, 2009. "I see Tommy's name but not Butch's."

"There," Dave said, leaning over and pointing his finger at the name Barry Dearing. "Butch came with me on the 'Bottoms Up' but I had to scratch Tommy after he got hit with food poisoning the night before."

"Yeah, I heard. But other than this paper, do you have anything else to prove that your brother was here?"

"Just our word, but I'll keep looking."

"You, Butch and Tommy had dinner after they arrived?"

"Yep, went to a local joint, more bar than restaurant. I gotta believe that's where Montezuma got his revenge, hit Tommy pretty hard. Strange 'cause we all ate the same thing. Frankly, I think it's from the war. You know Tommy had his guts blown to bits from an RPG while flying a mission in Iraq. He's damn lucky to be alive."

"What'd you three eat that night?"

Cochinita pibil. It's pork flavored with *achiote* and sour orange, then wrapped in banana leaves. Probably a side of fried plantains and refried black beans."

Lenny looked up from his notes. "You've got one helluva memory."

"I live to eat, besides that's what the place is known for."

As if on cue, the waitress returned with their coffees.

Lenny sipped his cappuccino. It didn't hold a candle to his mother's. "What'd Tommy do after he got sick?"

"I wanted him to lay low 'til we got back, but he wouldn't hear of it. Stubborn as a mule, and he's got this thing for history, so he ended up going to Chichén Itzá."

"I'm heading that way as soon as we're through here." Lenny glanced at his watch. "I've got a rental. Figure it'll take me three hours."

"Two and a half with a heavy foot. Tommy spent the better part of the day there, didn't return to my place till late that afternoon, pale as a ghost. I gave him a piece of my mind for not staying in bed, even thought about canceling plans for dinner; Diego and Gabriela came by that evening to meet him, but he wasn't much company. Tommy zonked out on the couch 'til it was time for him and Butch to go." Dave's gaze drifted off, he then seemed to catch himself and looked back at Lenny. "That war really did a number on my baby brother. Body and mind. Don't tell him I said so. He's got some kind of pride."

"What did Butch have to drink that night?"

"Wouldn't touch a drop. Said he had to fly."

Lenny glanced at his recorder to make sure it was still on. For the next thirty minutes he probed what Dave and Butch did that day, who may have seen them at the dock or fishing in open water, the number and kind of fish they caught and what time they returned to his condo.

"Why didn't Tommy stay the night if he was in such bad shape?"

"I tried but he wouldn't listen. There's no telling Tommy what to do once his mind is made up. Besides, there was a storm heading this way and apparently Butch had to get back to work and Tommy missed Jessie. If you ask me, she's got him by the cojones. He'll do whatever she says."

"What time did you take them to airport?"

"Around midnight, but it wasn't me. I was beat from being on the water all day. Diego and Gabriela were already going that way, so they gave them a lift."

"To Cozumel International?"

"No, the local airfield where the Cessna was already parked, and because Butch's a cheap sonofabitch, constantly complaining about landing fees. I spent two days with the guy eating *my* food, fishing off *my* boat, and he never once bought me a beer."

"Did Tommy ever mention a Red Armstrong, the owner of the Cessna? I've been trying to reach him, but he's hard to track down."

Dave shook his head. "Wish I could help. But his name never came up."

"Okay, that's pretty much it for now. I'm sure I'll have more the closer we get to trial." Lenny switched off the recorder and took another sip of his cappuccino.

Dave shook Lenny's hand and left.

For the next hour, Lenny questioned the Mendozas separately about the fishing tournament, their relationship with Dave and the time spent with Butch and Tommy that Friday evening before the two men left for the States. Their stories matched almost perfectly with Dave's, even down to the grilled chicken, guacamole, black beans, and rice Dave served for dinner. Too perfectly, Lenny thought.

After waving his goodbyes, Lenny picked up his rental at Playa del Carmen and raced off to *Chichén Itzá*, not that he had any interest spending time at old ruins. He hoped against hope to find something, anything, other than just the word of these witnesses and a piece of paper. But after spending the rest of the day talking with cab drivers, tourist guides and ticket takers at the popular tourist site, Lenny was no closer to answering his doubts about Tifton and his alibi. As soon as he returned to the good old U S of A, he would report back that the alibi was not nearly as airtight as Jake initially thought.

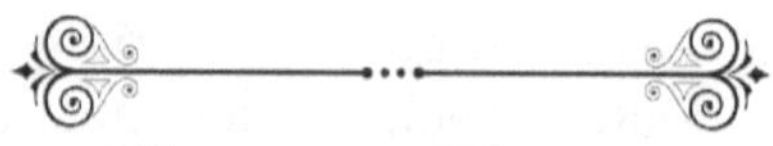

Chapter Eleven

While driving south on U.S. 1 toward the Homestead Air Force Base, Jake pressed the speed dial on his cell to his good friend, Mitch Bernstein, a former prosecutor with the Department of Justice's Strike Force and now in private practice. After Lenny's reaction in their meeting, Jake was eager to learn more about Tifton's lead prosecutor, Assistant U.S. Attorney Crawford Richter, and knew no better person to ask than Mitch.

"Jake Dalton!" Mitch shouted through the phone. "How the hell are you? You'd better be calling to split a fee or I'm hanging up. I'm overdue for a new Mercedes."

Jake chuckled at the thickness of Mitch's Brooklyn accent. "As a matter of fact, I did just score one, but nothing in the stratosphere you're used to." Jake pictured the fifty-something, former mob prosecutor with his ruddy round face, thick mustache, and unkempt hair, sitting with the worn soles of his penny loafers pressed against the edge of his antique desk.

"To what do I owe the honor?"

"I've decided to venture into your line of work, took on a drug case. I need the lowdown on an Assistant U.S. Attorney. The name's Richter."

Mitch's response was immediate. "Total dick. I've known the guy since our days at Rutgers Law and he was a prick then. Unfortunately, he's sneaky-smart with over twenty-five years' experience. Probably Mattson's best prosecutor."

"The U.S. Attorney?"

"Yeah, but Richter calls the shots. He's got his sights on being the next AG."

"Any words to the wise? I'm on my way to meet a DEA agent to check out a plane."

"Watch your back. Richter doesn't take prisoners. And don't let him bully you. About a year ago he got hosed by a fellow defense lawyer, whose name will remain anonymous. Richter now has a hard on for the rest of us."

"Sounds like fun," Jake said, trying to make light of the warning, but he knew better.

"You'll be fine. Richter doesn't have near your smarts. But be careful, when the two of you go at it, give the prick your best shot, then break free. It's the counter-punch that'll kill you."

After clearing the checkpoint at the Homestead Air Force Base, Jake drove to hangar 24 and killed the engine. He studied the turboprop, smaller than he envisioned, parked outside. Two men, both in charcoal gray suits, color-matched to the dreary skies, stood close by, presenting a picture of opposites. One was white, in his fifties, well-built with broad shoulders and Marine-cut hair, the other was a shorter black man, slender with a close-cropped afro, who appeared to be ten years younger. His small eyes darted behind wire-rimmed glasses.

"Agent Nettles," Jake said, extending his hand to the Marine-cut. "I'm Jake Dalton. Two grim faces stared back at him.

"So, you're Dalton," Marine-cut said, his tone icy, ignoring Jake's hand. "And the name's Richter, Assistant U.S. Attorney."

"I'm Special Agent Nettles," said the shorter man with glasses, shaking Jake's hand.

Jake stared back at Richter. "I didn't expect you here. Have we met before?"

"Before you board the plane," Richter said, ignoring the question, "we need to discuss prospective trial dates and report back to Judge Henry. A status conference has been scheduled in two weeks."

"Judge Henry?" Jake's stomach lurched. He had forgotten to ask Isora which judge had been assigned the case and she apparently hadn't the nerve to tell him. As former state-wide prosecutor, Henry was known for running a tight ship, and handing down maximum sentences every chance he got. A prosecutor's dream.

"That's right," Richter shot back. "Then you know this judge won't tolerate delays."

"Assuming there is a trial. What's your position on a possible plea?" Jake studied the prosecutor, trying to gauge just how confident Richter was in his case.

"In cases of this kind, we don't negotiate, that is, unless your client is prepared to plead guilty to all counts and provide complete cooperation."

"You can't be serious?" Jake was stunned by the prosecutor's arrogance. "Even if my client were guilty, where's the incentive for him to bend over like that?"

Richter scoffed. "What's the matter, counselor? Not ready for prime time? In any event, our mandate is to prosecute these cases to the fullest extent of the law. No exceptions."

"That's it? That's all you have to say?" Mitch was right. The guy was a dick.

"See you in court." With that, Richter did a one eighty and marched inside the hangar, leaving Nettles to oversee Jake's inspection of the plane.

Unnerved by Richter's attitude, Jake stood for several moments in front of the aircraft to collect his thoughts. He then climbed the steps into the Cessna and was instantly hit by the overpowering smell of kerosene. Jake covered his nose with his hand and moved to the cramped cockpit to study the complex instrument panel, marveling at the skill it must have taken to fly through a tropical storm. He could only imagine Tifton's abject fear that night. On his right, he noticed a smear of blood caked on the inside of the passenger's side window and recalled Tifton mentioning that he had smashed his nose. Ducking as he left the cockpit, Jake walked on the exposed metal floor into the passenger cabin. No seats, yet plenty of room to stack bags of cocaine. "This is bad," he muttered to himself. Lenny was right; any fool could see the aircraft was outfitted for transporting drugs, and no way to explain this away to a jury. As he walked through the empty cabin, a dark spot on the floor near the plane's rear wall caught Jake's eye. He knelt and rubbed his finger along a dry rusty stain.

An hour later, as Jake drove from the Air Force base, his mind drifted back to the acrimonious encounter outside the hangar, recalling Mitch's words about Richter having it in for defense attorneys. Yet, Jake sensed there was more to it than that, much more. This federal prosecutor seemed to have it in for him personally, and Jake was at a loss to understand why.

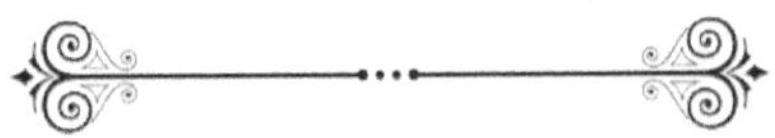

Chapter Twelve

Over the especially humid summer, Jake spent countless hours transitioning his practice from personal injury to criminal defense, and now he could breathe a sigh of relief. With fees from Tifton and other smaller criminal cases Lenny helped bring in, his firm was at last on a solid footing. That, coupled with news of Drew's steadily improving health, gave Jake reason to believe that his life had indeed turned around. Even Elena seemed more relaxed and affectionate, less in fear that their financial Armageddon was just around the corner.

For the Labor Day weekend, he drove with Elena and the kids to Sanibel Island, which had been one of Jake's favorite spots to hunt for sea shells as a boy. As waves gently lapped onto the shore, Jake snuggled against Elena, enjoying the feel of her warm body. From a distance, he gazed longingly at Drew and Nicole, who were busy erecting a sandcastle, giggling at each other non-stop.

Jake planted small kisses on Elena's bare shoulder, inhaling her heady perfume. "You were incredible last night."

She twisted her head around and kissed him softly on the lips. "You weren't so bad yourself. But next time we're definitely taking my parents up on their offer to take the kids. I couldn't stop thinking we were about to wake them in the next room."

Jake laughed. "We? I was about to cover your mouth so—"

"Shush!" Elena's face reddened. "You have only yourself to blame for that," she added with a laugh. She glanced at her watch. "We should be getting back. Alligator Alley will be a madhouse, especially on Labor Day."

Jake sighed. "I can't believe how fast the weekend flew by. Back to the grind."

"Tough week ahead?"

"Not particularly, but next month's a whole different story. I start this monster of trial. Lenny's already prepping witnesses."

"What's it about?"

Jake hesitated. He'd been dodging her questions about Tifton's case ever since Jake took him on as a client. This was the time to come clean, but he knew that if he told Elena he had taken on a drug case, especially one the size of Tifton's, she'd go apoplectic; the entire weekend would be ruined, if not more. Jake understood he'd soon have to make it up to her for his deception, but now was not the time. "I'm representing a real estate developer charged with filing fraudulent tax returns. Some nut job from the Department of Justice is in charge. He seems to have it in for my client."

Elena's eyes narrowed.

"Nothing to worry about," Jake added. "It's my client's problem, not mine."

Jake bolted from Tifton's pretrial conference and furiously punched the number to Lenny's cell. After the second ring, his PI answered.

"L.B., you're not going to believe this fucking judge. Everything I heard about him is true. For the entire hearing he was practically cheering the government on. I'm sure he already has our guy convicted and only sorry he has to go through the charade of a trial before throwing the book at him. And, of course, Richter was there, self-righteous as ever." Jake pulled his car keys from his briefcase and took a deep breath. "I need a stiff drink."

"You got it. I'm heading into the restaurant as we speak. What's your ETA?"

"I'm leaving the courthouse now. Be there in twenty."

Jake pulled into the Spanish-styled entrance of La Noche, Lenny's favorite restaurant in Coconut Grove to brainstorm cases and satiate his appetite for eye candy. The attractive hostess in a long flowing dress greeted Jake and showed him to a table overlooking the flower garden. Fresh-cut red and orange hibiscus adorned every table. He surveyed the restaurant and, feeling self-conscious, straightened his tie. Business types in designer suits filled every seat. Lenny, bent over and munching an appetizer, had yet to notice him.

"Glad you went ahead without me," Jake offered, as he settled into the empty chair across from his PI. "Traffic was a bear."

Lenny looked up, crumbs from the shrimp roll clinging to his lip. "Probably from the drive-by," he said, chewing as he spoke. "Everyone's talkin' about it. Couldn't have been more than a couple blocks from here. Driver took one in the head, can't even identify what's left of his face. SWAT's tearing up the Grove lookin' for the shooter or shooters unknown."

"You seem pretty blasé about it."

"You forget, it's Miami."

The shapely waitress sashayed over, placed a vodka on the rocks in front of Jake's ornate place setting and left. Lenny's eyes stayed on her like a heat-seeking missile as her hips moved side to side. He grinned at Jake. "Now *that* should be our next receptionist."

"Yeah, sure. I can only imagine how much work you'll get done."

Lenny pulled a notepad from his pocket. "I did more checking after I got back from Mexico. Here's the update from our last meet."

Jake nodded. "Bottom line. Will the alibi hold up? We might as well hang a sign 'gone fishing' if it doesn't."

"Bottom line. Wish I knew."

Jake felt the muscles in his neck tighten. "I don't like the sound of that."

"Wish like hell I could say more. The Mexican couple seem credible enough, and they're well respected in the community. And as I told you before, brother Dave's a little too smooth for my taste, as if he's reading off a script. We only got their word, no receipts, photos, to document their trip. Zip. Nada. The senor and his exquisite senora go into great detail about their time with Tifton, but then again, they could be bought and paid for. After all, it is *Meh-i-co*," he said, imitating a thick Mexican accent. "Everything adds up. Too perfectly. It's just that I don't like that the hair on the back of my neck rises up whenever I think that these people could be playing us."

"We've got no choice but to go with the alibi unless we *know* different. That's our solemn duty to the client. Do you know different?"

Lenny shook his head. "I'm working on it."

"You keep doing that. What else?"

"After trading a half dozen calls the past two weeks, we finally got a report from our expert."

"Cunningham? What'd he say?"

"The guy spent the better part of two hours crawling through the Cessna on his hands and knees, no less. I don't know how the guy does it, given his age."

"For Chrissakes, what did he say?" Lenny's idea of getting to the point was to fly from Miami to New York by way of Seattle.

"He confirms the Cessna was clearly outfitted for an extra fuel bladder." Lenny rolled his eyes. "No surprise there, and no use arguing the plane couldn't make it from Colombia, Peru, Bolivia or wherever the hell they grow the stuff."

"Does Armstrong have an answer?"

"Red? I tried reaching the guy too many times to count. He doesn't have an office and is never in town. I even called your poker buddy to see if he could help. If you ask me, we're getting the royal run around."

"I'll call Pendleton, see what gives. We need to button Red down. Trial starts in a month.

"There's more. Cunningham also studied the radar findings from the MacDill Air Force Base and the nearby height finder. I just hope he's around for trial."

Jake shot up in his seat. Cunningham was critical to their defense. "What the hell does that mean?"

"The guy's ancient, easily north of eighty and the first black guy to graduate from MIT with honors in engineering and aeronautics. He's crazy qualified, but I gotta warn you, the guy's bent like a pretzel over testifying in a drug case. Says he's never done it and practically wants a written guarantee he won't have a problem."

"L.B., you're killing me. What does he say about the radar?"

Lenny's face opened into a wide grin. "Our good doctor will testify that there's a glitch of some kind, probably from the storm. The height finder was totally fucked up, impossible to measure a plane's altitude. In fact, it shows a radio tower sticking up in the air at four thousand feet. If I were the government, I'd be shittin' bricks." Lenny separated his hands by several inches. "Big ones. And that's not all. He'll also swear that radar lost the plane on three separate occasions and that the Customs aircraft, a Citation II, was miles from our plane when the coke was allegedly tossed. That means they can't account for the Cessna for a full twenty minutes, and given where they found the coke, no way Customs could have seen the bags tossed."

Jake slapped his hand on the table. "That's fantastic!"

Nearby guests stopped eating and stared at Jake.

Lenny smiled. "It gets better."

"Keep it coming, I'm loving it. Man, I can't wait to try this case."

"I asked Cunningham to check and see if radar picked up other aircraft in the vicinity that night. Would you believe three, all coming south to north and along an almost identical track as our guy. It fits perfectly into what Tifton's been saying all along, that Customs got the wrong plane."

Jake couldn't stop smiling. "If you weren't such a cynic, I'd kiss you. Our expert has turned out to be worth every dime. In fact, Tommy says spare no expense, his brother's footing all costs."

"Where they getting this money?"

"Who cares? Len, you've met our war hero. The fact that you didn't come into my office screaming 'the sonofabitch's guilty' tells me something, right?"

"Tifton's a tough read, I'll give you that." For Lenny, that was huge.

Jake swallowed the rest of his drink. "Then it's decided. We go with the alibi. There's a chance he might be guilty, but that's the jury's job to decide, not ours. Besides, I like our odds that he's not."

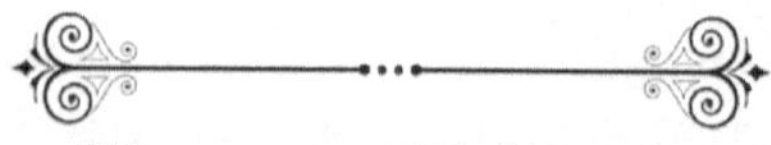

Chapter Thirteen

Less than twenty-four hours before the start of U.S. vs. Tifton, Crawford Richter looked up from reading a secret grand jury report and grabbed his phone on the third ring. He pressed the button to his private line. "Yes?"

"Didn't know if I'd catch you in on such a perfect Sunday afternoon," began the familiar female voice.

"It's hot and muggy here, and I'm sure nothing like the Potomac this time of year. What's on your mind? I start trial in the morning."

"I know." She hesitated. "I need a favor."

"If I can."

"Forget Tifton, plead him out if you have to. In the scheme of things, he's nothing more than a nuisance, a small one at that. There'll be others to make you look good."

Richter kneaded the back of his neck. "You couldn't have called me with this months ago? I've already committed valuable time and resources to this case. Besides, he's not the one we need to worry about."

"The rookie," she scoffed. "He doesn't know anything."

"We can't be sure."

"This isn't like you, Crawford. You need to keep your eye on the bigger prize."

"I am, but I've got too much at stake to take any chances. No promises, but I'll see what I can do."

"Listen," she said, her tone turning icy, "we can't afford for our little enterprise to get out in the open. If you continue with the case, you risk ruining everything over one guy. Tifton's nothing to us, do you hear, *nothing*. Just do as I ask and deep-six the goddamn file. I won't have your paranoia destroy what we've worked hard to get." She hung up.

"Fuck you," Richter screamed into the dead line. He stared at the phone for several moments, then ripped it from the wall and flung it across the room.

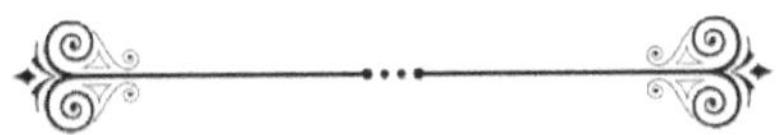

Chapter Fourteen

The next morning, Jake led Tifton and Lenny past a throng of spectators into Courtroom 8-1 of the Miami U.S. District Courthouse, minutes before jury selection and the start of trial. Bright lights, recessed high over dull gray-colored walls, gave the long rectangular room its intended somber effect. Jake took his seat at the defense table and tried to appear relaxed, but inside he was anything but. He smoothed his burgundy striped tie, making sure it lay snug inside his blue suit, and patted his dad's pocket watch for luck.

Tifton, seated between Jake and Lenny, appeared confident. He looked sharp in a dark gray suit and fire-engine red tie over a crisp white shirt. Jake had put the fear of God into him if he didn't do exactly as Jake said.

Richter and Nettles, whispering to each other, were seated side by side at the prosecution table several feet away.

Tommy leaned over to Jake. "I've seen funerals more alive than this."

"Tell me about it," Jake said, trying to keep a straight face.

Minutes later, Judge Henry settled behind his raised bench and called potential jurors to their seats inside the jury box and began the process of determining their qualifications to serve. He questioned the jurors generally about their background, education, work experience, and whether there was anything that would prevent them from being fair and impartial in reaching a verdict.

"Juror number two," the judge called, leaning back in his tall chair, "in view of the unusually high publicity surrounding this case, do you hold any preconceived notions regarding the guilt of the defendant that would prevent you from being objective?"

An elderly white man with eyelids drooping halfway over his eyes shook his head. "No, Judge. I can be fair."

"Juror number seven. Is there anything that would keep you from being open minded as you listen to the evidence?"

The juror straighten her short gray hair and smiled. "No, Your Honor."

"What about you, juror nine?"

Juror nine stared down at her lap, hesitated for several seconds, then shook her head.

Jake knew that this kind of questioning—mechanical, generic— would never expose a juror's hidden bias, and if left unchecked would leave Tifton with little chance of a fair trial. He glanced at the answers to the jurors' questionnaire handed in before trial and stood.

"Your Honor, I'd like to question juror number six about her son's recent cocaine addiction and whether that would affect her ability to be fair and impartial."

The judge squinted at Jake, obviously annoyed at the interruption. "Counsel, I've already ruled on that matter at pretrial. The *court* will conduct *voir dire*. Are we clear? If there is something in particular, you'd like for me to ask, put it in writing and I'll consider it. Now let's move on, I intend to seat a jury before lunch."

At ten past noon, having exhausted all of his preemptory challenges, Jake sat back and anxiously watched eight men, four women and two alternates sworn in to decide his client's fate. Two of the men in the front row, both retired military with buzz-cut hair and wearing replicas of American flags pinned to their lapels, sat tight-lipped, making it impossible for Jake to get a good read.

After precisely one hour for lunch, the judge took the bench. "Is the government ready to make its opening statement?"

"Yes, Your Honor." Richter rose from behind his counsel table, buttoned the jacket of his brown three-piece suit, and marched to the lectern. He raised the microphone several inches to accommodate his height, then faced the panel.

"Members of the jury. The case before you today represents a testament to the government's never-ending battle to win the war on drugs. This past summer, during the early morning hours of June twentieth, the defendant Thomas Tifton and one Barry Dearing, alias Butch, did knowingly conspire to import approximately one thousand kilos of cocaine, with a street value of over sixty million dollars, into the United States. They did so in the black of night, trying to use the cover of a tropical storm to escape detection. Thankfully, the brave men of the Air Force and U.S. Customs were there to make sure that didn't happen. But these drug smugglers were cunning, and more than a little experienced in their nefarious ways. The evidence will show that after being forced to land at the Opa-Locka regional airport, the defendant Tifton, Dearing and their Cessna aircraft were searched and no drugs were found. At the time, the defendant believed his ruse had worked and foolishly assumed that by tossing the load of cocaine from the plane before landing, he'd be home free." Richter took a step toward the jury. "We're here to prove him wrong, dead wrong. Because of tireless efforts of federal and local law enforcement, the cocaine pitched from the Cessna was found days later, strewn across the Everglades. Through expert analysis and visual observation, the government was able to connect the cocaine to the very plane flown in by the defendant. And who are the people that this defendant conspires when he smuggles dangerous drugs into this great land of ours? None other than the most violent criminal enterprise in the Southern Hemisphere: The Santolisma cartel, known for slicing off the heads of innocent women and children for no other reason than they enjoy it."

A few jurors winced.

Jake rose from his chair. "Objection, inflammatory."

"Sustained. Dial it back, counselor," the judge cautioned.

Richter nodded, but his point was made. Tifton was no run of the mill drug runner, he, and the cartel he worked for represented a threat to the American way of life.

"Ladies and Gentlemen," Richter continued, "you will also hear from members of the Air Force and Customs as well as aviation experts who will testify that the Cessna in question was specially outfitted for trafficking. I am confident that once all the evidence is in you will reach the only proper verdict—that the defendant is guilty of all charges in the indictment."

Several jurors nodded in agreement.

Judge Henry peered down at Jake. "Counsel, do you wish to address the jury?"

"Thank you, Your Honor. I'll be brief." Jake walked to the lectern, then waited for the coughing in the packed gallery to stop.

"Good afternoon. My name is Jake Dalton and I represent Tommy Tifton. Now that you've heard the prosecution's side of the story, and I emphasize story, let me tell you what the *evidence* will really show. First and foremost, my client readily admits to being on the Cessna Conquest during the night in question. He further admits that the seats of the plane were stripped out but you'll learn that he didn't know that such was the case until he boarded the Cessna for the very first time only days before. The evidence will further show that after he and the plane were searched, no drugs were found. Why? Simple. He wasn't carrying any."

Several of the jurors chuckled.

"That's what the *evidence* will show," Jake repeated. "If there was a plane transporting drugs through the storm that night, it wasn't the one Tommy Tifton was on. The defense will also show, even though the judge will instruct you that the burden of proof always remains with the government, that it was physically impossible for my client to have smuggled drugs into the country that night." Out of the corner of his eye, Jake caught Richter's puzzled look. "You, ladies, and gentlemen of the jury, will also have an opportunity to examine the personal and professional life of Army Special Forces Specialist E-4 Tifton—a badly wounded and decorated hero of Desert Storm, a tireless fleet manager at Florida Electric for the past seventeen years, and a loving husband to his wife, Jessie. I'm confident that once y'all hear and evaluate the evidence, you will return the only verdict that is just: a verdict of not guilty. Thank you." Jake returned to sit beside Tommy who gave Jake a satisfied smile.

"All right," the judge said, gesturing to Richter. "Call your first witness."

The prosecutor stood. "The government calls Colonel Clifford Stevens, United States Air Force."

A stout, square-jawed man in uniform, his chest adorned with a row of medals, marched down the center aisle, past the spectators, and stood at rigid attention in front of the witness stand. He tucked his hat under his arm and gazed at the flag, his eyes never leaving Old Glory while the clerk administered the oath.

"Nice touch," Jake whispered to Lenny. "I wonder if Richter opens all his trials with the Star-Spangled Banner."

"Colonel Stevens," Richter began, "let me draw your attention to the early morning hours of June 20. Were you on duty at that time?"

"Affirmative. Beginning at 1800 hours I was in charge of the Command Center at MacDill Air Force Base."

"Please tell the jury what you observed."

"At approximately 01:15, the airman monitoring the control tower informed me of a breach of the ADIZ, that's the Air Defense

Identification Zone. A single unidentified aircraft, flying eighty miles west of Cuba and maintaining a speed of two hundred and eighty knots, heading north by northeast, was approaching the southwest coast of Florida."

"What action did you take?"

"I confirmed the intruder's track and speed and ordered my staff to full alert. I needed to make sure Castro hadn't lost his damn mind."

The gallery roared with laughter.

The judged banged his gavel. "I'll have none of that in my courtroom."

Richter waited for the room to turn quiet and continued. "What did you do then, Colonel?"

"I ordered Homestead to scramble two F-16s, intercept the target and report back to me before taking offensive action."

"Did the F-16s comply?"

"Of course. Thunder One, the lead pilot, notified that interception had occurred at 01:36, and that—"

Jake rose to his feet. "Objection, Your Honor. Hearsay."

Judge Henry shifted his eyes to Richter, who wasted no time.

"Your Honor, the government is simply trying to elicit from the Colonel a history of relevant events to explain why he did what he did."

"Overruled. I'd like to hear more."

Jake's gritted his teeth. This trial was going to be *very* long. He needed to use his objections sparingly so not to alienate the judge or the jury, but on the other hand, he couldn't let Richter have free rein.

Stevens further testified that the fighter jets intercepted an unidentified turboprop over the Gulf of Mexico and that the intruder had no lights or transponder. The fighter pilots verified the target was not equipped with weaponry and posed no threat to national security. The Colonel therefore ordered the F-16s to withdraw but not before notifying U.S. Customs to take up pursuit.

Tommy bent toward Jake. "That wasn't me."

"I know," Jake whispered back, "but keep your eyes on the witness. I can't have the jury think you're bothered by his testimony."

Richter soon concluded his direct. Jake debated whether to ask the Colonel any questions, believing no real harm had been done. However, he did have a few points to make and rose from his chair.

"Colonel, just a couple of questions. Were the radar systems in good working order that evening?"

"Affirmative, except for the height finder. It had been temporarily impacted by the storm but was fully operational by 0400."

"Then you would agree that its findings regarding the height of aircraft flying in the vicinity, between the hours of midnight and four A.M., were not reliable? True?"

Stevens didn't answer.

"Colonel, did you hear my question? I'll have the court reporter read it back, if you like."

The Colonel avoided Jake's stare. "The height finder for a very brief time was not fully operational."

"That doesn't answer my question."

"Not reliable during the hours questioned."

"Thank you. One last thing, sir. How many aircraft did MacDill radar pick up between midnight and three that morning, and, if you know, their heading?"

"A total of three. All tracking south to north."

"All in the identical direction as the target aircraft, correct?"

"Affirmative."

Jake nodded in agreement. "No further questions."

Richter next called Captain Harry Gunter to the stand. The Customs pilot with thinning gray hair, beefy cheeks and a protruding belly stepped nimbly past the seated spectators, through the railing's waist-high swinging doors, stopping in front of the raised bench to be sworn in. His nostrils flared like a bull's.

Tommy grabbed Jake's arm. "That's the SOB I told you about. He loved sticking a shotgun in my face the second me and Butch landed."

"Captain Gunter." Richter's began. "How long have you been flying for the Air Branch of U.S. Customs?"

"Ten years. Fifteen years Air Force before that." Gunter sat erect in his chair; his broad chest pressed tight against the too small uniform jacket.

"And while serving our country any luck catching drug smugglers?"

Jake bolted from his seat. "Objection! That's—"

"Relax, Mr. Dalton," the judge said before turning to Richter. "Why don't you rephrase the question? I assume you're seeking to establish the law enforcement expertise of the witness?"

"Precisely, Your Honor."

And while you're at it, might as well try Richter's case for him, Jake muttered to himself. He passed a note to Lenny. *Are drug trials always like this?*

Lenny gave an emphatic nod.

Richter continued. "Captain, would you tell the jury what you observed in the early morning hours of June 20 of this year?"

Gunter leaned forward and adjusted his microphone. "Me and my crew were playing a friendly game of poker at the air base in Homestead. At approximately 01:40, the phone began ringing off the hook. I was having one helluva night, but I had to grab the call."

The jurors laughed.

The witness put his hand against his ear as if holding a receiver. "'Gunter here.' I learned that Control had intercepted an incoming aircraft, identified only as a turboprop with probable contraband, heading north by northeast toward the Florida Keys. My orders were to intercept ASAP. I hung up, grabbed my crew, and raced to the tarmac, but not before throwing down my hand, a full boat, three queens and two aces. I wanted my guys to know that phone call saved them a shi—uh, bunch of money." Gunter waved his hand to apologize.

Several jurors, including the two ex-military in the front row, turned to each other and smiled. They truly liked this guy. Concerned, Jake began to rise, then sat back down. Most of what Gunter had said was objectionable, but Jake would let it go. It'd be worse for the jury to think that his testimony had hurt or that the defense had something to hide.

"I cranked up the turbojet, a Citation II," Gunter continued, "and while we taxied, my co-pilot jotted down the speed and coordinates of the target given by Control before taking off." The Customs pilot squirmed in his seat as though reliving that night. "Those winds were somethin' else, never flown in anything like 'em before. But the Citation gave us superior speed and soon we caught up to the turboprop, flying without lights, over the Florida Straits, fifty-five miles southwest of Dry Tortugas. My co-pilot had on infrared goggles and was the first to spot 'em. But he couldn't get a fix on the target's N number on account of the storm."

Richter turned to the jury. "Captain, explain to the jurors what an N number is?"

"N means North America, followed by the plane's serial number."

"Please continue."

"The rain was coming down in buckets, making it impossible to see. Every couple of minutes I wiped condensation off the windshield, asking for the target's location, 'cause we were practically flying blind."

Jake jotted down the captain's last comment.

"Then all of a sudden, my co-pilot starts shouting that the target was at four o'clock. The winds were so loud I could hardly hear myself think. I dipped the nose of the Citation and aimed straight for the target. But I've gotta give props to that pilot, he knew what he was doing, mixing up his speed and altitude, using the clouds to his advantage."

"Captain, would it surprise you to learn that the man flying the Cessna that night, Barry Dearing, who goes by the name Butch, is a former Navy pilot, in fact a graduate of Top Gun, a Navy fighter weapons school?"

Gunter nodded. "That certainly explains it."

"What did you do next?"

"I ordered my crew to set up the FLIR. It's the Forward Looking Infra-Red recorder to capture nighttime activity. Then, before long he started hollering at the top of his lungs." 'Captain, those guys aren't ditching their plane, it's the load they're ditching! Bags are flying out like bombs over Baghdad!' I immediately radioed Control the coordinates of the drop, but we never did get his N number."

"Captain Gunter, did you eventually catch up to the target?"

"You bet." Gunter gloated. "We chased that plane for better part of an hour and landed minutes behind him at the Opa Locka Airport, twenty miles northwest of Miami." He went on to recite that his crew searched Tommy and Butch, and their plane, for weapons and contraband, but found none. The two were then released for lack of evidence.

"Captain, can you point to anyone in the courtroom who was on board the Cessna when it landed that night?"

Gunter stabbed his finger at Tommy. "That's him. No doubt about it."

The judge looked down at the court reporter. "Let the record reflect that the witness has identified the defendant, Thomas Tifton."

Jake slid Tommy a note. *His ID proves nothing.*

"One final question, sir. Prior to going off duty that morning, did you confirm with your superiors the coordinates pinpointing where the bags had been thrown from the Cessna?"

"Yup. And they matched up perfectly to where the cocaine was later found on the ground. It confirmed what I saw—that the contraband came from the very Cessna Conquest we chased and caught up to that night."

Richter pivoted to Jake. "Your witness."

Jake buttoned his suit jacket and stepped to the lectern, his eyes never leaving the jury. He couldn't wait to wipe the smirk off Richter's face.

"Captain Gunter. Sounds like you had a pretty unforgettable night."

"You can say that again. I've never flown through anything like it and hope to never again." The captain eased back in his chair.

"And during this hour or so you were in the air pursuing the target, you never did get a positive ID of the aircraft or its occupants. Is that correct?"

"Well, we think—"

"Sir, I didn't ask what you think. I'm asking what you're sure of. Let me remind you that you're under oath."

Gunter shook his head. "No, can't say we did."

Jake's confidence grew. "In fact, you lost sight of the plane you were chasing on more than one occasion that night. Isn't that also a fact?"

"But we always found it minutes later." Gunter loosened his tie.

"What you found was an aircraft, but not necessarily the same one. By your own admission the plane had neither lights nor a transponder to help you track it. Isn't that true, sir?"

"True."

"Wouldn't you agree with me that the radar reports during the night in question represent a more accurate record of the varying distances between you and the target, more so than your recollection?"

Gunter fidgeted in his chair. "I guess so."

"And for the record, you personally didn't see the bags dropped from the plane you were chasing, correct? It was your co-pilot, because he was the one wearing infrared goggles?"

"That's right."

"And when your co-pilot told you the bags were being tossed from the plane, 'like bombs over Bagdad,' how do you explain that radar had you positioned eleven miles from the target?"

Gunter shifted in his chair and stammered. "I-I can't."

"Your visibility during the storm wasn't eleven miles, was it?" Jake stole a glance at the jurors. A confused look spread across their faces.

"I don't think so."

"It was more like *one* mile, correct?" Jake knew he had him.

Rivulets of sweat appeared on Gunter's brow. "I'm not sure."

"You're not sure. And how many years have you been flying?

"Many, many."

"Well then. What's your best estimate?"

Gunter lowered his eyes and said nothing for several seconds. "'Bout a mile."

Jake paused to let the words sink in and repeated them to the jury. "'Bout a mile." He smiled inside, pleased that the jury would go home with this last piece of evidence on their minds, knowing that the testimony of custom's pilot could not be trusted. Jake looked up at the judge. "That's all I have, your Honor."

Judge Henry glanced at Richter, whose shake of the head indicated he had no redirect. "We stand adjourned until tomorrow at nine." The judge slammed down his gavel and scurried from the bench, unlikely seeing Jake turn to Lenny with a wide grin.

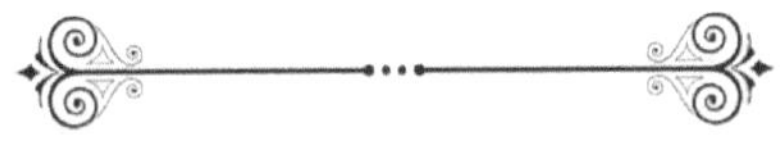

Chapter Fifteen

Jake pushed through the courthouse's revolving doors, pausing at the bottom of the steps to take in the fresh air. "Aren't you loving this?" He called to Lenny a half-step behind.

"Take it easy, Boss. It's only day one. We've got miles to go."

"God, I feel so alive, but you're right. This trial is moving like a rocket. Richter will most likely wrap up his case in a couple of days, so we've got to be ready to go by Thursday. Get Cunningham on the horn and tell him to study the radar reports once more and fly in Wednesday. The guy's more important than ever. He's got to emphasize the radar can't be trusted, and that Customs was more than ten miles from their target at the time of the drop. No way they coulda seen the bags tossed. They're making it up to cover their ass."

"Got it." Lenny's face beamed with excitement.

"Like I keep tellin' ya, they got it all wrong," Tommy said, almost tripping down the steps to keep up.

Jake reached the sidewalk and lowered his briefcase. "Len, put Cunningham up at the Sonata on Key Biscayne. I'll meet him there for breakfast first thing Thursday. Make it seven. Have the Mendozas fly in Thursday. We may get to them Friday, but probably not until Monday."

Jake turned to Tommy. "You'll testify last. I'll get with you and Jessie tomorrow night to make sure your memories match. I can't have you blowing up under Richter's cross."

"I've faced plenty worse."

Jake nodded. "I'm sure you have."

"Jessie, then Dave will go on after Cunningham," Jake added. "I need her to talk up your Bronze Star and Purple Heart and the pain you live through every single day. OK?" Jake didn't wait for an answer. "I've already subpoenaed the VA records custodian to back her up. You're a war hero for chrissakes, so milk it for all it's worth. I don't have to remind you what's at stake."

Tommy glanced at Jessie behind the wheel, who had already pulled up to the nearby curb with the engine running. "She can do that."

"She also needs to discuss that the two of you go to church regularly and that you're trying to have a baby. That's important." Jake intended to paint a picture of a God-fearing, apple-pie-eating all American couple.

Tommy reached into his pocket and popped a pill.

"What the hell is that?" Jake asked, startled.

"Antidepressant, afternoon dose. I use 'em to take the edge off." He pulled the plastic bottle from his pocket and showed Jake the label. "I got a scrip."

"I don't give care if the Surgeon General signed off. Take 'em when the jury's not around. We got enough drugs to deal with."

Jessie smiled at Jake as Tommy opened the passenger door. "You were awesome, Mr. Dalton. Way better than TV."

Jake closed the door behind Tommy as he settled in his seat and adjusted his seatbelt. "We had a decent first day. The jury's not great, but I've seen worse. They're still checking you out, not sure what to think, and that's a good thing. Remember, we don't have to prove you're innocent, just plant enough doubt about your guilt."

Tommy reached through the open window and squeezed Jake's arm. "You've got my back and I won't forget it." Tommy slapped the roof and they sped off.

Lenny winked at Jake. "Damn, you even had me believing they may have gotten the wrong plane."

"L.B., keep an eye on Richter. I don't trust that snake, not for a moment. It's only a matter of time that he pulls some crap."

For the next day and a half, the government continued its parade of witnesses, including the two Air Force F-16 fighter pilots who had intercepted the mysterious plane over the Gulf of Mexico. And while their testimony was relevant, it failed to inflict any real damage since they were unable to confirm that the intruder was, in fact, Tommy's Cessna. And when Richter called two fishermen and a hunter to testify about discovering locked duffel bags with Spanish markings scattered over the Everglades, Jake wasn't concerned. Even though the canvas bags contained record amounts of cocaine, with a street value of over sixty million dollars, the government couldn't connect them to Tifton.

Then, without warning, Richter stood and announced, "Your Honor, we request that the courtroom be secured."

"Granted." Judge Henry motioned to the U.S. Marshals. "Secure all doors."

The courtroom turned deadly quiet. Two loud knocks sounded at the rear.

Jake could only sit back and watch. As though scripted, six armed DEA agents rolled in two railroad baggage carts loaded with eighteen duffel bags and stopped when they reached the well of the courtroom. In moments, a noxious chemical odor filled the room and burned Jake's eyes, causing them to tear.

"Your Honor," Richter said, "the government calls Special Agent Nettles. We also have a DEA chemist on stand-by should that become necessary."

Agent Nettles left his seat at the prosecution table, promptly took the stand, and identified that the nine hundred and eighty-two kilos of seventy-percent pure cocaine was the same he'd inventoried from the various duffle bags found strewn across the Everglades.

Jake rose. "Judge, we don't object to any of this. In fact, if Mr. Richter would have informed me of his plans, I would have immediately stipulated to this evidence without the necessity of a Hollywood production, or the presence of toxic fumes unnecessarily infecting the jury. However, I'd like to reserve a few questions for cross."

The judge turned to the clerk. "Promptly mark the items into evidence, then remove them from my courtroom."

As the cocaine was wheeled away, many on the jury glared at Tommy. Richter's stunt had worked.

After the lunch recess, Jake rose to begin his cross-examination. "Agent Nettles, you are the lead agent in U.S. versus Tifton, is that correct?"

"I am."

"We first met at Homestead Air Force Base back in July when you allowed me to inspect a confiscated Cessna Conquest. True?"

"Yes sir."

"And since June 20 of this year when the Cessna landed in Opa Locka, and for each day thereafter, I assume you've been at work tirelessly investigating this case. Is that also, correct?"

"Yes."

"And for the entire time, the resources of the DEA, FBI, and U.S. Customs have been unable to produce any finger prints or other types of forensic evidence linking my client, or this Cessna, to the cocaine just marked into evidence. Correct?"

"To the best of my knowledge, that's correct."

"Thank you. That's all I have." Jake returned to his seat.

Richter then called an aviation expert as his next witness. "Sir, I show you what's been marked as government's twenty-three through twenty-nine. Did you personally inspect the Cessna aircraft and take these photographs?"

"I did."

"Please tell the jury what they depict."

The expert leaned forward and spread the color photographs on the edge of the stand. "Twenty-three through twenty-six portray the interior of the aircraft. Except for the cockpit, all seats in the aircraft have been removed, even the carpeting." He held up one photo and swiveled to face the jury. "See the bare metal flooring running throughout the passenger cabin?"

"Has any equipment or operational system of the aircraft been altered?"

"Yes, sir. Exhibits twenty-seven, twenty-eight and twenty-nine reveal an open valve under the cabin floor, suitable for attaching a fuel bladder. It is clear that the aircraft had been illegally fitted to fly above its normal range without the need of refueling."

Richter had saved his best for last.

Tommy grabbed Jake's arm. "I didn't know about that. I'd never been on that plane before that weekend, I swear."

"Sir, was there anything else that you found to be unusual?"

"There were two caked reddish stains, one on the cockpit's right-side window and the other on the cabin floor at the rear. The FBI lab later confirmed those to be a DNA match to that of the defendant, a residue of his blood."

"That's all, Your Honor." Richter returned to his table, a smile across his face.

Jake sensed a change in momentum. He would kill for a recess and a stiff drink.

"Sir, I have just one question," Jake said, half-rising from his chair, "with all the time spent on this case and from all the tests conducted, did you or any other government representative find any evidence of drugs? I mean even the slightest trace."

"Not that I'm aware of."

"Nothing further, judge." Jake quickly sat down. Then to his surprise, Richter stood.

"At this time Your Honor, the government rests."

Jake rose and handed Richter a notice of his alibi defense and then turned to the judge. "Your Honor, in view of the lateness of the day, I respectfully request that we adjourn until the morning. I've been told that my next witness, a Dr. Arthur Cunningham, is on route but that his flight has been delayed, and quite frankly I didn't expect to begin my case this afternoon."

"That's not my problem," the judge snapped. He looked over at Richter. "What does the government say to this?"

Richter looked up from reading Jake's notice of alibi. "We have no objection. In fact, there's a matter I'd like to take up with the Court, outside the presence of the jury."

The judge nodded his approval. After admonishing the jurors not to discuss the case, he dismissed them until ten o'clock the next morning.

As soon as the jury filed out, Richter spoke. "Judge, we have a serious problem that I am compelled to bring to the Court's attention."

Judge Henry's brow shot up.

"Defense counsel has just handed me a notice under the rules of his intention to present an alibi defense. Ethically, he is prohibited from doing so."

Jake had no idea what game Richter was playing and turned to Lenny to see if he knew. "Your Honor, the prosecutor is—"

"Don't interrupt, counsel. Let him finish."

Jake held his tongue.

"During pretrial discovery, defense counsel and I, along with Special Agent Nettles, met to facilitate counsel's inspection of the Cessna. At this meeting, Mr. Dalton informed me in no uncertain terms that his client desired to change his plea to guilty."

Jake couldn't contain himself any longer. "Your Honor—"

"Counselor, I told you not to interrupt. One more time and I'll hold you in contempt."

Jake clenched his teeth. He imagined Richter grinning and couldn't bear to look.

"Naturally," Richter continued, "I won't disclose the details of the negotiations, but suffice it to say that Mr. Dalton admitted to me and Special Agent Nettles, that his client was, in fact, guilty. Therefore, he is prohibited, both ethically and legally, from putting the defendant on the stand and having him testify to a fabricated alibi. Such conduct would undoubtedly constitute subornation of perjury, a felony."

Jake glanced at Tommy, who sat stunned at the defense table. Jake emphatically shook his head, trying to convince him not to believe Richter's distortion of what took place.

The judge turned to Jake. "Mr. Dalton, these are serious accusations. Care to respond?"

"Absolutely untrue, Judge. Before I examined the Cessna, there was a brief hypothetical...and I repeat 'hypothetical' discussion. At the time, I was merely attempting to assess the strength of the government's case and raised the possibility of a plea. At no time, did I ever suggest that my client was guilty. I would never do that. Now, in a blatant attempt to prevent the defendant from exercising his constitutional right to testify, Mr. Richter has totally mischaracterized what occurred. It's nothing but a ploy to undermine the defense."

"Well, counsel, your duty as an officer of the Court remains the same, to represent your client to the best of your ability within the bounds of the law and not to participate in any perjury or fraud of any kind. Are we clear on that, sir?"

"Perfectly clear."

The judge looked back at Richter. "I certainly do not intend to hold an evidentiary hearing on a conversation that would be inadmissible in this trial. Sir, is there anything further you wish to bring before the Court?"

"Just so we're clear, Your Honor. I maintain that any attempt by defense counsel to put forward an alibi defense would constitute a crime, the prosecution of which I intend to pursue to the fullest extent of the law."

The tiniest of smiles appeared on the judge's lips. He peered down at Jake. "There you have it, counselor. You're on notice." He tapped his gavel. "With that, we stand in recess until tomorrow morning."

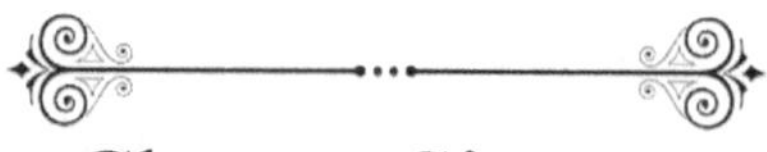

Chapter Sixteen

Jake left Lenny to deal with Tifton and raced to his car. He needed time alone. He had tried to explain to Tommy that Richter was lying about what had occurred but Tifton wasn't having any of it. An hour later, Jake unlocked the front door to his home and stepped inside.

"Elena, I'm home."

"In the kitchen," she called, "working on a Spanish mackerel. My folks took the kids for ribs. Wanna fix me a drink?"

"Sure," he said, walking toward her. "Think I'll have one myself, a double." He entered the kitchen and saw her standing over the sink, holding a bloodied fillet knife. How fitting, he thought.

Elena turned and blew him a kiss. She must have caught the concern spread across his face. "Baby, what's wrong? Bad day in court?"

Jake paused, not sure how to answer. His mind screamed that he should finally come clean, level with her about Tifton once and for all, and deal with the fall out. Why was he so terrified of what she'd do? But fear ruled and once again he went with the lie.

"Nah," he answered, "it's just that I'm dealing with a nut job of a prosecutor. The guy's a lunatic, Mitch had warned me but I had no idea. Not more than an hour ago, smack in the middle of trial, he tells the judge I admitted that my client was guilty, and worse yet, I'd be committing a crime if I had him testify. Absolutely insane!"

Elena moved closer. "Why would you do such a thing?"

"That's just it, I didn't. He's making it up. And--"

"And what?" She laid the knife down on the counter and wiped the blood off her hands with her apron.

"The way he looked at me…it was scary…his eyes. I gotta tell you. It was stone-cold chilling, like he wanted to do me harm." Jake opened the cabinet, grabbed the half empty bottle of vodka and a couple of glasses.

"Who is this jerk? He needs to be reported to the Bar."

"Total waste of time. He's with DOJ, nothing would ever come of it." Jake started pouring them drinks. "Believe me, I can't wait for this trial to be over."

"What'd your client say? Can't he see that this guy is up to no good?"

"Yeah, he gets it," Jake said, trying to convince himself. "But he's really pissed."

"Not at you I hope." After a long pause, she asked, "Your client, he's not violent, is he?"

Jake swirled the vodka in his glass as he mulled over a response, averting her gaze. How well did he really know Tifton? "No, no, not at all. Why would you think that?"

Crawford Richter slumped low in his passenger seat as the late afternoon sun cast a shadow across the hood of his government-leased sedan. Since his promotion two weeks ago to lead the federal task force on narcotic trafficking, he'd had precious little time to deal with witnesses. But this was no ordinary witness. He glanced at Special Agent Nettles, sitting grim-faced behind the wheel. For the past twelve years, he and the agent had worked closely together trying to shut down major drug operations in South Florida; each knew there was no one they'd rather trust.

Richter wiped away beads of sweat forming on his upper lip. A stiff breeze off Biscayne Bay cut through the suffocating humidity, making the wait almost bearable. Across the street, a white-haired, bespectacled black man stepped gingerly from a taxi, half-crouched over a cane.

"Let me see that," Richter said, snatching from Nettles' hand the grainy photo transmitted by the FBI an hour earlier. "That's him alright."

Nettles continued to stare out the window and said nothing.

"We'll stay put until the old man enters his room." Richter waited for Nettles to face him. "Make damn sure you don't say or do anything to fuck things up. As soon as this trial is over, we move on the lawyer."

"You sure you want to do this?" Nettles cautioned. "If Tifton goes down as planned, you'll have some explaining to do to the cartel."

Richter shook his head. "They wouldn't dare touch me. They have too much to lose."

As a car was about to pass, Richter shielded his face. It wouldn't be smart to be seen talking to a defense witness in the heat of trial. Moments later, he watched as the old man hobbled down the Sonata Inn's exterior walkway into Room 139. "Okay, let's go."

After two loud knocks Cunningham cracked open his door. He appeared weary, and wore a hearing aid in his right ear.

"Dr. Cunningham. My name's Richter. This is DEA Special Agent Nettles. We're here on official business." Richter nudged into the room and eyed the Chicago Cubs sports bag and several files lying on the queen-size bed.

Cunningham stumbled back. "How'd you know my name?"

"That's not important."

"How'd you know I was staying here?"

Richter ignored the question and signaled Nettles to close the door behind them.

Cunningham adjusted his suspenders and leaned on his cane, trying to straighten up. "Mind showing me some identification?"

Richter flipped open his wallet and flashed his photo embossed by the Department of Justice insignia. Nettles followed suit.

"What right do you have to be here?"

"Sir, have you noticed anyone suspicious following you the past few days? Anybody milling outside your Chicago townhouse or office who seemed out of place?"

Cunningham's blood-shot eyes flashed open. "No, not that I know of. Why?"

"We have information that you could be in grave danger, sir. We're aware you've come to testify for a high-level member of the Santolisma cartel," Richter lied, keeping his voice low. "We've been tracking Tifton's operation for over a year. We doubt Attorney Dalton has explained to you the seriousness of the situation, that his client is involved in trafficking large amounts of cocaine for the most notorious cartel in Mexico. Am I right?"

"No-not exactly," Cunningham stammered. He shifted his cane to better balance himself. "Mr. Dalton assured me it was a run of the mill drug case, nothing to concern myself with, that I would be in and out of court in a couple of hours, then on my way."

"Sir, we're here because the United States government fears for your safety. It wouldn't be the first time a witness has been murdered in a case such as this. I should know, one of my witnesses was found floating in a river with his throat cut not long ago. I'm not surprised a lawyer like Dalton hasn't told you the type of people you're dealing with. I'm afraid he has put you and your family in very real danger."

"Lord, I had no idea. Mr. Dalton only asked that I testify about radar reports. I see nothing improper about that." Cunningham's eyes hardened. "You're being here, like this, seems highly irregular. Isn't there some rule against *ex parte* communications with an opposing expert? I'd better call Mr. Dalton, see what he has to say."

"He's already left to meet his client."

"How'd you know?"

"Sir, it's not the first time a man like Dalton has gotten too close to his client, if you catch my drift. We're in the middle of a criminal investigation targeting a global conspiracy. We're talking bankers, lawyers, real estate brokers, even PhDs like yourself. Do I have to draw you a picture?"

Cunningham stepped back and reached for the phone on the night stand. "Then I'd better speak to his investigator."

Richter marched around the bed and yanked the phone from Cunningham's hands. "Look, you're not hearing me. I'm doing my best to keep you safe. The last thing I want to do is charge you as an accessory or with obstruction of justice. Don't force my hand."

"I—I have nothing to do with those people." Cunningham's left eye started to twitched. "From the beginning I explained to Mr. Dalton that I was reluctant to get involved in a drug case. I don't need this; it'll ruin my reputation. He should have told me what this case was about in the first place. I can't be seen helping a drug cartel."

Nettles stepped around the bed and placed his hand on Cunningham's shoulder. "We can see that you've had a long and distinguished career. We're just trying to keep you from making a big mistake. It's clear you had no idea who you're dealing with. You haven't been subpoenaed, so you're not required to stay. Let me call you a cab for the airport before it's too late. We don't want to see anything happen to you or your family."

Richter glanced at his watch. "Please heed our warning, sir. These drug dealers have no conscience. They'll eliminate anyone who gets in their way. I've no doubt your life would be at risk if you continue on this case. I suggest that Agent Nettles wait here while you pack your belongings to ensure your safety. I'm just thankful we were able to reach you in time."

Cunningham's face collapsed. His eyes darted around the room as though he were lost.

"Sir," Richter added, as he re-opened the door to leave. "The government appreciates your cooperation. If you receive any threatening phone calls once you return home, please don't hesitate to contact my office so we can further protect you."

Late that evening, Jake turned over in bed and grabbed his cell on the second ring. He stared at the caller ID. Lenny. This couldn't be good. He pressed the receiver against his ear and spoke in a hushed voice, "What's the matter?"

"Boss, I'm sorry to call you this late." Lenny sounded out of breath. "But it's important."

Jake swung his feet off the bed. He glanced back at the clock radio, then at Elena, who appeared fast asleep. "What is it," he whispered as he tiptoed into the hallway.

"I dropped by the Sonata to make sure Cunningham had everything he needed before your meet tomorrow. He's gone. I looked everywhere. Musta got cold feet."

"What! That's impossible. Maybe he never got in. Did you check the airlines?"

"First thing I did. His plane got in at five, two hours late, then he checked into the Sonesta half-past six. I slid by his room just before nine but he wasn't there. The desk clerk said Cunningham checked out an hour before, bags and all. Saw him helped into a cab by a wiry black guy in a coat and tie, wearing glasses. The description fits our DEA agent to a T. I'm heading back there now with a snapshot of Nettles to see if the clerk can ID him."

"Jesus, I'm not believing this!" Jake moved further down the hall, fearing his outburst may have woken Elena or the kids. "Check the nearby bars, restaurants, even hospitals. Try his cell." Jake caught his breath. "L.B., we need this guy."

"Already did. That's why it took me this long to call." Lenny paused. "Boss, I think we lost him."

"We're screwed." Jake raked his fingers through his hair. "No wait. Pull the file and have Isora prepare a motion enforcing his subpoena. Cunningham won't dare disobey a federal court order."

Lenny remained silent.

"What's wrong? You did get him under subpoena?"

It took a lifetime for Lenny to answer. "Didn't think we could. The dude lives and works in Chicago. Sorry, I fucked up."

"Are you nuts? We're in fucking federal court," Jake yelled into the phone. "You can tag a guy's ass surfing in Hawaii for God's sake. How do we get him back now?"

"Baby, what's wrong?" Elena called from the bedroom.

He stuck his head back inside. "It's okay. Go back to sleep. Everything's fine." All he needed now was for Elena to start asking questions.

From the hall, Jake closed the bedroom door and spoke softly. "Tifton won't believe Cunningham bailed like this. He'll find a way to put it on me."

"Go tell the judge. Even he won't let 'em get away with witness tampering."

"Yeah, sure. Unless we can get Cunningham to say what happened, we can't prove squat." Jake chewed on his lip, pondering his options. The judge was useless, practically cheering the government on. In fact, he might even use the opportunity to make Jake look bad for failing to have Cunningham under subpoena.

"Len, call Tommy. Go by his place if you have to. Tell him there's been a change of plans. Jessie's going on the stand in the morning, then him. In the meantime, keep trying Cunningham on his cell. Promise him anything but get him back."

"What else?"

"Yeah. Watch my back. There's no telling what else Richter will do."

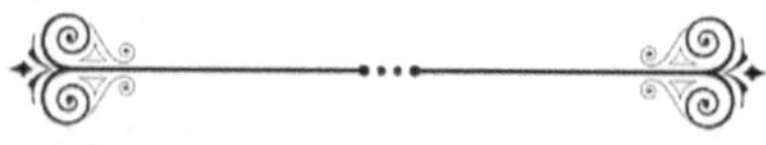

Chapter Seventeen

Jake winced as Elena slapped the front page of Herald on the breakfast table as he sat drinking his coffee. "What the hell is this?" she shouted. "You're defending a drug dealer? I can't believe it. After looking me in the eye and swearing you wouldn't."

Jake avoided her stare. "Baby, I can explain," he said, trying to think fast. After Lenny's call last night, it had slipped his mind to grab the paper from the driveway in the event Tifton made the headlines again.

"Don't you baby, me," she snapped, her lips trembling with rage.

"Keep it down, the kids will hear."

"I don't give a damn if the whole neighborhood hears. You lied to me. How can I ever trust you again?"

Never had he seen her this angry. He sat up and spoke in a calm voice. "I tried to tell you but there was never the right time. I'm sorry, I really am. But to be perfectly honest, the fee was simply too good to pass up."

She hovered over him. "Honest? You've no idea what that word means." Elena pointed to the headlines. "Have you lost your mind?" She paced the length of the kitchen, shaking her head. "These people are *loco*. If anything goes wrong, they'll kill you, then come after me and the children. Do you ever for once think of your family?"

Jake gripped the table. "All I ever do is think of my family." Jake could hear his voice rise with emotion. "Why do you think I took the frickin' case to begin with? Get rid of some bills, give us some breathing room. There isn't a minute that goes by that I don't worry about Drew, that he'll get sick again. I can't get out of my head him lying in that hospital, hooked up to God knows how many wires." Jake felt himself choking up. "For crissakes, Elena, I *live* for my family." He wiped the moisture from his eyes with his sleeve and grabbed the newspaper. The headline read: "Drug Cartel Secures Foothold in South Florida." He swallowed hard as he read on.

"Considered the most violent criminal organization in the southern hemisphere, the Mexican Santolisma cartel has reportedly gained a foothold in Miami's lucrative drug trade. For the first time, government sources confirm, the cartel has successfully spread its tentacles into South Florida. Unnamed sources close to the federal task force on drug trafficking say that Thomas Tifton, currently on trial in a Miami federal court for importing a record one thousand kilos of cocaine, is credited with the recent spike of cocaine importation and distribution throughout the region. Local attorney Jake Dalton represents Tifton and has steadfastly maintained his client's innocence."

Jake seethed. "This is absolute crap!"

Elena slammed the coffee pot on the table. "It's terrifying, that's what it is. I might as well put a sign out front saying 'My husband takes orders from Mexican drug lords.' I won't live like this. I won't!"

Jake raised his hand in the air for her to wait while he continued reading:

Tifton is further alleged to have played a leading role in the cartel's extensive air operations over the past decade. Government sources refuse to comment on the whereabouts of Barry Dearing, Tifton's co-defendant, and alleged accomplice. Dearing is also wanted by the State of Florida for the brutal slaying of a government informant found floating in the Miami River several years ago.

Jake wadded the paper and flung it across the room. "Total bullshit. Richter timed it to coincide with the trial. He's trying to taint the jury. That maniac will stop at nothing."

Elena's face turned pale. "*Dios Mio*! We have two small children," she screamed. "Can't you see what you've done?"

Desperate for money, it never crossed Jake's mind that taking on the case would rip his family apart. "Take it easy. It's only one—"

Elena's chest heaved. "I'm not taking it easy. Your children might as well find out what their father does for a living. I won't live like my mother, I won't. Scared out of her mind that her children will get snatched off the street, never to be heard from again."

"Elena, I know how you feel, I respect how you feel, but it's only one case. I don't plan on making a habit of this."

She stood over him, her face a deep crimson. "You've changed. From the day I said fine, do criminal law if you must, you've become so secretive, like there are things you don't want me to know. And last night, trying to tell me nothing was wrong after getting off the phone, but I knew better." She paused as though deciding whether to continue. "How is it that all of a sudden, our credit cards have been miraculously paid off and we're no longer behind on the mortgage?" Her tone turned accusatory. "What the hell is going on, Jake? Is there money I don't know about?"

He waved her off. "Now you're being ridiculous. "I've been doing pretty good lately and wanted to surprise you. I had no idea you'd be auditing our damn bills, you never concerned yourself with them before. And for the record," he said, his raised voice matching hers, "I don't share some of the shit that goes on in my cases because it would only freak you out more than you already are."

"Mommy, Daddy, why are you fighting?" Nikki called from her bedroom.

Jake heard Drew moving around in his room, probably too scared to come out.

The smell of burnt toast filled the kitchen.

"God, I never want to see you like this," he said, his voice barely above a whisper.

She tilted her head toward him. "You're not hearing me. You never do. I still have nightmares of my mother pulling me and Miquel inside, double locking the doors, hiding us in the basement every time there was news of another kidnapping. Do you want that for our children?"

"Elena, we're not in Colombia."

She waved her arms in the air. "That's it, the minute Drew and Nikki finish their breakfast I'm taking them to my parents where they'll be safe."

Jake recoiled. "Jesus, I don't want that." He stood and reached for her but she pushed him away. "Listen, you're upset, I get it," he said in as soothing a tone as he could muster. "Think of the kids. Haven't they been through enough? You want them traumatized even more?

Don't do something we'll both regret." He looked for a reaction, any reaction, but there was none. "Just hold off 'til the case is over," he pleaded. "Only a few more days. Then we'll sit down and talk. Give me a chance to explain everything. Will you at least do that for me, for our family?"

For what seemed like an eternity Elena stared at him without speaking. Finally, her breathing slowed. She sat in a chair next to him and with her hand wiped tears from her eyes. Then, and only then did she give him the tiniest of nods.

As Jake swerved the Saab into his office garage, he punched the numbers on his cell to the office of the US Attorney. A secretary finally put him through to Richter.

"What do you want?" Richter hissed.

"What'd you do with my witness? That's what I want to know."

"Why counselor, I thought for sure you were calling to say your client had a change of heart and decided to plead guilty after all."

"Cut the crap." Jake slammed his car door shut and ran towards his office. "I've tried to reach Cunningham but he won't return my calls. What'd you threatened him with?"

"I have no idea what you're talking about."

"You can't intimidate my witness and get away with it. I'll subpoena the motel clerk. He saw you and Nettles put Cunningham into a cab." Jake knew from speaking to Lenny earlier that the desk clerk was useless, that even after being shown a photo of Nettles and Richter he couldn't ID either, but Jake thought it was worth a bluff.

Richter scoffed. "Nice try. And speaking of subpoenas, you shouldn't have any trouble getting the judge to enforce yours. It's done all the time."

Jake froze. Richter must have checked the court records before going to see Cunningham. Jake tried to catch his breath but couldn't. "What's with you? First, the crap about my admitting Tifton's guilt, and now this."

"Sit tight my friend. The fun has only begun."

"What the hell does that mean?"

"Butch Dearing was arrested two days ago and has agreed to testify. So, chew on that. And if you continue with your trumped-up alibi, I'm coming after you with the full resources of the federal government." He hung up.

Jake's hand shook. His only expert witness was gone and now Tifton was about to face the sworn testimony of his co-defendant, who'd undoubtedly cut a deal to bury him. Jake pressed the speed dial on his cell to call Lenny with the latest bombshell.

As Jake rushed to the courthouse to start trial, his cell phone rang. Could it be Elena telling him she was leaving with the kids after all. An image of him coming home to an empty house seared his brain.

"Yes," he finally answered without looking to see who it was.

"Did you see that fucking story in the Herald?"

"Sam?" Jake asked before recognizing his voice.

"It's total horseshit," Sam continued. You've got to do something. The client's going fucking ballistic."

"You speak to Tommy?"

"Just tell that fuckin' judge there's no way he can get a fair trial. Not now. And if the judge won't do anything, get another judge."

"Thanks, I hadn't thought of that." Jake was sure Sam hadn't caught his sarcasm. "Besides, that's not how it works. Getting a different judge isn't do easy."

"How's the case going?"

What a time to ask. "We're in the thick of it, anything can happen. I'm on my way to court now. And while I got you, my investigator's been trying to nail down Red Armstrong. I called you last week and left a detailed message. What gives? I need to speak to him ASAP. Tifton takes the stand in a matter of hours."

"Ok, ok, but listen. You got to take care of this, Jake, for both our sakes. Do whatever you got to do. I don't give a fuck, just win the goddamn case. Do you understand? Just win the fucker."

Jake lost the connection. He stared at his cell. What the hell was going on? Why was Sam freaking out? And why did he send Tifton to him in the first place?

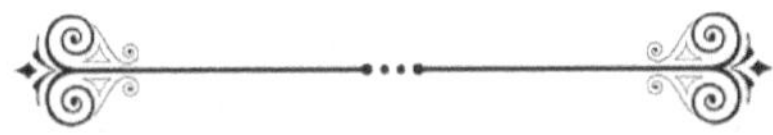

Chapter Eighteen

Jake walked briskly along Biscayne Boulevard toward the courthouse, his mind swirling with thoughts of Elena. Was she really going to leave, all because of a stupid lie? It wasn't like he was having an affair or gambling again. Sure, he had deceived her, wished now that he would have been truthful from the start, but was that it? Really? A broken promise not to do drug cases? There had to be more to it.

Upon turning the corner Jake froze. A mob of reporters stood camped on the courthouse steps waiting. As though rehearsed ahead of time, together they made a mad dash toward him, shouting questions.

"Mr. Dalton, care to comment on the article in the Herald?" one reporter hollered at him. "Is it true your client's the cartel's number one importer of cocaine in the state?" yelled a second as Jake shouldered his way through the herd.

"My client maintains his innocence," was all he could think of to say. Jake shielded his eyes from the glare of TV lights and pushed up the steps through the revolving doors, opened his briefcase for security, then raced for the elevators before stopping to catch his breath. Thank God cameras weren't allowed inside. He caught up to Lenny outside the attorney's conference room.

"You tell Tommy about Butch?" Jake asked.

"Yeah, didn't blink an eye. You'll like this. Says, 'Butch's a snitch, all snitches lie.' Speaking of which, the guy's got a rap sheet ten miles long, and a dishonorable discharge from the Navy, to boot. But I still think you should bitch like hell to the judge. It's crazy to let Richter spring him on you like this."

"I will but it'll get nowhere. The government has him in their hip pocket."

Jake glanced at the wall clock. "Showtime in ten minutes. Is Jessie ready?"

Lenny nodded. His face then turned solemn. "You're not going with the alibi, not now with Butch testifying, and not with Richter hurling his threats. Remember, it's your career we're talking about."

"You bet your sweet ass I am. You think for a second, I'm about to cower to that maniac's threats? Screw him. Tommy's alibi is rock solid, and more important than ever. Butch doesn't change a thing. Everybody knows he'd testify against his own mother to stay a day out of prison. What about Cunningham?"

Lenny's look said it all. Cunningham would remain MIA.

Jake marched with Lenny past the marshals manning the rear door, pushed through the low swinging gates into the well of the courtroom, and settled beside Tifton at the defense table. Tommy sat with his back turned toward Jake, staring at some distant object.

"Don't swallow Richter's crap," Jake began. "From day one I've believed in you. Richter's behind that story in the paper, and Cunningham, too. He's hoping to nail your ass by dividing us. Don't let him do that."

Tommy said nothing.

"You know about Butch," Jake added.

Tommy finally turned to face him. "He's nothing but a scum sucking lying bottom feeder who will say anything now that he's got his deal."

"And I intend the jury knows that. Now put aside whatever feelings you have for me. We've got a case to try."

Minutes later, the marshal called the court to order and before the jury returned, Richter rose. "Your Honor, I need to bring an important matter to the court's attention, and move to re-open the government's case."

Judge Henry nodded for him to continue.

"This morning I advised defense counsel that Barry Dearing, AKA Butch, has been arrested and has agreed to cooperate. I am mindful that Mr. Dearing had not previously been listed as a prosecution witness, but only yesterday did I learn of this development."

The judge turned to Jake. "Counsel?"

"We strenuously object. This surprise witness had been sprung on the defense not two hours ago. Obviously, I haven't been accorded sufficient time to prepare and consult with my client, much to our prejudice."

"Mr. Dalton, I fail to see any substantial prejudice to the defense compared to the overriding interests to be served by permitting such testimony. Under the rules you would not have been allowed to take the witness's deposition anyway. The government's motion to reopen its case and for Mr. Dearing to testify is granted. Bring in the jury."

The prosecutor stood. "The government calls Barry Dearing."

The courtroom's side door swung open and a short, burly man in his early thirties appeared, a deputy marshal on each side. His sun-weathered face contrasted sharply against his starched white shirt. After being sworn in, Butch settled into the witness stand, refusing to look at Tommy.

"Mr. Dearing," Richter began. "You are the co-defendant of Thomas Tifton, is that correct?"

"Sure, whatever."

"And you were a fugitive from justice until your capture two days ago, correct?"

"My girlfriend turned me in for the reward. Go figure."

"And yesterday you changed your plea to guilty and have agreed to testify for the government."

"The deal was I'd get max eight years."

Richter glanced at his notes. "Let me direct your attention to the weekend of June 19 of this year. Did you fly a load of cocaine from Colombia to Florida?"

Butch leaned back in his chair. "Hell, I'm no good at dates, 'cept about that time Tommy and me took off from Medellin for the Keys. It was our biggest load yet, about a thousand keys. It was gonna be Tommy's last trip. He swore to his ole lady he was getting out of the business."

Jake bolted from his chair, and before he could object, Judge Henry glared at the witness. "Sir, you are to answer only the question that is asked. Do you understand?"

Butch shrugged his shoulders.

Richter continued. "And when you say Tommy, you're referring to the defendant Thomas Tifton, correct?"

"Who else?"

"And the ole lady?"

"Jessie, his wife."

"When you say keys of coke, you're referring to kilograms of cocaine? Correct?"

"Yup."

"Please tell the jury who were you working for at the time?"

"Some guy named Red. He runs air transport for the Mexicans, who in turn buy from the Colombians. When the product is ready, we pick it up and deliver, sorta like Fed Ex."

Several jurors chuckled.

"When you say Mexicans, I assume you're referring to the Santolisma cartel?"

"Hole in one."

"That's a yes."

Butch nodded. "Yup."

"What's your relationship with this Red?"

"Zippo. He and Tommy are tight. I think they're related somehow, maybe cousins of some sort. I tried to get closer to the Man but Tommy would have none of it. Didn't want me invading his turf."

Tifton moved his chair closer to Jake. "That's a goddamn lie."

"I know," Jake replied, irritated. "But write it down. I need to focus."

"And how long have you and the defendant been working for this Red?"

"Maybe five, six years. Since I left the Navy, Tommy a bit longer. But I like I said, I'm no good with dates."

"I understand you were once a Navy fighter pilot? Even flew missions over Baghdad during the Second Gulf War."

Butch laughed. "Does me a lot of good now."

Jake caught the smiles from a few of the jurors and didn't like it. In his own peculiar way, Butch was making a powerful witness.

Richter continued. "Let's talk about that night you were stopped by U.S. Customs. Go ahead and tell the jury what you and the defendant were doing just before that."

Butch still hadn't looked at Tommy. "We started out just before dark from El Retiro, some shithole not far from Medellin. Everything was cool until that storm came up, kicked us in the teeth, knocked us way off course. Had plans to land on a dirt strip south of Key Largo. I was at the wheel and Tommy riding shotgun, making sure the product was secured."

"When you say product, you're referring to the cocaine?"

Butch shot Richter an are-you-fuckin'-stupid-look. "Right. We had to fly low to conserve fuel and avoid radar, but it did no good. Northwest of Cuba, two Air Force jockeys made us in their F-16s. Tommy broke his nose from the wake and started hollering that they were going to blow us out of the sky. But I knew better. They were just toying with us 'til Customs got there."

"Did U.S. Customs eventually intercept you?"

"Yeah, a Citation II, right after we landed."

"What did you do with the cocaine?"

"Tommy and me got into a fight over that. We had already ditched the extra fuel bladder, but he didn't want to toss the coke. Started freaking out that that the Mexicans would kill us and our families if we lost their load." Butch snickered. "But I was more concerned with going to jail and knew the feds couldn't do zilch if they didn't find anything on us. Finally, I won out. But the storm musta messed with our avionics, 'cause when I gave Tommy the signal to toss I thought for sure we were over water."

"Eventually you landed at the Opa Locka airport and were searched by Customs."

"Like I said, without the product they had to let us go. I then got the hell out of Dodge and never looked back. Thought I was in the clear until my girlfriend—" Butch lowered his gaze.

Jake glanced at Lenny, who sat shaking his head.

Richter moved to the clerk's table and lifted numerous brass locks with Spanish writings, previously marked into evidence. "Mr. Dearing," he said, "let me hand you Government's Composite Exhibit Fifteen. Can you identify these eighteen brass locks?"

Butch examined the locks. "Sure. These were on the duffels when we picked up the coke. It's standard procedure to lock the bags during transport, to keep the product from spilling out."

Richter smiled and turned to Jake. "Your witness."

While rising from his chair, Jake fired off his first question. "Mr. Dearing, you say you reached a deal with the government to testify against my client and for that you would serve a maximum of eight years in prison, did I get that right?"

"Figured I'd only do six after time off for good behavior."

"But that's only with regard to this case. Surely, that doesn't include all the other times you've smuggled drugs for the cartels?"

"My deal covers everything."

"*Everything?*" Jake's voice shot up an octave. "That's pretty remarkable, don't you think?"

Butch smiled.

"How much did you typically make on any given load of cocaine?"

"Quarter mil."

"And in your illustrious career, how many trips had you flown?"

Butch stared up at the ceiling, as though counting in his head. "Give or take, twenty."

"By my calculation you've made roughly five million dollars for the few years of doing such work. Fair to say?"

"Sounds 'bout right."

"And it's fair to say that you've never paid a dime of this income to the IRS."

Butch smiled again. "You got me there."

"And has the government indicated that you would be charged with tax evasion."

Butch shook his head. "Like I said, my deal covers everything. Pretty sweet, don't you think?" For the first time he looked at Tommy.

"And your deal with this federal prosecutor," Jake said, looking over at Richter, "even includes dismissal of the state charge of murdering a government informant. Correct?"

Loud chatter filled the courtroom.

Butch squirmed in his chair. "That was a bum rap. I never laid a finger on the snitch, didn't even know where the feds were hiding him, although I did hear through the grapevine that they had him squirreled away in a safe house somewhere."

"And to have all charges against you dropped and avoid a lifetime in prison, all you had to do is make up some story about my client, right?"

"I told you what I know. Let the chips fall where they may."

"And if you told the truth, that Tommy Tifton was *not* running drugs with you, the government never would have given you such a sweetheart deal. Isn't that a fact?"

Richter jumped out of his seat. "Objection."

"Sustained."

"And just so we're clear, sir," Jake continued, "you didn't just voluntarily leave the Navy. You were booted out, given a Dishonorable Discharge, correct?"

"I got a raw deal."

"You mean the same raw deal that my client is getting today."

Richter bolted from his table, but before he could speak the judge shouted, "No more of that counselor."

"By the way," Jake pressed, ignoring the judge's scowl, "I assume you have agreed to also testify against other members of the cartel?"

"Nope."

"No?" Jake asked. "You've been smuggling drugs for years and the government hasn't insisted that you provide them with the names and whereabouts of others for future prosecution. Is that what you're telling this jury?"

"I'd nothing else to give."

Jake glanced at the jurors. They weren't buying it.

"One more question, has the government ever threatened that if you didn't cooperate and point the finger at my client, that you would face an even harsher punishment than your eight years?"

"They made it clear that if I didn't flip, I'd be spending the rest of my life behind bars."

Jake had made his point. "No more questions."

Richter had no redirect and once again announced that the government rested.

"We're in recess," the judge announced. "When we resume, I expect the defense to call its first witness."

Tommy grabbed Jake's arm as he was about to leave. "You still believe me, don't you?"

Jake ignored the question. "Tell Jessie to get ready. She goes on when we get back." He grabbed Lenny by the arm. "Let's get some air."

Once outside, Jake turned to his right-hand man. "How'd I do?"

"Definitely wounded the guy. Any fool can see the government gave away the farm to get him to talk. But the jury may think that's okay."

"And Richter dealing away the murder charge, letting this guy get off with eight years? That's also okay?"

Lenny shrugged. "That's how the game is played. Feds make these deals all the time, but nobody gives a shit."

"And Tifton? How bad does it look?" Jake searched Lenny's eyes and got his answer.

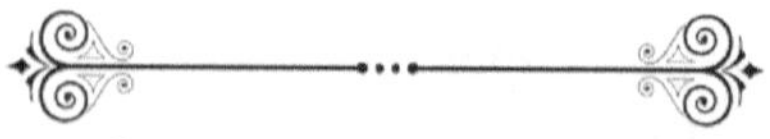

Chapter Nineteen

At the defense table, Jake took his seat beside Tifton. "Look," he began, "I know you're bent out of shape over Cunningham and you have every right to be. All I can say is that Richter got to him. I don't know what he said but I'm sure it amounted to obstruction of justice and witness tampering. The problem is that without Cunningham we can't prove it, at least not until your trial is over."

"Then for both our sakes you'd better beat this case so whatever the fuck went down can be written off as a bad memory."

Jake nodded. "Is Jessie ready?"

"She was born ready."

In minutes, court was called to order. The judge adjusted the sleeves of his robe while the jury settled in their seats, and peered down at Jake. "Counsel, call your first witness."

Jake stood and pivoted to the rear of the courtroom. "The defense calls Jessie Tifton."

In a powder blue cotton dress that stopped just below her knees, Jessie walked with head held high past the spectators to the witness stand, leaving a whiff of perfume in her trail. Her red hair, tied back by a gold ribbon, shimmered. A small silver cross hung from her neck, brushing the high neckline of her dress.

Jessie took her oath and stepped effortlessly onto the stand, all the while smiling at the jury. Two elderly women jurors in the back row smiled back.

"You are the wife of the defendant Thomas Tifton, is that correct?" Jake began.

"For two and a half wonderful years."

"Are you familiar with your husband's military service on behalf of our country?"

"I am."

For the next hour, Jessie testified about Tommy's time in the Army Special Forces, the injuries he suffered in Iraq during the First Gulf War, as well as his PTSD and bouts of depression.

"Mrs. Tifton, please explain to the jury what PTSD is and how it has impacted life with your husband."

"It stands for post-traumatic stress disorder. I hear soldiers get it because of the horrible things they see in war. Tommy's got it bad. He wakes up most nights screaming from nightmares and then just sits there, doing nothing, actin' real depressed."

To Jake, Jessie seemed to be pouring it on a little thick, but the jury appeared to be eating it up. And as Jessie answered each of his questions, she seemed to gain confidence, making him wonder if her small-town charm was a mask to something more.

Halfway through, Jake changed his line of questioning. "Mrs. Tifton, where were you during the early morning hours of Saturday, June twentieth of this year?"

"At home in our Coconut Grove condo."

"Please tell the jury what occurred."

"Tommy came home around four, maybe five that morning, soakin' wet, shivering from head to toe."

"When was the last time you saw him before that?"

"Two days before. I packed his bag for his trip to Cozumel. He was excited to go fishin' with his brother, even though he was scared to death of flying. Tommy hates planes."

Richter stood. "Objection, hearsay."

"Sustained."

Jake leaned on the lectern. "Your Honor, I'm simply trying to show—"

"I've ruled, counsel. Is there another question?"

"Mrs. Tifton," Jake continued, "only tell us what you know from your personal knowledge. You can't talk about what was told to you."

"I'm awful sorry." Jessie smiled at the jury. "But I know Tommy hates to fly, ever since he almost died when his helicopter got shot down in operation Desert Storm."

What a pro, Jake thought. She not only got to mention Tommy's war service a second time but also slipped in his fear of flying.

"Have you ever known your husband to deal in narcotics?"

Jessie directed a solemn gaze to the jury. "Never."

"Travel to Colombia or anywhere else in South America where they grow cocaine?"

"No way. Tommy hates drugs, even the ones the doctor makes him take for his depression."

"Was your husband ill when he returned from his weekend in Cozumel?"

"Boy, was he. Had diarrhea, real bad. I had to run to the store and get one of those giant bottles of Kaopectate. Lasted three days. My Lord, he's skinny enough as it is."

Several jurors chuckled.

More than satisfied, Jake announced, "No further questions."

For the next two hours, Richter pounded away at Jessie, to no avail. She remained adamant that Tommy had left home on a fishing trip and that he wasn't dealing in drugs.

"Mrs. Tifton, you don't work. Isn't that right?" Richter asked, leaning on the lectern.

"Tommy asked that I stay home, we're planning to have a family."

"So, the only income you and your husband have is the seventy thousand dollars he makes annually at Florida Electric, correct?"

"That's right. Tommy always says it's better to be rich in spirit."

Richter's face reddened. "Mrs. Tifton, just answer the question. No editorials."

"Editorials? I don't work for no newspapers."

The entire jury joined Jake in loud laughter. Even the judge couldn't suppress his smile. The grimace on Richter's face spoke volumes.

"And the only property you and your husband own is your home in Coconut Grove?"

"That's right. My folks gave us the money for the down payment, otherwise we never coulda bought it."

"Nothing further." Richter said, shaking his head.

Jessie stepped off the stand and as she walked by Tommy whispered, "You were awesome, baby."

"Your Honor," Jake announced, "the defense next calls Thomas Tifton."

Tommy buttoned his suit jacket, then straightened his tie as he strode to the stand and turned to face the clerk for the oath.

Jake started the questioning. "Mr. Tifton, have you ever served in the armed forces of the United States?"

"Yes, sir. Specialist E-4, U.S. Army Special Forces. 1987-1992."

"Ever seen combat?"

"During the First Gulf War, I was an electronics specialist assigned to covert operations in Kuwait and Iraq. During our last op, my squad's chopper took a direct hit from an RPG." Tommy made eye contact with the jury as Jake had instructed him to do. "That's a rocket propelled grenade. I lost two of my buddies and got tore up pretty bad. Spent nine months in an Army hospital in Landstuhl, Germany."

"Has your country bestowed upon you any medals for bravery in battle?"

The two retired military leaned forward in the jury box, their eyes fixed on Tommy.

"I received a Purple Heart for losing half my stomach and two of my fingers." Tommy raised his left hand. "Doctors say I got a bad case of PTSD, so I see a shrink once a month at the VA. I take antidepressants when my moods get real dark."

"Please go on."

"Also got a Bronze Star. They say I jumped back into the chopper, burning and all, and pulled out my buddies. Saved two, they tell me. But I don't remember much. In fact, I try not to."

"Mr. Tifton, are you now or have ever been involved in smuggling drugs?"

Tommy twisted in his chair toward the jury. "Never."

"Have you been employed since you got out of the Army?"

"I've been with Florida Electric, going on seventeen years. I'm now the Fleet Manager over the South Florida region." Tommy's face lit up. "I'm real proud of that. Also, while holding down my job I took out student loans and attended night classes at Southeast Methodist College. Eventually got my degree in military history. First in my family to do that."

"Please tell the jury where you were from June 18 thru June 20 of this year?"

Tommy recited exactly what he told Jake in their first meeting. He had flown to Cozumel with Butch to fish with his brother, Dave in a big game tournament, but came down with food poisoning, and visited *Chichén Itzá* instead. Then, after leaving Mexico, he and Butch were forced to land in the tropical storm and later questioned before being released by U.S. Customs.

"That night at your brother's just before flying back home, did you meet Diego and Gabriela Mendoza?" Jake kept his eye on the jury to gauge their reaction.

"Yes sir. I didn't know they were going to be at Dave's, but I'm sure glad they were."

"And it was the Mendozas who gave you and Butch a ride back to the airport?"

"Dave was bone tired from fishing and the couple was nice enough to give us a lift."

"After you landed in Miami, did you explain to Customs that they mistook your plane for another?"

"I tried, but they wouldn't listen. They kept pointing their guns and cursin' even after they found no drugs."

"Have you ever been on board that Cessna Conquest before taking the trip to Cozumel?"

"No, sir. Butch borrowed the plane from a friend of his. Never met the man."

"When you boarded the plane for Cozumel, did you notice anything unusual?"

"Sure did. All the seats except those in the cockpit had been stripped out."

"Did you ask Butch, that is, Barry Dearing, about it?"

Tommy nodded. "I tried but he got real upset. Told me to mind my own business, so I never brought it up again."

A loud murmur swept through the gallery.

"Mr. Tifton, were you anyway involved in removing those seats?"

"Absolutely not. Like I said, I didn't even know about it till I step foot on the plane."

Jake gathered his notes. "One last question. Have you ever flown from Colombia or any other place in South America to smuggle drugs?"

"I would never ever do something like that and risk losing Jessie and our chance to have a baby."

Jake turned to the judge. "No further questions."

The judge leaned over his bench. "In view of the time, we stand adjourned until tomorrow morning at ten o'clock." He rapped his gavel and left the bench.

At his counsel table, Jake stuffed papers into his briefcase, anxious to get home and spend time with Elena and the kids. He stiffened from a prickly sensation at the back of his neck and turned to see Richter smiling at him. To Jake's surprise, the prosecutor marched toward him, his face flushed.

"Sleep tight, Dalton." Richter then turned and stormed out of the courtroom.

Jake's mouth turned dry. He looked over at Lenny. "I don't like the sound of that. Not one bit."

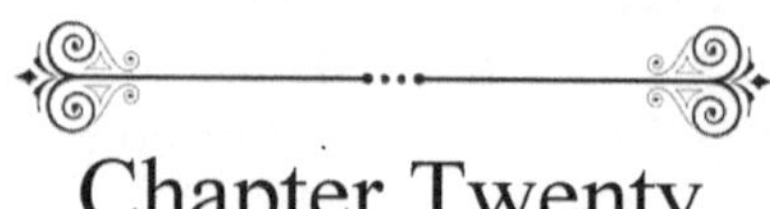

Chapter Twenty

Jake couldn't sleep. He felt strangely alone even as he snuggled against Elena's supple body. There was a time he wouldn't have thought twice about cuddling against her until she would turn to him, eager to make love. But that seemed like ages ago, before Tifton came into his life. Now, he lived knowing that her feelings for him had changed. It didn't take a rocket scientist to see. She spent more time with the kids, would often ignore him, barely acknowledging his presence. And when the latest round of bills arrived from Drew's blood work, tests, and doctor's visits, Elena said not a word. She simply slapped a note on the refrigerator: "$7,435 past due."

He quietly opened the sliding glass doors and slipped from their bedroom onto the back patio. A brisk breeze swept across his face, signaling Miami's long, hot summer was nearing its end. His thirty-first birthday was only days away and yet he felt ten years older. All he could think of was Richter and his smirk. The guy definitely had it in for him and still Jake had no idea why. Tommy's testimony had been rock solid, forceful, better than expected. Nonetheless, Richter's parting remark troubled him to no end. All Jake could do now was wait.

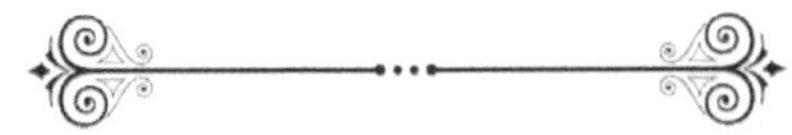

Chapter Twenty-One

In the morning, Tommy retook his seat on the witness stand and poured himself a glass of water. His face was pale and bags had formed under his eyes.

Richter stood erect behind the lectern. "Mr. Tifton, I understand you own a home with your wife. Correct?"

"Yes, sir."

"Have you ever purchased real estate for yourself or anyone else other than your home?"

"No, sir."

Jake slid Lenny a note. *Where's Richter going with this?*

Lenny shrugged.

Richter then abruptly changed the subject. "You say you didn't fly from South America on June 19 and 20, but instead came from Cozumel, Mexico. Is that your testimony?"

"It's the truth."

"And you say you have witnesses, your brother and Diego Mendoza and his wife, Gabriela, who will corroborate your whereabouts."

"Yes, sir. Like I said, I didn't expect to run into the Mendozas but I'm glad I did."

"I bet you are," Richter shot back, his tone laced with derision. "The Mendozas, did you get to know them well?"

"Not really. All I know is that Mr. Mendoza is active in the local chamber of commerce."

Jake sat back, impressed at how well Tommy was holding up.

"And referring to your testimony yesterday, you don't know the owner of the Cessna, is that your testimony?"

"I only know him as Red. Never met him."

A grin spread across Richter's face "Then I guess it's just a coincidence that the two of you are partners in a real estate venture in Lake City, Florida?"

A loud buzz swept the courtroom.

Tommy shook his head. "I don't know nothin' about that."

Richter stepped over to Nettles and grabbed a document from his outstretched hand. "May I, Your Honor?"

"You certainly may," Judge Henry replied, rocking back and forth in his tall chair.

Richter handed both Jake and Tommy a copy. "Isn't that your signature where it says Thomas Tifton, purchasing partner?"

Jake and Lenny exchanged looks.

"Your Honor," Jake called out while rising to his feet. "We object. The defense has never been shown this document before just now."

"Judge," Richter quickly replied. "This is offered strictly for impeachment, since the witness has previously testified that he has never dealt in real estate other than his own home."

"Objection overruled. Answer the question."

Tommy flipped the pages of the exhibit and then looked up, indignant. "I see my name, but that's not my signature. It looks like Dave's."

"So it's your brother, not you, who smuggled over sixty million dollars' worth of cocaine into this country. Is that what you're telling this jury?"

Jake erupted from his chair "Objection! Misleading. That's not what my client said."

"Sustained. You know better than to try to put words into the witness' mouth, counsel."

Richter eased back. "You're saying Dave Tifton signed your name to this exhibit, the one dated December 13, 2007, that shows Randall (Red) Armstrong as the managing general partner, this same Red Armstrong who owns the Cessna that you used to smuggle drugs?"

An alarm exploded in Jake's brain. Red Armstrong, who owned one hundred percent of the stock of Loesha, Inc., the record owner of the Cessna, now mysteriously surfaces in a real estate deal bearing Tommy's name. Jake didn't believe in coincidences.

"I didn't run no drugs," Tommy shouted back. "Dave had been going through a rough divorce and probably signed my name to keep what he had from going to his ex-wife."

For the next several hours the federal prosecutor peppered Tommy with a wide range of questions, exploring every detail of his flight through the tropical storm. Richter also used Tommy's bank records to question his ability to make the hefty mortgage payments on his half million dollar condo. Then Richter again changed the subject, intending to throw Tommy off balance, wear him down.

"You heard prior testimony that traces of your blood were found at the rear of the Cessna," Richter pressed. "What were you doing back there if you weren't throwing bags of cocaine from the plane?"

"The turbulence got so bad I smashed my face against the window and went looking for something to stop the bleeding."

Richter handed Jake yet another document, then approached the stand. "Mr. Tifton, let me show you government's composite exhibit thirty-one, dated May 12, 2008, also offered for impeachment. All I ask is that you examine the document and tell us whether that is your signature over your typed name?"

Tommy studied the exhibit for what seemed like an eternity then looked past Jake to Jessie, fidgeting in the front row.

"Well, Mr. Tifton?"

Tommy's grimace signaled trouble. Jake scribbled Lenny a note. Where'd he get these documents?

Lenny's expression told Jake that he didn't have a clue."

"It's not mine," Tommy finally answered. "As best I can tell, it's Dave's."

"Are you saying you know nothing about this transaction, even though your name is plastered all over it?"

Several jurors snickered.

"As I told you before, Dave was trying to keep money from his ex-wife."

"Can you tell us what composite exhibit thirty-one represents?"

"It's a legal document of some sort, something about buying four thousand acres in Valdosta County, Georgia."

Jake gripped the edge of the table and stared down at his legal pad, trying not to appear concerned, while his heart pounded against his chest. Tommy couldn't get off the stand fast enough.

Richter pressed ahead. "Attached to this contract for sale is another document, a partnership agreement. Who's the managing partner in this document?"

Tommy stared down at the exhibit. "Red Armstrong."

"You said it was Dave's deal. How did Red Armstrong get involved? And I thought you didn't know him."

"Ask the lawyer. I've got no idea why his name's there," Tommy said, squirming in his chair.

"Really?" Richter asked, mocking Tommy. "What was the cash price paid for this tract of land?"

Tommy hesitated. "It says three and a half million."

"Dollars? We're not talking Mexican pesos are we?" Richter asked. "Although I'm sure you've got plenty of those as well."

"Objection, Your Honor, argumentative," Jake said, halfway out of his chair.

"Mr. Richter," the judge cautioned, "you're stepping close to the line."

Richter wheeled toward Tommy, ignoring the admonition. "How does a manager making seventy thousand dollars a year come up with three and a half million dollars cash to buy land?"

"I don't know how many times I have to tell ya. It was Dave's deal, Dave's money. You'll have to ask him."

"And attached to the sales contract you have in your hand is a receipt made out to *you*, not your brother, for the sum of three and a half million dollars cash. Right?"

Tommy looked at the paper, then slowly nodded.

"Speak up, Mr. Tifton. Cat got your tongue?"

"The receipt was given to me but it wasn't my money, it was Dave's."

"Where'd he get all that cash?"

Tommy shook his head. "I know he's done pretty good with his investments, plus he owns a charter boat business."

"But when I asked you before whether you bought any other real estate, you said no."

"That's true. I didn't buy a thing, simply handed over Dave's money."

"And we're supposed to believe you didn't ask any questions when you turned over three and a half million dollars in cold hard cash?"

"I figured if Dave wanted me to know he'd tell me."

"To whom did you hand over this cash?"

"To Dave's lawyer."

Jake's head shot up from taking notes. Pendleton?

Richter waved the exhibit in the air. "Why doesn't your brother's name appear anywhere on government's thirty-one? Why only Red Armstrong as the managing partner and Sam Pendleton as Power of Attorney. How do you explain that?"

"I'll say it again for the umpteen time, ask the lawyer." Tommy slumped in his chair. "I've no idea how these things work."

"All of a sudden you don't seem to know much of anything, do you?"

Jake stood before Tommy could answer. "Objection. Argumentative."

"Withdrawn. One last question. Whose signature is that on the receipt of the three and a half million dollars?"

"Sam Pendleton."

"And who referred you to Mr. Dalton, your defense lawyer?"

"Sam Pendleton."

"One big, happy family," Richter said to no one in particular as he returned to his seat.

The judge leaned toward Jake. "Redirect, counsel?"

Jake was numb. His mind continued to reel from Tommy's testimony, making it impossible to think straight.

"Counsel, I asked if you had any redirect."

Jake stared at Tommy, knowing there was no way to undo the damage that had been done. "No, no, Your Honor. No questions."

The judge banged his gavel. "We'll stand adjourned until ten o'clock Monday morning."

Tommy moved off the stand and walked straight toward Jake. "How'd I do?"

"Are you serious?" Jake asked, then flicked a look at Lenny, who avoided looking at him. "I'll call Pendleton when we get outside, see if he can somehow explain away your testimony."

"He's not around."

Jake froze. Blood rush to his face. "And how would you know that? You've told me I'm the only lawyer you've ever dealt with. What gives? Wait, save your breath. I've already heard more than enough from you." Jake grit his teeth and felt he was about to explode. After several tense moments, he spoke again. "Tommy, it's time we sat down, mano a mano, and this time leave out the bullshit."

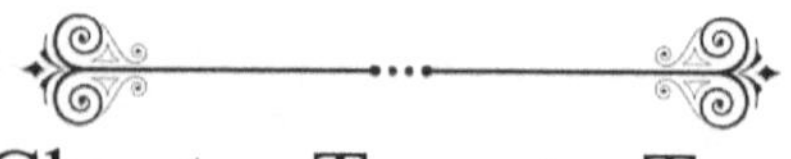

Chapter Twenty-Two

As soon as the cab dropped Sam Pendleton off at Miami's International Airport, he stuffed his ticket to LaGuardia into his briefcase and pulled out the one to George Town, Grand Cayman. As he was about to clear security, Sam glanced behind him to make sure he wasn't followed. At Gate 37 he took a seat among fellow passengers, a mix of business-types and flower-shirted vacationers waiting to board the Cayman Airways flight. Nothing appeared out of the ordinary.

An hour after take-off, the pristine waters of the Cayman Islands appeared outside Sam's first class window. Breezing through Customs, he strode through the rectangular, one-story terminal building, passing a well-dressed man in a white straw hat reading a newspaper while getting his shoes shined. Outside, natives selling their wares and tourists wearing bright colored shirts filled the narrow streets. Sam glanced around one last time before stepping into a cab with his overnight bag.

"The waterfront," he called to the driver from the back seat. "A quick stop at the harbor, then the Grand Hyatt."

"No problem, mon. Welcome to Grand Cayman, finest jewel in the Caribbean."

Fifteen minutes later, the taxi arrived at the bustling harbor across from Don Foster's dive shop. The cabbie shut off the engine but left the meter running. Sam watched the divers lining up their scuba tanks and made a mental note to return soon, with Gregory, his oldest, to dive among the marine life at Stingray City.

"Be only a minute," Sam called over his shoulder as he sidestepped puddles in the alley, before climbing the wooden stairs to a dilapidated door marked Law Office. He looked back one last time at the fish market two blocks south where vendors were hawking today's catch. Everything seemed as it should.

Sam knocked twice on the door and as usual let himself in. He looked inside, loose papers were strewn everywhere—over the solitary desk, a torn corner chair, and across the water-stained parquet floor. Inexplicably, the shades were drawn. A small antique lamp sitting atop a pile of books provided the only light. He wheeled at the sound of water flushing from inside the tiny bathroom.

"Good morning, Mr. Pendleton," the Cayman lawyer greeted him from the opened door, his lilt modulated by years of schooling in Great Britain. He sauntered toward Sam, drying his hands with a brown paper towel. A broad smile spread across his weathered face.

"Jesus. Were you robbed?" Sam scanned the cluttered office for the documents he had come for, fearing the worst.

The lawyer chuckled. "You must be referring to my filing system. Sorry, I didn't expect you this early. I had meant to tidy up and apologize if you were alarmed."

"I need the documents on Cheshire Ltd." Sam said, getting to the point of being there.

"Of course. Give me a moment, I'll look for them," the lawyer said, as he combed the room for papers on Cheshire, an entity Sam had set up for the sole purpose of laundering Red's profits.

Sam drummed his fingers on the desk. "Take your time. My plane doesn't leave for another week."

The lawyer shot Sam a baffled look, then continued his search. After several minutes, the Caymanian slowly straightened up. "Got them," he said, handing Sam a manila envelope. "You Americans, always in a hurry."

"Time is money, my friend," Sam said, tearing open the envelope. What he held in his hands would provide him access to Red's bearer bonds, monetary documents bearing no specific name, ensuring anonymity, and negotiable as cash. Sam scribbled his name on the receipt, handed it back to the lawyer and turned to leave.

"Before you go, Mr. Pendleton," the lawyer called as Sam was halfway out the door. "I thought you should know that a man rang up yesterday inquiring as to the time of your arrival."

Sam spun back around. "A man? Did you get a name?"

"I'm afraid not. But he did sound rather official."

"Perhaps someone from the bank?"

"I asked but he wouldn't say. But he did say he would try back later."

Sam's pulse quickened. In all the years he'd been visiting the islands, such a call was rare. Trying not to appear concerned, Sam left with the envelope tucked under his arm back to the waiting cab.

After checking into the Hyatt, Sam rode the elevator to the penthouse suite overlooking the famed seven-mile beach where perfectly tanned bodies populated the perfectly-white sand. Perhaps there would be time to snorkel, even hook-up with a lonely tourist. Marilyn would never know. He tossed his bag on the bed and pulled out his heavily-stamped passport, documents needed for the bank, and his Nikon.

Rested, he ambled down George Town's teeming streets, acting like hundreds of other camera-toting tourists while speeding scooters and bicyclists weaved in and out of honking traffic. After an hour of meandering and snapping photos, Sam stepped inside a small café on Queens Street. His mouth watered at the smell of barbecued shark and peppery cracked crab. He loved Miami for its posh restaurants, but nothing beat island cooking. A smiling hostess led him to a patio table where he spent the next hour sipping a Red Stripe and savoring grilled tuna, spicy black beans and rice. A Reggae band starting up next door reminded him to check his watch. Time for business.

He settled the bill and left to wander the side streets, casting occasional glances over his shoulder. The anonymous phone call continued to rattle him. That and the large man in a tan suit sitting on a bus bench across the street. Even without the white straw hat he bore an eerie resemblance to the man at the airport having his shoes shined. Was paranoia getting the best of him?

Sam continued his walk before stopping outside a jewelry store. He gazed at the glass display, hoping to catch a reflection of the man, but he had dropped from sight. Retracing his steps, Sam quickly ducked into the entrance of the Royal First Bank and approached a regal-looking woman in a tailored white uniform. She offered him a practiced smile.

"Excuse me," Sam said, studying the photo ID displayed on her lapel. "Miss Watkins. My name is Sam Pendleton, a preferred customer of your bank."

"Good afternoon, Mr. Pendleton. I thought I'd recognized you. How may I be of assistance?" Her voice was soft but the hardness in her eyes left little doubt that she was all business.

He pulled out the corporate documents and his passport from the envelope and handed them to her. "I'd like to get into my safety deposit box."

"Follow me." She stepped over to her desk and examined his ID, a notarized letter from the Cayman lawyer and legal papers to Cheshire Ltd., granting Sam entrée to the secured area. She then nodded her approval and escorted him down the marble stairs, unlocked a wrought-iron gate and stopped in front of a row of metal boxes. Without speaking, she inserted her key into Box 2441 and waited for him to do the same. Once both keys were in and the box unlocked, she turned to leave.

"Uh, before you go, Miss Watkins. Would you happen to know if someone from the bank tried to reach me? A man called yesterday but didn't leave his name."

"I'm sorry, sir. Without more I wouldn't be able to help. We have dozens of employees here." She offered the same cool smile and climbed the stairs, leaving him alone.

The shiny black box slid effortlessly from its rectangular tomb. Sam opened it and smiled. Staring back at him were sixteen anonymous bearer bonds, each imprinted with an official seal and worth a million dollars that he'd previously purchased with cash. No matter how many times he risked a trip for Red, he loved the feeling it gave, and the money he made: four and a half million over the past six years. After a few more trips, he'd be able to march into his father's study, mimic the old man's shit-eating grin, and unleash the rage he'd kept pent up for a lifetime, telling Travis Pendleton to take the trust money he doled out to his eldest son like crumbs to starving park pigeons, and shove it up his ass. Sam would then laugh in the old man's face and walk out of his life for good.

The next day, after wiring a million dollars to a separate construction account at his Coral Gables bank, Sam caught the two o'clock flight back home. At Miami International, he proceeded down the glassed-enclosed corridor to claim his bag before heading to Customs. He watched as several armed agents combed through piles of luggage, gripping the leashes of their drug-sniffing German Shepherds. In the past year, the airport had been put on a heightened alert for drug trafficking.

Sam's stomach churned. He grabbed his Louie Vuitton bag from the carousel, slipped into the line marked U.S. Citizens and moved to a uniformed officer behind the glass booth where Sam handed him his documents. The officer studied the completed immigration form, then electronically scanned Sam's passport. After several long moments, he looked up at him with an icy stare.

"Sir, I'm afraid you'll need to go with them," the officer said, pointing to two women positioned a few feet away. Both stood erect and poker-faced. One was tall and lean wearing a Customs uniform, the other was particularly fit and wore a handgun strapped to her hip, partially concealed by a blue parka with bright yellow letters across her chest: DEA. "And take your bag with you."

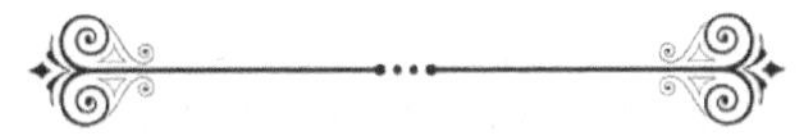

Chapter Twenty-Three

After Tifton's debacle on the witness stand, Jake couldn't get away from the courthouse fast enough. A horde of reporters tried to flag down Jake with questions, questions he couldn't answer. He summarily waved them off and kept walking with Lenny by his side.

"I can't believe I never saw it coming."

Lenny remained silent.

"Thanks for not rubbing it in."

"You're doing plenty without my help."

Jake kept moving, crossing North Miami Avenue before he stopped and faced his investigator. "The sonofabitch really played me. About Red, Pendleton, and that small detail of laundering millions in drug profits. Oh, right, he knows nothing about it. Who's going to swallow that? As far as I know, he could have masterminded the whole goddamn thing." Jake wanted to scream. "This is so fucked up."

Tommy and Jessie ran across the street and caught up to Jake and Lenny at the corner. The four looked at each other without saying a word.

Jake spoke first. "Let me get cut to the chase. I can't, I won't put your brother or the Mendozas on the stand. I just won't."

Tommy's face reddened. "Wait just a goddamn minute. It's my ass that's lookin' at thirty years." He must have seen the fury in Jake's eyes. "Can't we just talk about it?"

"There's nothing to talk about. I'm not going to do it. End of story."

"Just give Tommy a chance to explain," Jessie chimed in. "It's not that bad."

Jake stood momentarily speechless. "Are you serious? Weren't you in the courtroom? Didn't you see the look of the jurors? Yes, Jessie, it's that bad."

"What 'bout my alibi? I got no chance without it."

"You should have thought of that before. I'm not chucking my career on perjured testimony." Jake turned to leave, then looked back. "Did you think I was so stupid that I'd never figure it out?" He waved Tommy off as he walked toward his car.

"At least give me a chance to explain, Tommy shouted. "You owe me that."

Jake wheeled back around. "I owe *you*? That's rich. How do you expect me to argue your innocence now that you've practically admitted to laundering millions for Red Armstrong, the very owner of the plane you flew in that night?"

Tommy avoided Jake's stare and remained silent.

"I thought so."

Like never before, Jake needed to be alone. He half-walked, half-ran toward Bayfront Park, the pulse of his heart roaring in his ears. He didn't trust himself to get behind the wheel. As he approached Biscayne Bay, his cell phone rang. He fumbled to pull it from his pants pocket, not bothering to look at the caller ID. "What!" he yelled into the phone.

"Jake, is that you?"

"Elena, I'm sorry...for everything," he said, choking up. Did he dare tell her his worst fear was about to be realized: that a ruthless federal prosecutor, with the help of a major drug dealer, might be coming after him?

"You sound awful. Are you okay?"

"I'll explain when I see you. Is Drew, okay?" he asked, realizing that a call from Elena in the middle of trial was rare.

"He's fine. It's not that." She hesitated. "I just got this weird call, really creeped me out. Some guy with a thick Spanish accent wanted to know if you lived here."

Was the cartel already sending a message to play ball? "Who was it? How'd he get our number?"

"That's what I wanted to know. When I asked he just laughed, a real sickening laugh. I told him to stay the hell away, that I've got a really bad temper and an even bigger gun. Then he hung up."

"Jesus." He loved Elena's nerve.

"It has something to do with your case, doesn't it?"

He chose his words carefully, not wanting to frighten her any more than she already was. "I'm not sure, but to be safe, lock all the doors. I'm on my way home now." Jake ended the call and sprinted to his car.

As he pulled out of his office garage, Jake decided to avoid the heavy traffic on U.S. 1 and instead drive across the Brickell Avenue Bridge toward South Miami Avenue and the Grove. After driving for fifteen minutes, he glanced into his rearview mirror and spotted the same late model black Trans Am he'd seen a several cars behind leaving downtown. Jake slowed to get a better look and the Trans Am did the same. Jake then sped up on South Bayshore Drive, passing the entrance to Mercy Hospital before coming to a stop at a red light. His grip tightened on his steering wheel. Who was it? Once the light turned green he gunned the Saab until the road narrowed to two lanes, and then slowed. Again, the Trans Am appeared, two blocks behind. This time Jake pulled onto the shoulder and waited. Within seconds the Trans Am sped by before making a hard right, tires screeching, onto 22d Ave. toward Tigertail Ave. Jake caught only a glimpse of the driver: middle-age male, dark-complexioned, wearing a non-descript baseball cap pulled over aviator sunglasses.

Tifton and friends meant business.

Thirty minutes later Jake unlocked the front door and entered his home. He immediately found Elena seated at the kitchen table, smoking a cigarette. "I haven't seen you do that since grad school."

She remained silent, methodically blowing rings of smoke into the air.

He moved a chair close to her and sat down, stroking her hair. "We need to change our phone number. Having it unlisted hasn't done a damn bit of good."

Elena simply nodded. After several moments, she finally looked up at him. "Don't you think it's about time you tell me what the hell is going on?"

He squeezed her hand. "I'll tell you everything I know." Jake began from the beginning, describing the encounter with Sam at the courthouse minutes after Carmen settled, followed by his getting slammed at poker and Sam's phone call the next day. Jake shared in detail the initial meeting with Tifton and Jessie, the hundred thousand dollar retainer, half by check, half in cash, using a portion to replenish the kids' college fund he had previously taken to pay the home mortgage. He even shared Lenny's warnings and his own misgivings about Tifton and how he let the large fee cloud his judgment. Jake described Tifton's feigned ignorance on the witness stand and what it meant as well as learning of Sam's involvement in money laundering.

After he finished, Elena took another drag of the cigarette and dropped it lit into a half-filled glass of water. Moments later she dipped her finger into the glass and swirled the water for several seconds until it spilled onto the table, making no effort to clean it up.

"Sounds like you've got yourself into one God-awful mess," she said, her voice flat, lacking all emotion. "I could get all hysterical, but frankly, Jake, I'm just don't have it in me anymore. So excuse me if I just sit here and do nothing." She turned away from him.

"I don't know what to say except I'm sorry. I never imagined it would come to this. I thought I was doing the right thing."

Elena half-turned, her eyes burning right through him.

Jake waved his hands to clarify. "No, no, not about the lying, but by giving Tifton the benefit of the doubt. Frankly, I thought the case would be our meal ticket, provide a nest egg if, God forbid, Drew should get sick again. Instead, I could be in real trouble."

"Oh Jake, what are we going to do?"

He said nothing. There was nothing to say.

Elena finally spoke. "I don't get it. Isn't it your job to try to get your clients off, to keep them out of jail? Isn't that what you're paid to do?"

"Of course. But I can't put my client on the stand and help him lie about something I know is untrue. That's a crime."

Elena rose from the table. "Sam. That bastard. I had a bad feeling about that dirt bag the moment you told me he was giving you a case. Remember?"

Jake shuddered at the thought of Sam's inevitable arrest, and knowing Sam, the likelihood of his pointing the finger at him to stay out of jail.

Elena put her hand to her mouth. "Poor Marilyn. I've got to warn her about Sam. They could be in real danger."

"You do what's best. Right now I've got to finish the trial and prepare for the worst."

"You're still going to represent that man knowing who he is?"

"Got no choice. The judge would never let me off the case. In fact, Lenny called on my way home, says Tifton insists on a meeting ASAP. Wants to explain everything."

"Don't you dare. You don't know what he's capable of. You could get hurt."

"I doubt that. He still needs me...at least till the trial is over." Jake put his arm around her shoulder.

"Just tell that drug dealer to get another lawyer. I don't want you near him."

Jake said nothing.

She pushed him away. "There's no talking to *you*. You always do whatever the hell you want, like my opinion means nothing. Go ahead, go meet with your drug dealing client. I might as well prepare the kids that their father might not be coming home ever again."

"Please, baby. Let me get through this. I promise nothing will happen. Besides, Lenny will be there. I'll call the minute the meeting breaks."

Elena searched the open-air shopping mall and finally spotted Marilyn browsing in front of a kiosk. "Something for the boys?" Elena asked as she approached, trying to sound casual, even though it was eating at her insides what she had to say to her best friend.

Marilyn turned and smiled, then kissed Elena on the cheek. "I love your hair. Did you get it cut?"

Elena shook her head. "Maybe one of these days, I'll finally get up the nerve and go butch."

Marilyn laughed. She picked up a smart phone case that she'd been admiring. "Sam just got all three boys a new iPhone. I thought it was a bit over the top, but what the hell, you only live once." She reached over and squeezed Elena's hand. "What's going on? You sounded awful on the phone." Marilyn motioned to a nearby Mexican restaurant, nestled among the fashionable shops. "It's still Happy Hour. Let's grab a drink. The first margarita's on me."

Elena managed a smile and gestured to a small wooden bench in front of a rock waterfall. "It's so nice outside. Okay if we sit over there?"

After they settled on the bench, Elena spoke first. "I've got only an hour. Jake's watching the kids, then running back to his office. He's still in trial."

"Lord that man works harder than anyone I know. All Sam ever does is smoke pot and do real estate." She glanced down at her watch. "His plane from LaGuardia arrived an hour ago."

She gripped Marilyn's arm. "There's something I got to tell you. I don't know where to begin."

"You really *are* leaving Jake," Marilyn said, more a statement than a question, her Bostonian accent coming off thicker than usual. "I know the two of you have had your ups and downs, but hell, men lie. They just do."

Elena shook her head. "That's not why—"

"Honey, it's the nature of the beast. I'm not telling you anything you don't already know."

"But I never thought Jake would." Elena sighed and thought back to her senior year at the University of Miami when she rebelled against her controlling father and strict Catholic upbringing by dating a much older man who lied about being divorced. Embarrassed by her affair with a married man, Elena had told no one, other than Marilyn, who she had known since elementary school. Since then there were few, if any men, Elena trusted.

"El, let it go. Jake's a great guy. Everybody knows that. And he's heads over heels in love with you. I'd trade him for Sam any day."

"It's not that. But you're right, it did cross my mind, I was so angry." She slumped in her seat. "Boy, what a year. I could write a book."

"Well, all I can say is look before you jump. It ain't so pretty out there."

Elena's brow shot up. "You thought about divorcing Sam?"

"Thought about it, but you know me, I'm not one for change. Besides, I could never do that to my boys."

Elena briefly imagined life without Jake, but couldn't. "Lately, all we do is fight. It was never like that before. Drew and Nikki absolutely worship him…he's kind, not your typical macho type. When it's good, it's really good, but when…I don't know anymore. I guess deep down I still love the jerk."

"And he loves you, as damn well he should."

They shared a laugh.

Elena gazed at the passing shoppers, admiring the latest fashions in window displays as though they didn't have a worry in the world. She grabbed Marilyn's arm. "I have to tell you. It's killing me not to.

Please don't hate me for it. Jake just found out that Sam's been laundering money for the cartel and thinks it's only a matter of time before he's arrested."

"What?"

"I was as shocked as you are when Jake told me," Elena lied, trying to spare her friend.

Marilyn's hand flew to her mouth. "That's impossible, Sam doesn't need the money. My lord, he gets plenty from his father. Besides, he would never do such a thing and risk losing his boys!" Her eyes hardened. "You tell Jake he's got it all wrong. Who'd say such a thing? Some coked-up druggie, trying to score points. I know Sam better than anyone, and believe me, he'd have nothing to do with those people."

Elena hesitated. In all the years of knowing Marilyn, she knew better than to argue. All she could do was reach over and hug her dear friend.

Chapter Twenty-Four

Okay, Sam told himself, relax, it's just routine. Every umpteenth person in line gets pulled out. You can do this. No big deal, it doesn't mean a thing. As he approached the slender Customs officer, Sam tried to remember if he had anything in his bag that could be incriminating. The armed DEA agent, standing a few feet to his left, maintained her cold stare.

"Follow me." The Customs officer pointed to several adjoining metal tables behind a solid yellow line. She led him to the area, then turned and gestured to his bag.

"Please open it and kindly step back."

Sam complied.

The officer gave a cursory look inside, shuffled a few articles of clothing, including the Armani suit and tie Sam had packed to convince Marilyn he was traveling to New York, then examined his passport.

"Mr. Pendleton. Is that how you say it?"

"That's right," he replied, trying to remain calm.

"I see you've been to Jamaica, the Bahamas, and the Cayman Islands more than a dozen times this past year. Would you mind telling me the nature of your business there?"

"Not at all. I'm a lawyer, and I represent several real estate investors, both here and abroad." The Customs officer continued to stare at him while the DEA agent stepped to Sam's bag and slid her hands inside, feeling for hidden compartments. "They've retained me to look after their interests in the islands," Sam continued. "Been doing it for years." Sam knew he was babbling and clamped his mouth shut, angry at himself for volunteering too much.

"Is that so?" said the Customs officer as she examined the stamps on the passport. "My husband's in real estate. How do you find these investments?"

"I wish I could help, but I'd be divulging client confidences." Sam tried to keep his tone light but he didn't like where this was heading. "I'm sure you understand."

"Of course, Mr. Pendleton. Didn't mean to pry." She handed back his passport, then half-turned to the DEA agent, who shook her head. "Welcome home."

The DEA agent stepped back, making room for him to pass. He'd hate to run into her in a dark alley, Sam thought. One tough bitch.

Sam passed through the double glass doors sealing U.S. Customs from the outside world, lengthened his stride down the corridor and turned the corner, finally out of sight. He pulled his handkerchief from his pocket and wiped the sweat from his neck. Time to bring Red up to speed but Sam would leave out the bit about Customs. In fact, they'd hardly searched his bag; probably harassing him because he was a lawyer.

He pressed the numbers on his iPhone and continued to walk.

"Hey man," Sam said, keeping his voice low, "just got back in town. I took care of the wire this morning, should be sitting in the account, less my usual ten percent."

"About time you called." Red's raspy voice grated through the phone. "I need 50k right away. We've run into a snag with *your* friend."

Sam glanced at his watch. Half past four. His bank's drive-thru closed at six. "That doesn't leave me much time."

"Just do it. My guy's trial is going south."

"What happen?"

"Not over the phone. Be at the Italian joint at seven with the cash. Your poker buddy's becoming a bigger problem than we thought."

The call went dead. Sam stared at his cell. He had plenty of service but the connection was lost. Red Armstrong, one of a few *gringos* the Mexicans trusted to fly their cocaine in from Colombia, the one guy Sam never wanted to piss off, had just hung up on him.

Minutes before seven o'clock that evening, Sam bypassed the valet and pulled into the self-parking lot of Nick's Little Italy and cut the engine. He entered the crowded restaurant, walked past the hostess, and immediately spotted his client. The broad face behind dark sunglasses, shoulder-length, wavy red hair and matching mustache were impossible to miss. Sam hurried to the last booth in the far corner and slid in.

Red glared at him, his menacing eyes nearly concealed by the dark glass. "How many times do I have to tell you about the fucking phones?"

Sam froze at Red's tone. "Sorry, it won't happen again."

Red's face grew tight. "Tommy blew up in court."

"How'd you know?"

"I had someone in the courtroom. He was doing fine 'til they brought up shit about the land. He blames you."

Sam swallowed hard. "Me?"

"Yeah, *you*. Is there something the fuck wrong with your hearing? What were you thinking putting Tommy's name on those papers? The pea you've got for a brain couldn't come up with somebody else?"

"Wait a minute. Those deals were closed one, maybe two years ago. You told me Tommy would never work for you again. Those were your words. Never, ever. How was I supposed to know you'd bring him back in?"

Red shook his head. "I can't believe I let him talk me into it. I should have cut him loose long ago. Now the Mexicans are all over my ass."

"It'll blow over the minute he's acquitted."

Red leaned over the table, his face inches from him. "Then your poker buddy better get with the program. That's a problem, a big fucking problem. I got Mendoza and his wife ready to fly in but now your friend says he won't use them. Who the fuck does this clown think he is? Maybe I should put two rounds in his head. That'll get Tommy a new trial."

Sam's leg refused to stop shaking under the table. He knew full well what Red was capable of. "Come on, give the man some slack. Dalton's smart, he'll figure something out."

"He'd better." Red lifted his butter knife off the table and plunged it into the heart of garlic roll in front of him, "I got too much at stake."

Sam's mouth went dry. What had he done? Sam thought back to Red's call in the middle of the night right after Tommy's arrest. Since Tommy was part of his crew, Red had agreed to cover his legal fees and looked to Sam to find the right guy to handle

Tommy's defense. Sam's first thought was to hire one of two criminal defense lawyers he had used in the past. But at the time they had their own problems—looming federal indictments stemming from the crackdown on lawyers, accountants and bankers tied to the cartels. Nonetheless, Sam now knew he should have chosen someone with more experience and not have given in to Marilyn's nagging to help poor Jake.

Sam's eyes roamed the room for a waiter. "Can't anyone get a friggin' drink around here?" He looked back at Red. "Take it easy. You have nothing to worry about."

Red pulled the knife from the roll and slowly buttered it, as if nothing was wrong. "Do I look worried? I understand your friend's got a sick kid. That should make convincing him a lot easier."

Sam's jaw dropped. "My God, you're not going to hurt his boy?"

"That depends." Red took a bite of his roll and smacked his lips. "Man, these Italians sure know how to make great bread, don't ya think?"

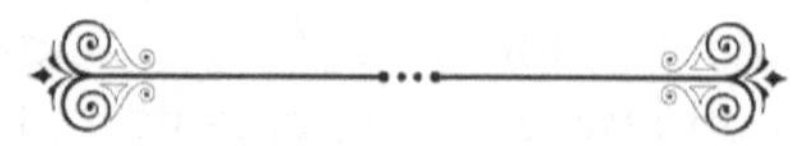

Chapter Twenty-Five

"Good to see you, counselor," Tifton called from the sofa inside Jake's office the moment Jake opened the front door, late for their meeting. Jessie sat beside her husband and smiled as if life couldn't get any better. One cool customer.

"Going somewhere?" Jake asked, eyeing the bulging Samsonite suitcase on Tommy's lap. "That certainly would save us a lot of trouble."

Tommy laughed. "I always did like your sense of humor." He patted the luggage. "Nah, but I did bring something for you to see."

"Where's Lenny?" Jake asked, already anxious to get the meeting over and done with.

"Your investigator let us—"

Jake turned toward the sound of Lenny's footsteps from the back office. "There you are. Let's get started."

"Tommy rose from the sofa. "What I got to say is between me and you, Jake. Your man can stay here and keep Jessie company."

"Lenny goes where I go. If you have something to say, say it to both or not at all."

Tifton hesitated. "Fine, let's do it."

Jake led the three down the hall to his office and quickly settled into his chair behind his desk. Lenny remained standing at Jake's side, his hands clasped in front of his body. Tommy and Jessie each took a seat across from Jake.

"What's so urgent that we had to meet this morning?" Jake asked. "Are you thinking of changing your plea to guilty?"

"You'd be doing all of us a big favor." Lenny quipped.

Tommy shook his head. "My story hasn't changed one iota. I just can't get into certain things. That would be unhealthy for the both of us."

Jessie nodded her agreement.

Jake and Lenny exchanged looks.

"All we're askin' is that you give Tommy a chance to explain himself," Jessie said, offering her worth to the conversation.

"This is how I see it," Tommy said, leaning toward Jake. The alibi is key. I've got little or no chance without it. The good news is that Richter hasn't laid a glove on it. I admit it hurt when he brought up the land, but that's all. He still hasn't tied me to the coke."

"Aren't you forgetting Butch's testimony and the three and a half million in cash that you gave to Pendleton, who invests for Red, the owner of the Cessna, who you swore you knew nothing about?"

"The God's honest truth is that the money isn't mine, never was. As for Butch, he's a lying sack of shit who won't be around for his next birthday."

Jake could only shake his head at hearing this. "Both of us would have been much better off if you'd been straight with me from the start."

"Well, I still like my chances, in spite of what you say. Dave and the Mendozas will make great witnesses."

Jake rose from his chair. "Tommy, you're not hearing me. Your alibi is crap, and I'm not about to risk my career putting on perjured testimony."

"But you don't know that."

"I know enough."

Tommy lifted his suitcase and dropped it on the desk. "I had a feelin' you'd see it that way." He snapped it open and pointed to its contents. "It's yours, fifty thou in twenties and fifties, and another fifty when we beat the case." The cash was tied with rubber bands in even stacks. Drug profits, no doubt. Jake would be crazy to risk disbarment, if not a conspiracy charge, by taking it.

"Consider it a bonus," Tommy added.

Jake waved him off. "No way will I take your money. It's not open for discussion."

"Well, thought I'd give it a try." He looked long and hard at Jake. "All I'm gonna say is that you'd better beat this case, counselor. For *everyone's* sake. I'm the last guy in the world who wants to see anyone get hurt, but understand that I'm not one to take this lying down." He slammed the suitcase shut, motioned to Jessie and they walked out.

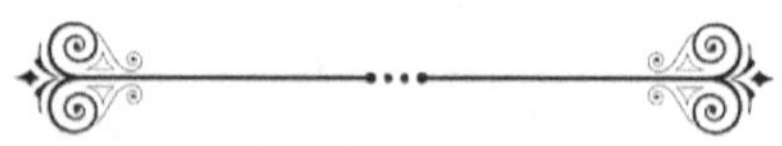

Chapter Twenty-Six

In the courthouse canteen, Jake played over in his mind the closing argument he was about to give. He had arrived two hours earlier to avoid the swarm of reporters and TV crews camped on the street for the first scent of a verdict. At 8:30 A.M., he glanced over his third cup of coffee and spotted his guy.

Lenny waved, paid for his coffee, then meandered over and sat across from Jake. He looked solemn in a double-breasted charcoal suit and black striped tie.

"Looks like you're going to a funeral," Jake said, pushing aside his files to make room. "Hope it's not mine."

"I normally don't wear such nice threads to court," Lenny said through a laugh, "but I wanna pay my respects to Tifton on his last day a free man."

"You that sure?"

Lenny blew at the steam rising from his coffee and took a sip. "Twenty to one, guilty. Those were the odds an hour ago."

"Ouch."

"You tell Elena about Tifton's stunt in your office?"

"Had to. I sure as hell wasn't going to keep anything from her after last time."

"What'd she say?"

"Freaked out, worried if Tifton was desperate to offer that much cash what else might he do."

Lenny nodded his head but said nothing.

"Great. My first drug case and already I'm thinking about doubling my life insurance."

Out of the corner of his eye, Jake saw Richter and Nettles enter the canteen. The federal prosecutor gave Jake a mock salute.

Jake rose from his chair. "I'm outta here. The Grand Inquisitor just arrived."

Jake noticed the tremble in Tommy's hand as he sat beside him waiting for Judge Henry to finish his final instructions to the jury. Jake thought his summation went well, under the circumstances. He even had a couple of jurors nodding in agreement when he pointed to several flaws in the government's proof—the height finder being down, evidence of three planes tracking south to north along the same path as Tommy's, and the eleven-mile distance between Customs and its target, making it impossible for Customs to have seen the duffel bags tossed.

In the corridor outside the courtroom, Tommy and Jessie continued to wait on the verdict while Lenny left to meet a witness in another case. Jake figured the jury would take their lunch on the government's dime, and then return a verdict in time to beat rush hour traffic home. However, four hours later the jury sent a note of a possible deadlock, proving Jake wrong. Then, shortly before five the jury filed back into the courtroom, their faces impossible to read. Jake envisioned NOT GUILTY! splashed across the Herald's front page, making Tifton's day and his career.

The judge glared down at the panel. "Members of the jury, I understand you have thus far failed to reach a unanimous decision. Therefore, expect a very long day tomorrow because we are not leaving here until I have a verdict. I shall expect to see each of you tomorrow morning promptly at nine o'clock." He banged his gavel and left the bench.

The jury collected their belongings and filed out, looking neither at the prosecution nor the defense.

For the first time in days, Jake smiled inside. Even a hung jury would be a major win in his eyes.

Richter's mouth remained locked tight as he left the courtroom. Jake was tempted to rub Richter's face in the possibility of an acquittal but thought better of it. He couldn't wait to be done with this case and get on with his life.

Tommy grabbed Jake's arm as he was about to leave. "Spare a few minutes?"

"Sure, why not." By tomorrow Tommy would be either led off to prison in handcuffs or set free. Either way, Jake had his fill of the war hero.

"Let's go under the flag." Tommy motioned to the far side of the courtroom where Old Glory stood. He gestured to Jessie to wait outside.

Jake followed his client to the secluded area where Tommy turned to face him. "Sorry about the other day. I told Jessie you wouldn't go for it, even with a sick boy at home." Tommy's eyes roamed the near-empty room. "What I did wasn't a sign of disrespect. As a matter of fact, I've come to respect you for giving me your all from the get-go. That hasn't happened to me since Desert Storm."

Several moments passed in silence before Jake spoke. "Why'd you bullshit me, Tommy? Did you think I'd cut and run if you'd told me the truth?"

"You wouldn't have taken my case otherwise."

"You're wrong. Everyone's entitled to a defense. I do what I do because I care about the system. It's bigger than both of us." Jake chose to leave out the part about needing the money.

Tommy's eyes turned distant, as though lost in thought. "I had you pegged the second we met, even told my brother later on you wouldn't have taken the case if you knew the truth."

Jake remained silent.

"You should feel flattered," Tommy added. "I saw right from the start that you had integrity. Believe me, that's rare in your breed."

Jake studied his client. Gone was his folksiness, replaced with a cunning intelligence not revealed before.

"You should have given the system a chance."

Tommy laughed hard. "Oh, brother, lemme tell you, I've tried that before. Got shot up, nearly ate it for a country I love, then for the next twenty years got screwed over by my own fucking government. It finally dawned on me to take matters into my own hands. But I'll level with ya, I owe you that much. It was my first and only trip. I tried a few years back but had to abort, too many memories. So, when I saw that article in the paper, when they said I 'played a leading role,' I nearly fell off my chair." Tommy gazed up at the Stars and Stripes. "You've no idea the shit that goes on every single day while God-fearing folks pay homage to this flag, are willing to spill their blood for this flag, no questions asked." He tapped his fingers on the side of his head. "But I finally wised up. I got buddies buried in Arlington who paid the ultimate price. For what? For a government that's fucking corrupt, that's for what."

"You mean Richter? He had no right running off our expert. I haven't forgotten—"

"I ain't talkin' about that. Man, that's chickenshit. It's way bigger, much higher up. It would blow your mind, what I know, all in the name of God and country."

"What the hell you talking about?" Jake felt the conversation had gotten away from him, that Tommy was talking in some kind of code. "If you know something about people on the take, I'd like to hear about it."

"That's all I'm gonna say for now. I'm just waitin' to see how much more the good ol' U S of A continues to screw with this soldier." He laughed again.

"What's so funny?"

"This whole fucking trial, that's what. Wasn't supposed to happen. Nothing but a parade. But instead of going down Main Street, it's heading straight up my ass. Trying to convince folks that the feds give a damn about the war on drugs, instead of what it's really about." Tommy rubbed his fingers and thumb together. "Power and money. Someday you'll open your eyes and see what I'm talking about." His face relaxed.

"What do you mean 'the trial wasn't supposed to happen'? What are you saying?"

Tifton shook his head. "Another time." He stuck out his hand and Jake took it. "Counselor, you're way better than advertised. I'll never forget how you gave that sorry ass of a prosecutor a run for his money." Tommy winked. "Who knows, the jury might surprise us all and come back not guilty."

"Let's hope so."

"You mean that?"

"Sure. Like I said when we first met, I'm not here to judge you, just give you my best shot."

Tommy nodded. "I'll remember that."

The next day came and went without a verdict. Jake envisioned coming home and cracking open a bottle of champagne with Elena; a great ending to his first and last drug case. However, two days later, heads bent low, the jury filed into the courtroom. They wouldn't look at Tommy, and Jake knew what that meant. As if in slow motion, the forewoman handed the verdict to the clerk, who passed it to the judge. Judge Henry opened and read the paper, his lips parting into a barely perceptible smile. He then returned it to the clerk, who read out loud the jury's unanimous verdict of guilty on both counts of the indictment.

At the defense table, Tommy stood motionless, his eyes closed, as though praying. Behind him, in the front row, Jessie sobbed.

Richter and Nettles congratulated each other. Then the prosecutor turned toward Jake and mouthed, "You're next."

After the judge polled each juror, confirming their guilty vote, Richter rose.

"Your Honor, in view of the jury's verdict, the government requests that the defendant's bond be revoked. Innocence is no longer presumed."

The judge nodded. "Based on the verdict, I hereby order that the Defendant's bond be revoked forthwith and that he be remanded to the custody of the Attorney General. Sentencing is set in this courtroom for December 14, 2009 at ten o'clock. Marshals, take the prisoner away."

Instantly, three huge deputies converged on the defense table and shackled Tommy with handcuffs and leg irons. He offered no resistance. Jake stood stunned by the swiftness with which Tifton was transformed from a free man to chained prisoner. Jessie leaped from her seat and ran crying to her husband, only to be shouldered aside by the marshals. Tommy twisted his body around and blew her a kiss as the deputies led him from the courtroom.

PART 2

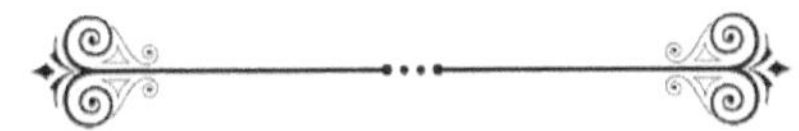

Chapter Twenty-Seven

Red Armstrong elbowed his way through the stands as powerful thoroughbreds stepped skittishly into the starting gate, waiting for the bell to sound for the sixth race at Calder Race Track. His burner phone buzzed.

"Yeah?" he shouted into his cell over the raucous crowd.

A woman wailed back.

"Jessie, is that you?"

"Tom…Tommy's going…." She stuttered through sobs.

The bell rang and the race was off. Red put his hand over his free ear to muffle the screams all around him.

"I can't hear you. Call me later." He had better things to do than deal with a hysterical woman.

"Tommy's in jail. They—"

"What!" Red wiped the spittle from his mustache.

"The bastards dragged him away in chains, like a dog!"

"What you calling on?"

"The phone you gave me."

"Hold on." Red ran down the stairs to a near-empty concourse where he could hear himself think. He glanced up at the screen to see how his horse, Magic Portion, was doing, then spoke low.

"Jessie, calm down. Everything's going to be okay. What'd the lawyer say?"

"Thinks Tommy's got a shot on appeal, but won't get out any time soon. Red, we're broke," she whined, "we don't have no money."

"I might as well kiss my Cessna goodbye," Red mumbled.

"Whatcha say?"

"Forget it. Lemme see what I can do." He glanced at the monitor to see if Magic Portion still had the lead. "Did my name come up?"

"Tommy—" She started to cry again. "Red, you gotta help."

"Get a grip, dammit. With all your bawling, I can't make out a word you're sayin'." Her breathing slowed until her sniffles were barely audible. "There, that's it. Now, go on. What was that?"

"A couple of times."

Red stopped in his tracks. "You're shittin' me."

"Tommy didn't tell---"

"Fuck no. Why should he? I only saved his sorry ass after he tossed the goddamn load."

"Don't be like that," Jessie pleaded. "He didn't say nothing the feds didn't already know."

"Sam's such a fucking moron," Red said, moving toward the exit.

"What am I gonna do? I can't live without Tommy."

"Relax, will ya, let me think. Can you fly a turboprop?"

"Huh? Yeah...sure, been flying since I turned eighteen." Her voice grew stronger. "Why?"

"I need you to get down to the executive airport...in Perrine. Ask for Chris at Marco Aviation. You got that, Chris at Marco Aviation. Take my King Air and land at the strip near my cabin. It's plenty long so you won't have a problem. There's better than two mil."

"Where's it at?"

"Back of the barn, stashed in burlap bags marked fertilizer. Then go to your step mom's and wait for my call. And Jessie, I know you won't get stupid seeing all that cash."

"Red—"

"What now?" The crowd cheered and the stands shook. Red ran up the stairs and watched the thoroughbreds kicked up dirt as jockeys fought on the rail for the home stretch.

"What if I'm caught? Tommy—"

"Just do as I say, dammit." Red snapped the cell shut. He scanned the lighted board to see if he had won, then tore up his ticket and stormed out, pissed that he'd blown ten grand so easily.

Driving south, Red glanced into the rearview mirror while he pressed the numbers on his cell to call Javier, the cartel's point man in Miami, and the same crazy-ass Mexican he'd reached out to spare Tommy's and Butch's lives after the coke was ditched.

He never figured Tommy, of all people, would turn out to be such a fuck up. But Red swore he'd never forsake his cousin, not after what Tommy's folks did for him and his little brother, Joey. The deeply religious couple had refused to let him and Joey rot in an orphanage after their own dead-beat parents took off in the middle of the night, leaving them to fend for themselves. Instead, Tommy's mom and dad took the two boys in and treated them like their own flesh and blood. From that moment on, Tommy and he had grown tight in Beizley, a town deep in Florida's panhandle. And when seven-year-old Joey got killed by some drunk in a pick-up, Tommy was there for him like no other. From that moment, Red swore he'd have Tommy's back, no matter what.

Red pressed the burner against his ear. "Hey, *chico*," he said when Javier answered. "Got news, but not over the phone."

"*Que pasa, mi amigo?*"

"We need to talk. Now, if possible." Red turned down the radio and waited.

There was an uncomfortable silence before Javier spoke again. *"Esta bien. Te veo hoy. El Café Havana, en una hora."*

The line went dead. Red checked his watch. Only an hour to get to Miami's *Calle Ocho*. He reached over and opened the glove box. A black .40 caliber semi-automatic stared back at him. He secured the loaded Glock inside his jacket, checked the rearview mirror once more and sped toward Miami.

After circling the area twice to make sure he wasn't followed, Red pulled into the rear parking lot of Café Havana and killed the engine. Minutes later, Javier—short, stocky, and wearing a sky blue guayabera— appeared from behind a parked car. The Mexican cupped a lit cigarette in the palm of one hand and fingered his pencil-thin mustache with the other. Could that be some sort of signal, Red worried.

Red stepped from his jeep and surveyed the half-filled parking lot and surrounding shrubbery. He didn't expect trouble, but with Javier he could never be sure.

"Thanks for coming," Red began the conversation, while checking Javier's guayabera to see if he was armed. "A federal jury just nailed one of my guys. I wanted to tell you face to face that you don't have a problem."

Javier remained silent. His small eyes darted behind tortoiseshell sunglasses.

"He's my cousin and solid as they come," Red added, knowing Mexicans have a thing for family. "Tell the Man I've known him my whole life. He's no snitch."

Javier took a long drag of his cigarette and exhaled a stream of smoke through his nostrils. "Before we get to that, my friend, I'd like to know why your people want to steal from me."

The steely edge in the Mexican's voice unnerved him. Red casually moved to scratch the small of his back and felt the semi-automatic snug under his shirt, inside the waistband of his pants. "Are we talking—"

"Who else would I be talking about? Last week one of my loads disappeared," Javier snapped his fingers, "just like that. My people are not happy."

"Could be one of your own," Red shot back. Javier constantly pissed and moaned about being ripped off by the CIA.

"I don't think so. Besides, I always said your government cannot be trusted."

"Ok. Give me a few days to look into it. There's someone I can call."

Javier smiled but it didn't reach his eyes. "I must insist on...how you Americans say...proof. Yes, proof your people haven't disrespected our agreement. That would be most unfortunate."

Instantly, Red knew the problem was Carlos, a field operative. Burned by Carlos once before, Red had wanted to kill the sonofabitch but was convinced by his station chief to let it go. Now, left unchecked, Carlos could fuck up Red's entire operation.

Red studied the Mexican. "Understand my cousin had nothing to do with whatever the fuck went down, but you have my word I'll straighten things out. In the meantime, do I have your word no harm will come to him?"

"I see no reason to end such a profitable friendship." He flicked the lit cigarette to the ground and crushed it with the heel of his boot. "At least, not yet. If, *en el futuro,* your cousin were to have an unfortunate accident, understand it was simply a matter of respect." Javier wheeled and left.

Red jumped back into his Wrangler; satisfied Tommy was safe for now. Doing business with this particular cartel, the Santolisma, had been lucrative but not without risk. For years, and at Red's insistence, the cartel had agreed to pay ten percent of its profits to U.S. counterintelligence in exchange for assurance that monthly shipments into the U.S. went off without a hitch. But now Carlos and others had apparently helped themselves to a load of coke to sell to third parties, threatening Red's relationship with the Mexicans. Carlos had to be neutralized and the coke returned ASAP, if Tommy were to stay alive.

As Red veered south on U.S. 1 toward Homestead, he punched the private number on his cell to his contact in Langley.

"Hey," Red said, trying to sound casual. "Can't talk long, just wanted to see if everything's cool. There was a verdict in Miami."

"This better be important." The woman's voice was unusually gruff.

"I wouldn't be calling if the matter had been taken care of like I asked."

"I reached out like I said I would but it did no good."

"Try explaining that to my guy."

Her tone softened. "It never should have gotten this far. I'll make another call."

"One more thing. I got a not-so-subtle message from our friends in the south. They're sure one of yours ripped 'em off. I wouldn't put it past Carlos. He needs to make good before all hell breaks loose."

"Just a sec, someone's coming."

Red pulled onto the side of the road, checking once again to see if he was followed.

"I'm back. If one of ours has his hand in the till, it's unauthorized. Get me a name."

"Already fucking did. Carlos."

"You'll hear from me." The line went dead.

Chapter Twenty-Eight

Jake gulped down his vodka and waved Mitch over the moment he entered O'Malley's.

"Man, this gotta be important," Mitch said, slapping at Jake's raised hand as if he'd just scored a touchdown, then slid into the booth across from him. He loosened his tie and eyed the iced tea with three lemons on the table in front of him. "You remembered." The former mob prosecutor's thick Brooklyn accent could easily be heard over the babble of the pub's regulars.

"Sorry to pull you out of your meeting, but I've been a bit crazed ever since that asshole of a judge threw the book at my client. Gave him thirty years."

"Yeah, my secretary said you sounded like you meant to call 9-1-1 and got me instead." Mitch chuckled.

Jake stared down at his empty glass.

"Aw, come on kid, don't take it so hard. Lose a few more and you'll get used to it. Besides, you said you're buying."

Jake managed a smile. "Elena was so right about my doing this shit. A drowning man never realizes he's in trouble 'til it's too late."

A red-haired waitress sauntered up and set two plates before them, a corned beef sandwich for Jake and a steak burger for Mitch. She nodded at Jake's glass. "Care for another, sir?"

Mitch tried to wave her off.

"You're reading my mind." Jake smiled back at her, ignoring his friend.

Mitch took a bite and talked around the burger. "You caught a bad break, that's all. Henry's one mean sonofabitch, and there's no bigger prick than Richter."

"I need a favor," Jake said, getting to why he called Mitch.

"Name it."

"I'd like you to represent Tifton on appeal. Money's not a problem."

Mitch straightened his shoulders, took his napkin and wiped the steak juice off his chin. "I particularly liked hearing that last part."

"Figured you would. I can't represent him any longer, you should only know the crap that went on in trial."

For the next hour, Jake shared with Mitch everything he knew about Tifton and the case.

"Smart move on your part," Mitch agreed. "Any lawyer worth his salt never would have let those folks testify. What'd you do after you realized the alibi was a crock?"

"My first thought was to take Tifton outside and shoot him, but I didn't have a gun."

Mitch threw his head back and laughed hard. "Now you're beginning to sound like some of my mob clients." He smacked the bottom of the ketchup bottle until his fries were smothered. "How's Elena taking it?"

"There was a time I thought she was out the door, but lately things have gotten better." Jake loosen his tie. "My lies nearly cost me my marriage."

"You underestimate how much she loves you. But getting back to Richter, I don't get why he'd waste his time going after you over such measly crap. Let's say you knew the alibi was as phony as a three-dollar bill; we're not exactly talking crime of the century. People lie in court all the time." Mitch paused. "Unless you're leaving something out?"

"I've told you *everything*. I'll admit that at times I had an uneasy feeling when Tifton's story didn't quite add up, seemed a little too pat. But that's it."

"One thing's for sure," Mitch said, looking at the Jake's empty glass, "that shit won't help. Take it from a guy who's already ridden that pony." He did Jake a favor by changing the subject. "To have a shot on appeal, Cunningham is key."

"Good luck with that, he won't return my calls. Richter must have put the fear of God in him."

"I'll get him to talk," Mitch said, confidently.

Jake pushed away his half-eaten sandwich. "What if Tifton thinks he's locked up because I failed to get Cunningham subpoenaed?"

Mitch scoffed. "Don't be ridiculous. Incompetence won't get you killed, that would eliminate half the Florida Bar." He started to laugh but stopped when Jake hadn't joined in. "Relax, kid. Tifton's talking appeal, right?"

"That reminds me. When I told his brother I wouldn't be handling the appeal, he mentioned the feds were holding Tommy here, instead of transferring him to Atlanta."

Mitch stopped eating. "That's not good. It can only mean one thing: Richter plans to put him in front of a grand jury. You could have a bigger problem than I thought."

Jake bit down on his lip. "What in God's name do they want with me?"

"Nothing sells papers more than indicting a lawyer."

"This is bullshit!" Jake shouted, causing those at nearby tables to stare at him. He lowered his voice. "Tifton knows I've done nothing wrong. He's better than that. Besides, I've never done a drug case before. Isora knows my clients. She'll back me up."

"Hold on, kid, you're getting way ahead of yourself. Let me go see him, take his pulse, so to speak. Wouldn't be the first time a felon tried to lie his way out of prison."

"Thanks, I'm beginning to feel better already." Jake sighed.

"Well, what are friends for?" Mitch gave him a broad smile.

Jake hesitated. "I'd hate to give you a bigger head than you already have."

Mitch waved him on. "Go on, you know I love hearing it anyway."

"You're as good as they come, ol' buddy."

Mitch winked at Jake. "Back at ya, kid."

Chapter Twenty-Nine

Into his hand-held cassette recorder, Mitch dictated a memo to his secretary while driving to see Tommy Tifton at the Federal Correctional Prison, making the familiar forty-mile trek southwest of Miami more times than he cared to remember. During his time in charge of the Strike Force's Miami Office on Organized Crime, he would arrive to interrogate convicted Mafiosos anxious to roll over on one of their own for a one-way ticket into the witness protection program. Now, in private practice, Mitch missed the special treatment the guards had once shown him and was resigned to stand in line like every other lawyer waiting to see their client.

A severe cold front, unusual for Miami even in January, dipped temperatures into the upper-thirties. Mitch breathed in the crisp cool air, a welcomed relief from Florida's oppressive humidity and more akin to Brooklyn, his hometown. He slid his Florida Bar card and photo ID through the two-inch opening of the glass-enclosed booth. The stoic face of a uniformed guard opened into a wide grin the moment he recognized Mitch.

"Who we got today, counselor? Another inmate whose name ends in a vowel?"

Mitch smiled. "Not quite. Thomas Tifton." Mitch peeked through the double-plated glass to see if his name had made it to Tifton's list of approved visitors, then glanced at a mugshot of Tifton he held in his hand.

The guard ran his fingers down the page and looked up. "Got him." He handed Mitch a visitor's pass. "Mighty popular client you got there. You're the third to see him this week."

After taking two steps, the heavy steel door emitted an ear-splitting electronic buzz, then a loud clunk, and unlocked. Mitch tugged on the door and walked through a metal detector and stopped. After the door snapped shut behind him, another grating buzz sounded as a second steel door, a few feet ahead, unlocked and opened. Two grim-faced guards, keys rattling from their thick leather belts, examined his day pass. Without speaking they led him down the narrow corridor to a dank, dimly-lit room furnished with a small rectangular table and two straight-back metal chairs. The smell of cement filler was everywhere. Mitch settled into an empty chair, pulled out his legal pad and waited.

Soon, prisoner 0117467 shuffled in with a guard by his side. Mitch watched as a gangly man with sallow skin, deep-set gray eyes and sunken cheeks moved toward him. Though incarcerated only seventy-five days, Tifton had not fared well.

Once the guard left, Mitch stood and extended his hand. "Mitchell Bernstein."

"Dave speaks highly of you," Tifton replied, shaking Mitch's hand before plopping into a chair opposite him.

Mitch knew to get to the point. "I understand you want me to take on your appeal."

Tommy nodded. "Like I said, my brother checked you out. Tells me you're no longer in the business of putting guys away. Decided to make a buck by coming over to the dark side."

Mitch laughed. He could see how Jake was taken in by this guy. "Well, before we get to that, there's something I need you to understand. Jake Dalton is a friend of mine. So, if you intend on causing him a problem—"

Tifton waved him off. "Jake needn't worry about me, but the feds, that's a whole different ballgame."

"How so?"

"Two agents paid me a visit earlier this week. DEA. Said I didn't need no lawyer, that the government was willing to offer me the deal of a lifetime, make my sentence practically disappear, if I turned on your friend." Tifton shook his head. "Imagine that. The feds now wanna be my new best friend."

"What'd you say?"

"Don't let the door slap you on the ass on the way out."

"Anything else?"

"Not with those guys. But just before the holidays I get this new cellmate, and before I could say Merry Christmas, he starts askin' all sorts of questions, about my case, my lawyer, even witnesses at my trial. The rat musta thought I had stupid tattooed on my forehead."

"You can bet he was wired. Anything you said the feds would want on tape." Mitch clenched his teeth, realizing he'd left his own recorder on the passenger seat of his Mercedes. "Well, expect a grand jury subpoena any day now. Richter will probably be doing the honors. He'll hammer you with all kinds of questions—who do you report to, where'd you get the cash for the land, did Jake help concoct the alibi, and so on."

Tifton snickered. "Let 'em ask."

"If you invoke the Fifth and refuse to answer, Richter will have a judge immunize you and order you to testify. You lose all constitutional protection against self-incrimination. Then if you still refuse to answer, you'll be held in contempt and—"

Tifton guffawed. "What they gonna do, put my ass in jail? You think I'm gonna fret over some bony-ass judge threatening me with contempt?"

"The feds could tack more time onto your existing sentence."

"Fuck 'em."

For now, Mitch thought, Tifton was talking the talk. How long would it last? He didn't like Jake's odds.

"I need to ask you something and it's important that you be straight with me."

"Go for it."

Was Jake in on the alibi?"

"Nah, at least I don't think so. But Dalton's a smart guy. Maybe he realized I was feedin' him a line and decided to go with it. Can't say I blame him. It's tough to say no to a hundred grand when your kid's sick."

"I just wanted to hear it from you."

"Then, you'll represent me?"

"On the appeal, sure. I'll need to review the record, get a statement from Cunningham—"

"Don't hold your breath."

Mitch's brow shot up. "What does that mean?"

"Last week I heard he got two in the head, execution style. So, unless you know a way of resurrecting the dead, he won't be much help."

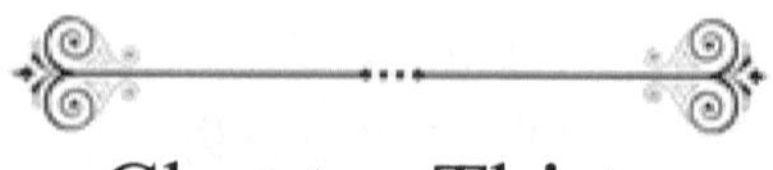

Chapter Thirty

On a cool February morning, Red parked his Wrangler and in the steady drizzle walked toward Merrie Christmas Park, inhaling the heady aroma of fresh gardenias. The flower's distinctive fragrance rekindled fond memories of his childhood days on the Tifton family farm. Then, like clockwork, every Sunday after church Tommy's evangelical father would lead his entire family, Red included, to their flower and vegetable garden out back, have everyone kneel on the smooth clay dirt, and recite the Lord's Prayer.

As he approached within a half-block of the park, Red unzipped his parka and checked the .40 caliber Glock snug against his side. He pulled down his Miami Dolphins cap and checked his watch: 0700. He could thank the Navy for learning to be on time.

Soon, he spotted Carlos alone, leaning against a giant banyan tree. Through the light drizzle, Red checked the barrel-tile roofed houses nearby, making sure there were no uninvited guests. The only sign of life was an elderly couple a block away, walking their yellow lab. What he came to do wouldn't take long.

Red slogged through the wet grass and called out to Carlos. "Been here long?"

The beady eyes of the operative stared back at him. "All night I've been asking myself what could be so fucking urgent to drag my ass out of bed and meet you at the crack of dawn."

"Cancun," Red bristled, studying the wiry, thirty-something man, more Cuban than American, to see if he was carrying under his parka. "When you going to fix the problem?

"Oh, that." Carlos's eyes narrowed, betraying his uneasiness.

"Yeah, *that*. Javier bitched to me non-stop that he's short a load of coke and wants to know when something's going to be done about it."

"All that coked-up Mexican ever does is bitch and moan. I'm surprised someone hasn't done us all a favor by putting that crack head out of his misery."

Red moved closer, feeling the Glock ride up on his hip. "I still haven't gotten an answer to my question. Already, I had to make good for losing one load, so I'll be damn if I take a hit on a second. That's on *you*."

"Man, we're talkin' peanuts. I'm surprise those guys even miss it."

"Not the point. That shit was consigned to me and until it gets delivered our business will be on hold. Comprende?"

Carlos let out a nervous laugh. "I'm working on it. Peter to pay Paul, you know how it goes."

"Work harder. Until you do, you're not getting another nickel out of me. Tell your pals at Langley I got a business to run. Do what you've gotta do and do it fast before both of us wind up dead." Red turned and left.

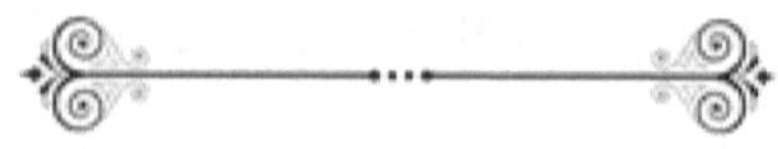

Chapter Thirty-One

Jessie swore she heard a sound outside her condo and looked up from blow-drying her hair. She switched off the drier. The bathroom's digital clock read 6:33. The knocking grew louder. Who could that be this early in the morning? She hastily fastened the buttons of her blouse over her swollen belly and hurried into the foyer, her breathing short and quick. Once she reached the front door, she called, "Who is it?"

"Mrs. Tifton, this is Special Agent Nettles. We'd like a few words with you."

Jessie stumbled backwards. "What do you want? I've got nothing to say to you." She peered through the peep hole at a squirrelly black man with small eyes set behind wire-rimmed glasses. A DEA photo ID hung from around his neck. She recognized him from Tommy's trial, sitting like a stone statue beside Richter.

"It concerns your husband. We believe you can help him."

"Go away. Leave me alone. I got nothing to say."

"Mrs. Tifton, please open the door. It's important."

She didn't trust this agent; knew he'd say and do anything to get what he wanted. Her hands trembled as she glanced around the room to see if she left anything out. Red would surely kill her if he knew she was talking to these people.

"Please, go away. I can't be seen talking to you."

"Don't make us come back with an arrest warrant. I really don't want to do that."

She gripped the doorknob. She couldn't let them do that. Not now, not with Tommy's baby.

"Mrs. Tifton," Nettles persisted, his voice becoming louder, "you're the last hope your husband has of getting out of prison anytime soon. I thought you'd want to help. Now, please open the door."

"Dear Lord," she muttered. Was it true? Was there a way of helping Tommy? Jessie slid off the chain lock, cracked open the door and caught a whiff of Nettles' sickly-sweet cologne. She stared at the blonde female agent next to him, then back at Nettles. "You need back-up to talk to me?"

Nettles shook his head. "Protocol."

"Come in before someone sees you." She shivered from the chill of the March morning and glanced at the nosy neighbor's house, then out into the street. "Come on, will ya, hurry up." She waved them inside and quickly shut the door.

The two agents stood in the living room surveying her home. She was proud at how neat she'd kept it since Tommy went away.

"There's nobody here but me," she volunteered, trying to appear calm. "What do you want? I don't see how I can help."

Nettles glanced down at her belly, then looked up at her with a wry smile. "You underestimate yourself, Jessie. What I brought with me is an offer you can't refuse."

Chapter Thirty-Two

In the Hollywood Hard Rock Casino, Sam stacked the four thousand dollars in chips he'd just won in the last round of Texas Hold 'Em, then glanced over his shoulder at the two men standing close behind. The broad-shouldered, buzz-cut white guy wore an expensive herringbone suit and silk tie; the shorter black guy with cheap wire-rimmed glasses had on a light suit with matching gray tie.

"Hey, guys," Sam said, as he rotated to face them. "You mind moving? I'm kinda superstitious."

Buzz-cut laughed, but in a menacing way. "You're one lucky guy, Pendleton."

Sam shot him a look. "Do I know you?"

"You're about to." Buzz-cut leaned closer to him and whispered. "The good news is that Red doesn't know we're here."

Sam froze. "Who?"

"Don't play dumb, asshole. The name's Richter, Special Assistant U.S. Attorney." He nodded to the accountant-looking guy beside him. "This is Special Agent Nettles, DEA."

Gamblers on each side of Sam slid away.

Sam rose from his seat and plowed his chips toward the dealer. "Cash me in." He then moved a short distance from the table and studied the two. "What's this about?"

"I think you know," Richter said.

Sam half-turned toward the shouts of gamblers at a nearby craps table. "Why don't we go somewhere private?"

Richter smiled, but his eyes remained deadly serious. "I know just the place."

Once he reached the parking lot, Sam turned to face the two. "I'd like to see some ID?"

Both flashed their photo IDs.

"Tell you what. Why don't I call your office and make an appointment next week?" Sam knew that without a warrant, they couldn't hold him.

Richter sneered. "What we have expires today, asshole. The next time you'll be leaving in handcuffs."

"For what? I've done nothing wrong."

Richter turned to his sidekick. "Why do they always say that?" He looked back at Sam. "Your name's all over land contracts laundering millions for the cartel. Or didn't you follow Tifton's trial? And if you continue with this charade, we'll return with an arrest warrant." The prosecutor moved a step closer. "Your call."

Sam removed his jacket, suddenly the heat became stifling. He could play hardball, remain silent but that would only insure his immediate and embarrassing arrest. On the other hand, it wouldn't hurt to hear what they had to say.

"Ok, let me grab my winnings and we can meet somewhere." Sam's eyes roamed the parking lot. His life would be worthless if Red spotted him with these two.

"I've got a better idea." Richter nodded at Nettles to lead the way, then grabbed Sam's arm. "Let's go. If you make it back, your money will be waiting for you."

In a beige government sedan, Nettles drove the three of them downtown before turning into the federal building's secure parking lot. Sitting alone in the back seat for the hour-long ride, Sam's mind raced, strategizing how best to handle these two.

Once inside Richter's office, surprising Sam with its plush carpeting, rich décor and expansive view of Biscayne Bay, they took turns questioning him. What did Sam tell Dalton of Tifton's operations when he referred the case? Was the alibi Dalton's idea? What other clients has Dalton handled for the Mexicans? Sam was stunned at how badly Richter wanted to nail Jake.

"I keep telling you," Sam insisted, facing the prosecutor sitting behind his desk, "I wouldn't call Jake a friend or associate. We're poker buds, nothing more. It's our wives who are tight. I didn't— wouldn't—tell him any of my business."

Richter swiveled forward and leaned over his desk and glared at him. "Fuck you."

Sam tried a different tact. "Look, I've no idea where you've been getting your info, but yes, I did refer Jake the case, but nothing more.

I felt for the guy. His kid almost died and I thought he could use the dough. If you saw how bad he played poker, you'd understand why." Sam started to smile but saw the two grim faces and stopped. He realized these guys weren't interested in the truth. How ironic. He actually was trying to help Jake dig himself out of a hole, and knew he'd score points with Marilyn for sending him business.

"We've got you on tape with Red bragging how the alibi will get Tifton off and even suggesting that Dalton get a bonus for the job he's done. So, stop the crap."

"Look, I was just pumping the man up. Red's got this special bond with Tommy since they were kids. The guy was going ballistic, saying Dalton was screwing everything up. I was only trying to calm him down. You don't want to see his temper."

Richter's face hardened. "He's not the only one with a temper, you prick." He then settled back in his chair and lowered his voice to a whisper. "I'm trying my best to be fair here, treat you like a professional, but you're making it real hard."

Sam fidgeted in his seat. Richter clearly had a screw loose. "Just talking to you puts me and my family at risk."

Richter shook his head. "Not my problem. You talk, we deal. Simple as that. Otherwise, you're looking at twenty years hard time, time away from your three boys. The train is about to leave the station, Pendleton. What's it going to be? You onboard or not?"

Sam felt bad for Jake, but not that bad, and knew that if he were in his shoes he'd do the same. "How do I know that once I give you what you want you won't toss me out like yesterday's trash? I know how you guys operate."

"Jessie and Tifton's brother have already fared quite well for themselves."

"Jessie's talking to you guys? I don't believe it."

"How do you think we're on to you?"

No fucking way, Sam thought to himself. Richter was bluffing. He made damn sure Tommy and Jessie knew nothing of his business. Time to call the bluff. "What exactly did she tell you?"

Richter motioned to Nettles. "Read the prick his rights."

Nettles stepped toward Sam and pulled a pair of silver handcuffs from under his suit jacket.

Sam half-rose from his chair. "Hey, boys, take it easy. Don't get your bowels in an uproar. I was simply asking a question."

"You don't get to ask questions," Richter snapped. "Any day now we expect Tifton to roll on Dalton, and once he does, all bets are off. We won't need your sorry ass anymore."

Nettles bent close to Sam. "Listen to him. He's trying to help."

Sam tried not to laugh in the agent's face. This doofus thinks I'm falling for that good cop bad cop routine. Yet, it seemed like no matter what Sam did, Jake was going down.

Sam slumped back in his chair and loosened the top button of his shirt. "Don't you guys believe in air conditioning."

"Get used to it." Richter smirked. "Where you're going there isn't any."

Sam stared down, trying to hide his fear of prison. "What we talking about?"

"Plead guilty to a one count conspiracy, pay a hefty fine plus all back taxes and penalties. That shouldn't be a problem. We understand you're loaded."

"My old man keeps a death grip on the purse strings. And tax fraud?"

"Everything will be rolled up into one neat package. No other charges."

With his father's connections, he'll most likely serve at best a few months, maybe a year, Sam thought.

"And if you cooperate," Richter continued, "we'll provide cover with your family. The plea agreement will recite that you got caught up in a dangerous criminal enterprise, that you tried to back out, but out of fear for your life and the lives of your family, you couldn't."

"Specific activities would be kept from my wife and kids?"

"Absolutely. Like I said, we're not out to hurt you."

"Then make me a deal where I don't serve time."

"No can do. Not with the millions you've laundered. I'll agree to a max of two years. You'll end up serving a year in a minimum-security facility, more like a tennis club. You'll get to work on your serve."

Sam shuddered at the thought of even a minute in prison. Now was the time to do what he did best. "I need a guarantee of no more than six months, that I'll be sent to a facility close to my family and given ample protection. Moreover, the information I provide pertains to Dalton, and Dalton alone. Otherwise, no deal."

Richter glanced at Nettles, then spoke. "We'll see what we can do. How do we know what you've got is worth what you're asking?"

"What I've got," Sam boasted, "will blow a hole in your Calvin Klein's. In fact, you don't have to sign off 'til you're satisfied with my proffer."

"There'll be enough to convict Dalton?"

Now was the moment he'd been waiting for. Sam leaned back and smiled. "Not just convict him. What I got will bury him."

Chapter Thirty-Three

In the prison cafeteria, Tommy sat on the hardwood bench and picked at the slop they called food. Across from him, two Cuban cellmates chortled, apparently telling each other jokes in Spanish. "My God," he muttered under his breath, "this is America, speak English." The foul-smelling breakfast caused waves of nausea to wash over hm. He didn't know how much more he could take.

In mid-sentence the Cubans stopped talking and shifted their eyes to someone behind him. Tommy twisted around and looked up. A beefy black guard stood over him, smiling.

"Tifton," he said in an friendly voice. "I know you'd hate to pass up such a scrumptious meal, but you got a visitor."

Tommy's eyes shot open. Normally, visitors were allowed only on Sundays and never in mornings. "Really?"

"Kid you not." The guard stepped aside for Tommy to stand.

Gathered in their respective gangs, inmates heckled Tommy as he marched through the cafeteria, one step ahead of the guard. After unlocking a reinforced steel door, the guard motioned Tommy into the courtyard where he could relish the warmth of a sunny spring day.

Tommy continued in silence as he and the guard moved through the courtyard and passed another steel door leading inside. In the four months since he'd heard the judge say, 'You are hereby sentenced to fifteen years on each count of the indictment, to run consecutive,' Tommy had learned to stifle all emotions, including recurrent thoughts of suicide.

After passing a row of empty cells, the guard led him into a room furnished with a worn suede couch, throw rugs, a table and two metal chairs. High above rays of light streamed through a window framed by iron bars, giving the room a soft glow.

"Who's here to see me?" Tommy implored, unable to restrain his excitement a moment longer.

The guard simply chuckled and left.

Soon a knock sounded and the door opened. Tommy spun around. A different guard moved aside as Jessie walked in. The morning light lit up her smooth face, giving her the look of an angel.

"Sweet Jesus," Tommy cried, spreading his arms to receive her. "I thought they'd never let us be together again."

Jessie ran into his arms. "Oh, baby, I forgot how good you feel," she said, snuggling her head against his chest. She looked up at him and stepped back. "My Lord, you're thin as a rail. Aren't they feeding you?"

He stroked her long hair while eyeing the guard at the door. The scent of her perfume made him hard.

"You've got thirty minutes," the guard called before shutting the door, leaving them alone.

"Baby," he said, leading her onto the couch and taking her in his arms. "You look amazin'. God, I miss you."

She rubbed his bony cheek and nestled close to him. "And I miss you, especially at night when I'm all alone."

"I can take care of that," Tommy said through a flurry of kisses to her mouth and neck. He put his hand inside her dress and stroked the enlarged breast, feeling her taut nipple.

She laughed and moved his hand away. "If you hadn't already noticed," she said, looking down at her swollen belly, "you've more than done the deed, thank you very much."

Tommy smoothed his hand over her stomach. "There isn't a day that goes by that I don't thank Jesus for our child and think of being with you."

"But we can. Soon."

Tommy's face lit up. "What do you mean?"

"Richter says if you testify against Dalton he'll go to the judge and get your sentence cut to one, maybe two years. Isn't that wonderful?"

"Richter? You've been speaking to that insect? Are you trying to get us killed?" All thoughts of sex vanished. Tommy rose and moved to the locked door, and listened for any sound on the other side. He turned to Jessie and put his fingers to his lips, then spent the next several minutes checking the room for bugs. Satisfied there were none he returned to sit beside her.

"Red knows all about me being here," she said in a low voice.

"He does? What'd he say?"

"I expected him to bust a gut but he was cool with it, said he was gonna help."

"How?"

Jessie ran her fingers through his short hair. "Dunno. He just wanted me to find out where Dalton lives."

"Dear, sweet Jesus. Red's not gonna hurt him? I don't want that."

"I don't think he would...unless he had to, I guess."

"What's Richter want with Jake?"

"Don't know and don't care." Jessie nudged closer to him. "All I care about is getting you outta this place. Richter has given us that chance."

Tommy shook his head. "Rat on Jake? I can't do that. Besides, it's my own damn fault that—"

"Will you stop already? He did you no favors. Look where you are. You don't owe him a goddamn thing."

"Baby—"

Jessie moved off the couch, away from him. "When you gonna start thinking about me and our son? Am I the only one here trying to have a normal life?"

"A son? I'm gonna have a son?"

"I wanted to surprise you, honey, but you know me, I've never been any good at keepin' secrets." She stepped close and took his hand and rubbed it over her belly. "I just pray our boy doesn't have that big nose of yours. I can't have folks thinkin' he's a Jew."

"Richter. Like dancin' with the devil, that's what it is. I'll have no part of that."

"Tommy, stop it!"

He stood and moved close to the door to see if the guard was coming.

"I want you home so we can be a family again."

"What about Jake's family? Doesn't that count for something?"

"Damn him and damn his family. He can take care of himself. If you give the feds what they want, you'd be free to see your son grow up, maybe even go to college. Before you know it, we'll have a second, and a third." She caressed his face and kissed him softly on the lips.

A dull ache gripped him. He had always wanted a family, but to start one like this?

"And you won't be the only one."

"What'd you mean?"

"Your brother's already cut a deal."

"Dave?"

"Pendleton, too."

"I can't believe it."

"Don't blame 'em. The feds know if they promise a man his freedom he's likely to say anything. They only care about their headlines." Her eyes began to tear. "Don't you wanna be home with me and our baby?"

"Jess, of course I do, but not like this."

"I wish you'd stop being so damn stubborn and just listen for once in your life. You're lookin' at thirty years. My God, you'll be an old man when you get out." She turned away. "You can't expect me to wait forever, I just won't."

"Oh, baby, you don't mean that." He knelt and put his head against her belly. The baby's movements made him feel alive. "You know I love you like no other, but what you're asking—"

"It's our last chance, we got to take it. Dalton's going down anyway. Besides, it's not only about you. The feds know about things I've done. I don't want—"

"Oh, Jess. This is happening so quick. I need time to think.

A knock sounded on the door and the guard poked his head inside. "Time's up."

Tommy glanced at him "Already?" He couldn't believe it.

Jessie leaned close and kissed him. "Baby, you've got to do something and fast."

"Why? I'm not going anywhere."

"Richter says time's running out, that you gotta act now or we'll miss our chance."

He stared at Jessie for several moments. "Baby, have you forgotten what he did to us? Don't do this. Don't ask me to crawl under a rock with that snake."

Chapter Thirty-Four

On a bright Sunday morning, Jake looked up from filling the ice chest to see Elena in a golden yellow sundress, smiling. "Wow, don't you look amazing," he said. With Drew's health and Jake's law practice improving day by day, he and Elena were finally able to recapture what they once had.

Elena moved close and tenderly pushed back strands of his hair. "Come on, *chico*. We need to go. The kids are waiting in the car." She grabbed a bottle of Hawaiian Tropic from the kitchen counter and glanced at ice chest stocked with food and drink. "We're only going for a few hours."

"Okay, okay. Let me grab one last thing." Jake slammed the freezer door shut and turned to put his arms around her. "Thanks for being there for me. I know I haven't been much fun lately."

"I'm always there for you, you just don't know it." She caressed his cheek and kissed him softly on the lips, then broke free. "*Vamanos.* It'll be good for you to get out and play."

She was right. With the indictment all but a fait de accompli Jake never felt so depressed. If it wasn't for his family, he didn't know what he'd do.

After stopping off at a bait and tackle shop, Jake drove his Saab over the Rickenbacker Causeway, the inviting sandy beaches of Key Biscayne on either side of him. He glanced into the rearview mirror and smiled at Drew and Nicole in the back, busy playing cards, and then at Elena in the passenger seat, adjusting the brim of her Panama hat. For that brief moment, he could put Tifton out of his mind.

In minutes, Jake stopped and paid the entrance fee at Bill Baggs State Park and found a place to park near the barbecue pit he had reserved a week before. "Okay guys," he said, turning to his kids. "Drew, grab the fishing poles and the bait from the cooler and show Mom what I taught you. Remember that sea wall over there? I hear the fish are this big." He held out his hands about two feet apart.

Drew's eyes grew large as he rose from his seat.

"Hold your horses. Don't go anywhere without your mom. And don't forget to put on tons of sunscreen. Nikki, how 'bout you and me rent some bikes and check out the trails? We might even get to see a squirrel or two playing hide and seek."

Nicole put her fingers to her mouth and giggled. She jumped from the car, grabbed her dad's hand and stood beside him.

Jake turned to Elena. "Honey, let's meet back for lunch in a couple of hours."

Elena smiled. "Sounds like a plan."

Hand in hand, Jake and Nikki headed for the bike shop. He was thrilled for the chance to spend the time alone with his daughter.

At the entrance of the state park, Red squirmed behind the wheel of the white Chevy van as he handed the five-dollar bill to the park ranger. Weeks ago, he took the precaution of ditching his Wrangler and anything else that could be linked to him. According to his CIA contacts, his whereabouts and current physical description were unknown to local law enforcement, but he couldn't be sure. The sight of a uniform always put him on edge.

Peering through dark sunglasses he drove the van through the park, making sure to stay under the posted 25 MPH speed limit. He licked the sweat off his upper lip where his mustache had once been, then looked with disgust in rear-view mirror at his receding hairline, more visible now that his hair was cut ridiculously short.

On his second pass around the park, Red spotted a shapely brunette with long dark hair and a boy of about seven fishing off the sea wall. He studied the faded snapshot of the Dalton family that Sam had mailed to his P.O. Box, then scanned the area to see if the lawyer was around. He was in luck. No Dalton, and only a handful of people nearby. He pulled down his Dolphins cap and rolled the van into a parking spot next to a camper outside the Lighthouse Café, killed the engine and rummaged through his gear in the back until he found what he was looking for.

"Hello there," he called to the woman and the pale-faced boy as he walked toward them, trying to appear nonchalant. He had to make his move before Dalton showed up. Swells from passing speed boats pounded against the concrete wall and splashed his face.

The boy looked up and waved.

"Catch anything?" Red asked, removing his sunglasses and wiping the water from his face while inching closer.

The boy reached down and slid his hands along the scales of two fish, tails slapping against the ground in the last throes of life, and proudly showed off his prize. "All by myself. I can't wait to tell my dad."

Red put his sunglasses back on and shook his empty rod. "A heckava lot better than me." He paused to study the boy, struck by how much he looked like Joey, his kid brother—the same round face, sparkling blue eyes, and even freckles running up and down the nose. He tried to refocus on what he came to do. "I used up all my bait and still couldn't catch a thing. You'll have to tell me your secret."

"Come on, Drew," the woman called, grabbing his shoulder and pulling him closer to her. "We need to clean up. Your dad will be here any minute." She hardly glanced at Red as she spoke to the boy, but the hardening of her eyes betrayed her fear. Perhaps she thought he was there to hit on her, or worse. Red reminded himself to play it cool, be natural. The last thing he needed was for her to scream.

The boy glanced at his mom, then back at him. "I used to fish here a lot with my dad before I got sick."

Red relaxed his shoulders and let the fishing pole lean against him. The woman still hadn't said a word to him, but continued to grip the boy like a hawk protecting her young.

"You got sick? Hey, wait a minute. Is your name Drew, and your dad, is he a lawyer?"

The pretty brunette shot him a curious look. "You know my husband?"

"Jake Dalton, right?" Red asked, as if guessing. "He mentioned in passing his boy's illness and showed me pictures of you and the kids.

"How do you know Jake?" she asked, her tone laced with suspicion.

"He handled a case for me a short while back. He's real proud of his family and how nice you look. But to tell you the truth, you're much prettier in person."

She closed the top button to her sundress and moved the boy back even more. "What's your name?"

"Smith. Randy Smith. But everyone calls me Red." He ran his hand through his hair, forgetting how short it was. "Your husband did a heck of a job when I got rear-ended in my truck, hurt my back real bad. Jake made a bundle for me and for himself when we settled the case for cash."

"Cash?"

Now he had her attention. "Yeah, the guy who hit me didn't have insurance, but he did drive a fancy Porsche and Jake found out he owned a string of pawn shops. You know how those guys always deal in cash. Anyways, your husband and I got together and agreed to discount the case for a quick settlement out of court. We each made over fifty thousand. Cash. Me, a little more, of course." Seeing her jaw dropped, he tried to keep from smiling.

"Please excuse my manners. I'm Elena, Jake's wife, but I don't remember my husband ever mentioning your case, especially one so…big. When did this happen?"

"Bout a month ago. He probably wanted to surprise you." Red continued to stare at the boy, then turned to the woman. "I don't mind telling you how much your son resembles my brother Joey. It's uncanny."

"That's nice," she said. Her tone remained guarded.

"Yeah, we were just kids when he got run over by a drunk driver, right before my eyes. There was nothing I could do. He was about your boy's age when it happened."

"My God, how awful." She tightened her hold on the boy. "Gather your things, Drew. It's time to meet up with your dad." She grabbed the line with the fish, pulling the boy with her.

Red gazed at the boy for several more seconds before finally taking the hint. "Well, best be going." He had already been here too long. One thing he didn't need was to run into Dalton.

"If you're going to be in the area, I'll tell Jake to look for you. I'm sure he'd like to say hello."

"I'd love to, but I'm goin' try another watering hole. Hopefully, I'll have better luck." He tipped his cap to her. "But do make sure you tell Jake how much I appreciate what he did for me. In fact, tell you what. If I get the chance, I'll stop by and thank him myself. You still live on that cul de sac off Kendall Drive?"

Her face turned ashen.

How he loved instilling fear. "But don't worry, I got your number so I'll make sure to call first. In the meantime, take good care of yourself and that handsome boy of yours." With that he grabbed his pole and left.

Walking back to his van, Red pressed the speed dial on his cell to Carlos's burner. He answered on the second ring, "What's up?"

"I called to say we're back in business since you made good with our friends."

"I said I would. What else?"

"I'm working on getting one of my guys back with his wife."

Carlos chuckled. "You playing marriage counselor now?"

"He wouldn't be where he is if the assholes in Langley had done as I asked."

There was a long pause before Carlos spoke again. "What'd you need?"

"How you with combinations and locks?"

Carlos laughed. "Happens to be my specialty."

"Good, I'll get you the address."

Jake carried Nicole on his shoulders as he meandered down the trail, enjoying the gentle breeze from Biscayne Bay. A perfect spring day. For the past two hours they had biked along the paths through the tall pines while Elena and Drew fished, reminding Jake what a joy Nikki was to be with. He made a promise to himself to do it more often. He spotted Elena and Drew packing up gear near the sea wall.

"Hey guys," Jake called, placing Nicole on her feet. "Whatcha catch for dinner?"

Drew jumped up and down, waving his arms over his head. Elena appeared subdued and didn't look his way.

As Jake walked closer, Drew stood over the ice chest and pointed. "Dad, look what I caught, all by myself!"

Elena stood at the edge of the seawall, staring out at the water.

"Mom, it was so fun," Nikki said, staying by Jake's side. "Daddy couldn't believe how good I did on my bike."

Elena turned toward Nicole and spoke in a flat tone. "That's nice, sweetie."

"My Lord," Jake said, peering into the ice chest. "You've caught enough for an army." He glanced over at Elena. "Baby, you see this?"

Elena edged alongside Drew and patted him on the back. "Great job, honey," she said, her voice flat, lacking emotion. "Now kids, get into the car, it's time to go. We need to get home before it storms."

"Storm? The skies couldn't be any bluer. I wanted to show the kids the lighthouse and then have lunch. It's such a glorious day."

"No, it's going to rain. We have to leave now," Elena said through pursed lips.

"Aw, Mom," Drew and Nikki groaned.

She started for the car, then wheeled back at Jake. "You coming?"

Jake approached Elena and whispered. "Is something wrong?"

She bit her lip. "You could say that."

Drew and Nikki climbed into the back seat while Jake stowed the fishing gear and ice chest in the trunk and slammed it shut. He wiped his hands on his shorts, settled himself behind the wheel and started the engine before turning to Elena beside him. "What's going on?"

Elena's face was taut. With head down, she twirled her hair with her fingers while Jake drove out of the park into light traffic. She shifted in her seat and pressed her head against the window with eyes shut.

"Come on, hon, get it off your chest. You'll feel better."

She slowly turned toward him. "I met a client of yours today." Her tone was ominous.

"You're kidding. Who?"

"Randy Smith."

"Who?"

"Randy Smith."

Jake could only shrug, the name meant nothing to him.

"He said everyone calls him Red."

Jake's voice caught in his throat. "Red? You met him?"

"So you do know him?"

"Not really. We had plans to meet but it got canceled." Jake did his best not to sound alarmed. "He's one of Sam's clients. His name came up when Sam referred Tifton, then again at trial. The guy supposedly owned the Cessna that was seized by Customs. What'd he look like?"

"Tall, well-built, in his forties."

"Mustache, long hair?"

"What does it matter if you don't know him," she snapped.

He glanced back at Drew and Nicole playing in the back, oblivious to the exchange between Elena and himself. "Just curious. Maybe it's not the same guy." Her eyes told him she wasn't having it. "Why are you being so argumentative?"

"Because you haven't been honest about the money you've been making. I knew it. That's what I get for letting my guard down, and to think I trusted you. This Red, ugh, gave me the chills. Started talking about his dead brother and how much he look like Drew."

Jake's hands blanched from gripping the steering wheel. "I never should have left you guys alone. What money we talking about?"

Elena stared straight ahead while they drove back over the causeway toward home. "So creepy, the way he looked at me, even knew where we lived."

"Jesus, why didn't you come get me or call for help?" Jake's temple throbbed. For the first time he thought of buying a gun.

"He didn't do anything physical. He was too smart for that. But he made a point of telling me he knew you and—"

"But he doesn't, I already told you that. I've never laid eyes on the guy, never had anything to do with him." Jake reached for her hand but she yanked it away.

"I pleaded with you not to do drug work, but you wouldn't listen. You never do."

I'm sorry, I really am. I never thought it would come to this."

"He said you got over fifty thousand dollars in cold hard cash on a case you did for him."

"You can't be serious?"

"You're damn right, I am."

"Keep it down, will you." Jake glanced back at Drew and Nicole still absorbed in their game. "It's bullshit, plain and simple," he hissed. "I don't know why he's lying but he sure as hell is. The only fifty thousand I know of is the cash Tifton brought to my office, but I already told you about that. It's crazy to think I have that kind of money laying around with Drew being sick and all. You can't believe him?"

"You don't exactly have an Olympic medal for telling the truth."

He shifted into fourth gear and fed the engine more gas. He couldn't wait to get home. The first thing he'd do is change the locks. "All I can say is that the SOB's trying to make me look bad. I don't know why but it's gotta have something to do with Tifton. As soon as we get back, I'm calling Sam."

"Great. More Sam. I warned you to stay away from him."

Jake veered onto the ramp toward U.S. 1 south. "I can't believe you'd take the word of a criminal over that of your husband."

"You've got to admit the whole thing's hard to swallow. Here we are pinching pennies and some stranger comes to me out of the blue and says he's a former client and gave you fifty thousand dollars, cash. What would you think?"

"I get it. You just need to trust me. Search the damn house if you want."

Elena picked at the ends of her hair. "I don't know who or what to believe anymore. If you've lied to me once, how do I know you won't do it again? And I don't want to even think there's money you haven't told me about. All I know is that I'm frightened, scared for me and the kids. And all because of your birdbrain decision to get involved with one of Miami's biggest drug dealers."

Chapter Thirty-Five

Inside the conference room of the federal correctional, Richter sat at the small metal table doodling on his legal pad. Even with his considerable clout, he had been unable to cut through the red tape and have Tifton transported to his office downtown. That is, not without the force of a grand jury subpoena. Besides, what he had to say was best kept off the record.

In minutes, Tifton—appearing twenty pounds lighter from when Richter last saw him at his trial—came through the doorway escorted by a guard. His skin was pasty and his cheeks sunken.

"Jessie asked me to remind you to take your meds," he started the conversation as soon as the guard left. "She's worried about you."

Tifton plopped into the empty chair across from him and said nothing.

"I assume you already know your brother and Pendleton have agreed to cooperate. It's now up to you. Any time now Jessie's going to have your baby and she wants you home with your family, where you belong."

Tifton raised his head and stared at him. "You think I don't know what you're doing?"

"Look, I'm trying to help. We already have more than enough to convict Dalton. You're either with us or you're not. What's it going to be? Once you agree, you'll be debriefed, then it's only a matter of my filing the appropriate motion informing the judge that your testimony has been invaluable in putting a huge dent into the operations of the cartel and asking that your sentence be reduced to a year. Most likely you'll end up with two. Even federal judges are sensitive to bad press. But hey, not so bad compared to what you're facing."

"Then I should lie?"

For a fleeting moment he considered that Tifton might be wired but knew better. "Not at all. It's simply a matter of having your memory jogged, refreshed. Point the finger at Dalton, then you can go home, in a manner of speaking, and be with your family. I know this has been hard on you."

Tifton sat up in his chair. "Ya think? Damn case never should have been brought to begin with. You know it, I know it, and those you report to know it. I haven't done shit for the Mexicans, so why am I here?"

"Wasn't my call," he lied. "Besides, there was too much heat not to go forward."

Tifton laughed, derisively. "You expect me to fall for your crap? You've got something up your sleeve, people like you always do. I haven't figured it out yet, but when—"

Richter grabbed his pad and stood to leave. He walked to the door, pounding on it several times for the guards to let him out. When the door finally opened, he glanced back at Tifton with a cold stare.

"You've got twenty-four hours to decide. For all I care you can rot in here for the rest of your miserable life."

Chapter Thirty-Six

Jake tore from the courtroom to retrieve a text message from Elena: 9-1-1 DEA AT R HOME. His hand shook as he pressed the speed dial to his home phone. After the fourth ring it went to voice mail. In a panic he tried Elena's cell. Same result.

"Dear God," he cried, causing lawyers nearby to turn his way. Feeling suffocated, he loosened his tie and hurried into the open elevator. Calm down. Think. Surely, the feds wouldn't have come to his home knowing he was at work if they intended to arrest him.

He sprinted off the elevator toward the exit, punching the numbers to his office. The phone kept ringing. Where the hell was everyone?

"Law Offices," a man finally answered.

"Lenny?"

"Hey, Boss." His tone was grave. "We've got a problem."

"Where's Isora? Why isn't she manning the phones? What the hell is going on?"

"She's occupied. Can't talk right now. I've got two DEA agents staring down my throat."

"What?"

"You didn't get my message?"

After reading Elena's text, he hadn't bothered to check for others. Jake reached the bottom of the courthouse steps onto the sidewalk, breathing hard. "What in God's name is happening?"

"Just before nine, four agents came with a search warrant, not exactly talkative types. Fortunately, no clients were here."

"What they want?"

"Anything to do with Tifton, Pendleton and a Randall Armstrong A/K/A Red."

Jake scurried around a crowd at the courthouse and charged across the street, dodging screeching cars. "This is crazy!"

"Tell me about it. Isora's in the back pulling documents called for in the warrant, making sure the feds don't rummage through other client files. I'm on the phones."

"Have you heard from Elena? There're agents at my home, too."

"About a half hour ago, looking for you." Jake could hear the stress in Lenny's voice. He fumbled through his pockets and finally found his car keys. "Said the feds were tearing up the house, looking for evidence. She sounds scared, Boss."

"L.B., take care of things there. I've got to make sure Elena's okay. Other than the warrant, did the DEA have an affidavit from Tifton?"

"First thing they stuck in my face."

"Waiving the attorney-client privilege? They can't see a damn thing without it."

Lenny's silence said it all. Tifton had flipped and was now a government witness, ready to play Jake as his get-out-of-jail card. Certainly no fool, Tifton would play the system for all it was worth.

Jake peeled out of the parking lot with his cell to his ear. "I'm gonna keep trying Elena. If she calls, tell her I'm on my way." He snapped his phone shut and ran through a red light.

As he sped home, Jake tried Elena's cell a dozen more times. No luck. The sight of federal agents at their home must have sent her into a frenzy.

Jake raced like a madman getting home. After turning into his cul de sac, he slowed at the sight of a marked Miami-Dade police car parked in front of his house, blue and white lights flashing. Two unmarked sedans sat in his driveway as neighbors milled around in their yards, no doubt wondering what kind of criminal lived next door.

Successive cracks of thunder sounded overhead, warning of a violent storm ahead.

Jake swerved just before hitting his mailbox and skidded to a stop. He jumped from his car and ran through the open front door and was instantly stopped by a uniformed cop.

"I'm sorry, sir, you can't come in here," said the muscle-bound man, extending his thick arms to block Jake's path.

"This is my home, get out of my way," Jake shouted before turning to the sound of footsteps coming from Drew's bedroom.

"It's all right, officer. Let him through," Nettles called, approaching Jake with a pen and notepad in his hand. "Counselor, you've arrived just in time."

"Lemme see your warrant," Jake barked.

"It's on the kitchen table. I already showed it to your wife."

"Where is she?"

Nettles gestured with his chin toward the master bedroom.

As he was about to step toward the bedroom, Jake saw the uniform cop start to follow. He spun around and held up his hand. "I need to speak to my wife. Alone."

"Sure, no problem," Nettles replied. "We've already searched that area of the house." He motioned to the officer to return to his post at the front door.

As Jake turned to check on Elena, he noticed Drew sitting in the family room watching a DVD of his favorite road-runner cartoon. He rushed to him. "Honey, what are you doing home? Are you sick?"

His son looked up, his eyes bloodshot from crying, and ran to him. "Daddy, daddy, there're policemen in the house."

Jake squeezed Drew tightly and felt his forehead. "You have a fever?"

Thunder boomed overhead and Drew huddled closer. "No, it's teacher work day. Nikki's still at school."

"Stay here, I need to speak to your mom. Everything's going to be fine." Jake turned to leave.

"Daddy, don't go."

He moved back to Drew, gave him a tight hug and kissed him on his brow. "It's ok, watch your cartoon. I just need a second with your mom."

Jake hurried to the bedroom and found Elena sitting on the bed, holding her head in her hands. Without saying a word, he sat beside her and put his arm around her shoulder.

Slowly, she lifted her head, her eyes reddened, her face gripped with fear.

"Don't be frightened, this is all a big mistake. I'm going to clear everything up."

"They said you're some kind of criminal, that the kids and I are not safe."

"Who said such a thing?"

She shifted away from him, her stare cold and distant.

"Baby, this is nuts," Jake continued. "Can't you see? Tifton's trying to use me as his ticket out of prison. That's what this is about."

"They seem so sure."

"It's bullshit. Nothing more than a power grab, the feds thrive on it." He reached to hold her closer but she moved away to the other side of the bed.

"I don't understand…people ripping up our home." Her voice rose with every word. "They've already searched the attic and tore out our beautiful garden. Jake, tell me, are you working for the cartel?"

"What? How can you even ask—" Jake wheeled to a knock on the bedroom door. Nettles stood, waiting to enter.

Jake marched toward him. "You've got some nerve barging into my home."

Nettles didn't flinch, but instead gestured over his shoulder. "One of my agents found a locked safe in the back. We need you to open it."

Jake nodded.

Nettles crooked his finger at him. "Follow me."

With Elena at his side he followed Nettles into the den where a blonde female agent stood over the three foot high safe. "Care to do the honors?" she asked.

Jake bent and worked the combination. "It contains my will and other personal papers, nothing more." He looked back at Elena; her eyes anxious.

After hearing the final tumbler click into place, Jake turned the handle and swung open the door. His brain froze. Inside, piles of cash stared back at him. From what he could tell, the money was bound with rubber bands in stacks of twenties and fifties, eerily similar to the cash Tommy had brought to his office.

Nettles clucked his tongue. "My, my, what do we have here?"

Jake gaped. "It's not mine, I have no idea how it got here," he blurted before realizing it was crazy to say anything during the execution of a search warrant.

"What the hell is that?" Elena shouted, pointing to the cash. "You swore you weren't hiding any money. What in God's name is going on, Jake?"

"I-I. We need to talk." Jake took her arm and led her to their back bedroom and spoke in a soft voice. "Baby, I swear on the lives of our children that money's not mine. It's a plant, to make me look guilty.

I would never ever bring drug money into our home." She broke his grasp and fled into the bathroom.

Jake followed right behind.

"I-I've tried so hard to believe you," she stammered, "but I don't know how I can anymore. You've changed. Ever since that damn case you haven't been the same. And that day at the park, when you didn't come right out and say who that creep was...Red and his money. God, I tried not to think about it." She held her stomach and took a deep breath. "Now I know what he meant about the cash. I feel like such a fool."

"I already told you," Jake pleaded, making sure to keep his voice low. "I don't know the guy. He lied about being my client." Jake tried to put his arms around her but she squirmed away. "Listen to me and think. If I didn't want you to know about the money would I be so dumb to put it in our safe? In our home? There are thousands of places I could have stashed it."

"You know I never use it. I don't even know the combination."

"That's because you keep forgetting it. Listen to me. Do you believe for one minute if I had that much money lying around I wouldn't use it for Drew? Think dammit. Use your head and think."

"Are you saying someone broke into our house and planted drug money, and I'm supposed to believe that?"

"That's exactly what I'm saying. I know it sounds crazy. But you don't know the kind of people I'm dealing with."

"And I never wanted to."

"Come on, baby, can't you see what's happening here? This guy Red shows up out of thin air and tells you about cash he gave me just weeks before the feds come barging into our house looking for it. Awfully convenient, don't you think? I know now he's probably a drug smuggler, but I didn't then. He lied about the money so you'd think I was as dirty as him. Can't you see what's happening?"

She spun around, her eyes flaring at him. "Even before today I thought about leaving, taking the children to my parents where they'd be safe. And now to my face you admit the money you know nothing about belongs to a drug dealer who could have broken into our home while we were asleep and just as easily slit our throats."

"Elena, look at me." He grabbed her arms so she couldn't move. "I know you're frightened, but I haven't changed. I'm the same guy you met waiting tables in New Haven. I could never do what they're accusing me of doing." He eased his grip and gently smoothed her arm. "Please believe me."

"As soon as these people leave, I'm pulling Nikki out of school and taking her and Drew to my parents. I'm not taking any more chances."

He stood stunned, groping for words. "You can't mean that."

"You're damn right I do. You're not the man I thought you were."

"But I've done nothing wrong."

She vehemently waved her hands at him, signaling that their marriage was over.

Chapter Thirty-Seven

In the dingy studio apartment, Jake tossed in bed, unable to escape the same terrifying nightmare, night after night. *Wearing gray and white prison stripes, he was being led by two U.S. marshals through the pouring rain onto a waiting train. In the distance, Elena stood on the platform with Drew and Nicole sobbing and clutching their mother's long black dress, forbidden to wave goodbye. Then, as the train lurched forward on the tracks, Jake was shoved into a darken railway car, never to see his family again.*

Jake awoke in a sweat. He crawled out of bed and stared at the illuminated dials of the cheap portable clock. "Three o'clock," he muttered. How he'd kill for a good night's sleep. He flicked on the overhead light and trudged to the bathroom, catching a glimpse in the mirror of his six-day-old growth. Since leaving his home three weeks ago, he'd had his fill of frozen dinners, canned soups and tasteless pizzas. For a week, he hadn't bothered to go into the office. He had instructed Isora to cancel all appointments, to say he'd come down with the flu. With his marriage in shambles and facing indictment, what was the harm in one more lie?

He turned on the faucet and stared down at the cracked porcelain sink, a stark reminder of how badly he'd screwed-up his life. The chance of a lifetime, Tifton was to have made his career. Now, this.

Depressed and alone, Jake had nowhere to turn except Lenny.

Under a cloudless blue sky, Jake sped across MacArthur Causeway past the cruise ships anchored in Government Cut to catch the high-speed ferry to Fisher Island. Once on board, he left his car and walked the deck, trying to steady his nerves. Lenny had told him to act natural, be himself, but that was near impossible. He was on his way to meet Albert Kellerman at an exclusive golf course. And Albert Kellerman was no ordinary man.

When the ferry docked, Jake drove past the clubhouse to the bag drop where he was greeted by a gangly teenager, clad in a Nike golf shirt. Jake waved at him through his open window and popped open the trunk. In seconds, the boy carried his bag onto an empty cart.

"How's it going?" Jake called out. "I have a 7:43 tee time with Mr. Kellerman. Any idea where I can find him?"

"On the practice green, sir." The teenager gestured behind him. "We call it his second home. You know him?"

"Only from seeing him on CNN."

"Well, you'd never know by looking, but the club just threw him a party for his eightieth birthday. He's tall and bald as an eagle."

"Thanks." Jake shifted into first, not wanting to be late.

"Oh, and when he speaks, the dude doesn't mean to shout." The kid pointed to his ear. "If you know what I mean."

After parking, Jake made his way to find his host, wondering how much Lenny had told Kellerman and whether the renowned lawyer would come out of retirement to take his case, and if he did, how Jake would ever manage to pay his fee. Soon, he found his golf bag strapped to a cart, embossed with initials 'AK', parked adjacent to an immense putting green. Jake pulled his dad's putter from his bag, recalling the rare times he'd played with him before his unexpected death from a heart attack. Then, Jake was always too busy building a practice that no longer mattered.

Jake turned to the sound of a deep belly laugh. On the manicured green, a large man, moving with a noticeable limp, pumped his fist and roared as his thirty-foot putt rolled into the cup. He adjusted his Brooklyn Dodgers cap and looked around to see if anyone had noticed, then met Jake's gaze and smiled. "You must be Dalton," his booming voice carried a distinctive New York accent, similar to Mitch's.

"Yes, sir." Jake approached the broad-shouldered lawyer and extended his hand. "I really appreciate your taking the time to see me, Mr. Kellerman. Lenny can't stop singing your praises."

Kellerman let his cane lean against his side and grasped Jake's hand, his grip firm and confident. His jutting jaw, intense brown eyes, and overall demeanor marked a man with a purpose.

"Call me Al. Mister makes me feel I'm about to be carted off to some nursing home. Besides, Lenny has to say nice things. I'm married to his aunt." Kellerman's grin spread across a deeply tan face.

Jake managed a smile. "Guess Lenny told you what I'm up against."

"Probably more than I need to know. God bless him. Maybe before they stuff me in a box he'll learn how to get to the point."

"Then you know Lenny. He's got good instincts though. I should have listened to him when I took the case. Funny how the mind makes you see only what you want to see—"

"And filters out the rest." Kellerman slapped him on the back. "Don't be so hard on yourself, son. You're simply not as jaded as the rest of us. Give it time, you will be." He scooped his ball from the cup and turned to Jake. "Kinda tragic, don't you think, how life finds a way of kicking the good guys in the nuts."

Five minutes and Jake already felt deeply connected with the man.

"Before we get down to business, and you do your best to convince me to give this up," Kellerman said, waving his hand out over the golf course, "I need to know your handicap. Mine's early dementia."

Jake smiled. "I used to play to a twelve, but that was a ways back."

"I love it, you're sandbagging me already." Kellerman laughed deep, throwing back his head. "If you don't mind," he said, sliding behind the wheel of his golf cart, "I'd like to drive." He handed Jake his cane. "There's no telling how much time I've got left before they take away my keys."

Jake guffawed and Kellerman joined in even louder. For a few precious moments, Jake gave himself permission to step away from the abyss he knew lay just ahead.

After a short drive, Jake walked up to the first tee, grateful no other golfers were nearby. He'd never played on a private course before. He teed up his ball and took a practice swing, his thoughts on Elena and how he wished he could win her back. Straight ahead lay the fairway, the soft inviting grass impeccably cut. Sweat trickled down his arms into his palms.

Jake swung hard and shanked his drive, causing egrets to take flight as the ball splashed into its watery grave. He looked over at Kellerman. "I hope that's not an omen."

Kellerman smiled and strolled to the tee box, and without fanfare hit his drive straight down the middle of the fairway. He took off his cap and wiped perspiration from his smooth head. "Federal prosecutors, righteous sonofabitches, always so full of themselves. Half of them don't give a damn about the truth. It's nothing but a blood sport to feed their ego."

"Never did I imagine it would get this far. I guess Lenny told you about my problem with the lead prosecutor? From the moment I met him, I got this feeling that it was personal."

"Richter, right? Never met him. But I say, always go with your gut." He threw Jake one of his golf balls. "This time hit the sucker but leave out the emotion. Don't mean to come off like a Tibetan monk, but anger clouds the mind. Think of Tifton and how he'll come after you, because you know he will. It's not complicated. He intends to destroy you and your family to save his own, and it's on you not to let that happen. The key is to identify his weakness and turn it into your strength."

Jake positioned himself over the ball and pulled his club back slowly, the spikes of his shoes gripping the Bermuda grass for balance. He thought of Tommy deceiving him from the start, of Pendleton lying about Red, and of Richter's icy stare as the club drove through the ball, causing it to jump off his driver and sail past Kellerman's, rolling to a stop on the right side of the fairway. Jake looked up and grinned. "Damn!"

"What the hell you expect, Dalton? You've got fifty years on me," Kellerman said, laughing hard. He turned serious. "That's exactly what I expect of you at trial. Be cold, be calculating. Unfettered emotion will only land you in prison."

"Does that mean you'll represent me?"

"I still need to hear more; about you. Lenny's already told me plenty about the case."

"I don't know where to begin. It's a long story."

"It's a long course, so let's get started." Kellerman started walking toward the golf cart. "You talk while I drive."

Jake slid his driver into the bag and settled back into the cart. He cleared his throat.

"I guess it all starts and ends with Elena. She is…was my everything. Never did I think I'd meet such a woman, much less marry one. Smart, witty, pretty, down to earth. I couldn't believe my luck. But, and there's always a but. Through no fault of her own I had this fear, insecurity if you will, that I'd never be able to measure up. Of course, it was all in my head. She was perfectly fine living in a small three-bedroom house without the trimmings or fancy cars." Jake could feel his eyes tear up. "I don't know why I couldn't see that. Perhaps, if I'm totally honest with myself, I was in mortal fear that Elena would one day do what my mother had done to my dad: get up and leave, just like that. And when Drew…our son, got sick and my personal injury practice went into the toilet and I couldn't pay the bills, I became desperate." Jake took a deep breath. "So, when Tifton came along, it was my chance to be somebody, to make Elena proud…that I could take care of my family. But that meant breaking my promise not to handle drug cases. So, instead of keeping my word I immediately broke it, then lied and lied again to cover it up." Jake felt himself choking up. "And now, she's gone."

Kellerman stopped the cart and looked at him, but said nothing.

"You know," Jake continued, "living in that hell-hole these past few weeks has given me time to sort things out. I realize that family is all that matters, and I know that proving my innocence would be a huge step in getting them back." Jake's eyes locked on Kellerman's. "Therefore, I'm asking you, sir, will you help me do that?"

Kellerman extended his hand. "As best I can, son."

Jake grasped it. "Then you'll defend me?"

"But you'll have to do the heavy lifting. I don't have sixteen-hour-days in me anymore. So, the first thing we have to do is notify the U.S. Attorney that you'll turn yourself in when the indictment comes down and get Mattson to agree to let you out on a personal bond."

"Thank you," Jake heard himself say. He barely recognized his own voice. "I don't have much, but—"

Kellerman waved him off. "You're welcome. And about your wife, she's frightened, and I don't blame her." He patted Jake's knee. "Just be there for your kids. She'll see that and be reminded of who you are, and not the villain the government will try to make you out to be. And what I want from you is to suck it up, be strong, cause we both know you're in for the fight of your life."

Chapter Thirty-Eight

Lenny waited, and waited. He tapped his fingers on the steering wheel of his 4Runner as darkness fell on the Key Largo home of Dave Tifton. For the past two hours, he sat parked down the street hoping to find something, anything to help Jake.

Voices from inside the house reached a fever pitch, followed by a piercing scream as the screen door flew open. Through night-vision binoculars Lenny watched a very pregnant Jessie running into the front yard cursing, "Fuck you, I ain't gonna do it!" She raced to her Ford Bronco while flipping her middle finger back at the house. At the sound of the truck's engine, Lenny tossed his binoculars into the empty passenger seat, paused a sufficient amount of time, then took off behind her.

As if stopping for gas forty-five minutes later, he pulled off U.S. 1 into the EZ-GO service station and parked alongside a rusted-out Ford F-150 pick-up. Across the road Jessie waved her arms wildly as she spoke on a pay phone adjacent to a truck stop. What's a pregnant woman doing out at night all alone like this?

A white guy, his face wrinkled with age, stuck his head through the open passenger window. "You a cop?" he asked, his breath reeking of booze.

Lenny jerked his head back. "No cop," he said, trying to think fast, "just a PI. My client hired me to tail his ol' lady." He nodded at Jessie across the street. "He's convinced the baby's not his."

"Hell, don't blame him one bit. With all the screwin' going on these days, he's probably right. Hope you find the bastard who did it." The curious drunk tapped the hood of the 4Runner and shuffled back to his truck.

"Be seeing ya," Lenny said, angry at himself for letting the cracker sneak up on him like that. He lifted the binoculars and continued to watch Jessie pace as far as the phone cord would allow, apparently pleading with whoever was on the line. Then without warning she slammed down the receiver, jumped back into her truck and peeled out, spraying gravel behind. Lenny raced after her, north toward Miami.

For the next hour, he kept his eyes glued to the Bronco's taillights as he followed her on Old Cutler Road, a meandering two-lane highway bordered by luxury homes. She seemed to be killing time circling the area, or maybe she'd spotted the 4Runner and was trying to shake him by turning back past Fairchild Gardens toward Perrine.

Careful, don't crowd her, Lenny mumbled.

He tailed the Ford for several more miles, keeping a safe distance between them. After a bend in the road, the Bronco's taillights disappeared. Lenny floored the 4Runner to catch up. No Jessie. He slapped at the steering wheel. "Fuck!" He lost her. He pulled onto the shoulder of the road and flicked on an inside light to check a map of the area. Only two places she could have gone: a string of abandoned warehouses or the seldom used executive airport. His money was on the latter.

Lenny killed the headlights and slowed the 4Runner to a crawl as he approached the opening in the airfield's front gate. The night was strangely quiet, interrupted only by a chorus of chirping crickets. He rolled for several hundred yards before spotting Jessie's truck, parked at the side of a building. The sign on top read Marco Aviation. Through his binoculars Lenny spotted her pacing in front of the hangar's double doors. He slouched low in his seat and pulled his .38 Special from its holster, and cradled it in his lap. No more surprises tonight.

Soon, the high pitch drone of a plane's engine could be heard overhead. Low in the sky a King Air appeared and within minutes touched down, taxied to the hangar and stopped while the twin propellers continued to spin. Had to be some kind of quick drop.

Lenny grabbed his infrared camera and through the telephoto lens watched Jessie stroking her swollen stomach. Before long, a tall, muscular man of about forty, clean shaven with short red or blonde hair, hurried down the plane's stairs with two suitcases. His shoulders dipped from the weight of what he was carrying. Lenny zoomed the Nikon 70-300m for a closer look. This had to be Red Armstrong, sans mustache and long hair.

Red grabbed Jessie by the shoulders and shook her, making her head bob uncontrollably. She tried to break free, to no avail. Instinctively, Lenny started to open his door to help, then stopped, not wanting to blow his cover. Jessie would have to fend for herself.

Before long, Red transferred both suitcases into the back of her truck, sprinted back up the steps of the King Air and took off. Jessie immediately gunned her Bronco for the exit. Lenny waited until the its taillights were barely visible and followed. He wasn't about to lose her again.

He tailed her for forty minutes past Coconut Grove when she abruptly turned into the parking lot of an all-night Taco Bell. She sure as hell hadn't come this far for a burrito. Lenny continued a block farther, turned down a side street and parked. He scrambled back to the parking lot and crouched behind a thick hibiscus hedge, only yards from where Jessie was standing. Lenny rose to aim the camera. Crack! Jessie wheeled at the sound of Lenny's shoe splintering a dead branch. He froze while she scanned the bushes, her gaze stopping at the exact spot he was crouched; so close he could smell her perfume. Finally, she turned and walked back to her truck and waited.

In minutes, a dark-colored Trans Am pulled into the dimly-lit lot. Lenny could only catch a partial of the Florida license plate as the Pontiac backed into a parking space two spots from Jessie's Bronco. Lenny recalled Jake telling him about a similar muscle car that had followed him half-way home from court.

It seemed as though an eternity had passed while the driver remained inside his car. "Come on, asshole, show your face," Lenny muttered as he ran his hand over his .38.

The door of the Pontiac sprang open and the driver stepped out. He was tall, lean and dark-complexioned. The guy stole a glance at the teenagers mingling in front of the drive-thru before moving straight for Jessie. Lenny activated the motor drive, hoping the clicks weren't loud enough to reach the parking lot.

Mystery man slid past Jessie and flung open the Ford's hatchback, pulling out the two suitcases. As he bent over, his tan parka rode up his back, exposing a handgun nestled inside the waistband of his pants, similar to the way undercover cops concealed their weapons. Without missing a beat, he returned to his car with the suitcases in hand and took off.

Jessie stood for a full minute as if in a trance, chewing at the ends of her hair. She then climbed back into her Bronco and left.

First thing tomorrow he'd call Jake and tell him his hunch proved right: The Tiftons were still in business with the cartel.

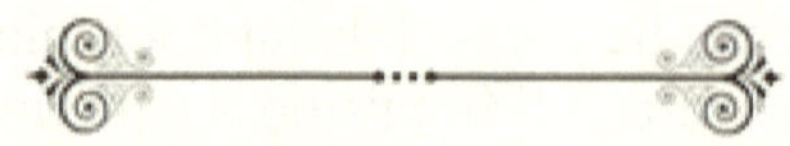

Chapter Thirty-Nine

As Jake and Kellerman approached the rear entrance to the federal courthouse, Jake's cell phone went off again. It was Lenny's third call this morning.

"Dammit, Len, not now." Jake eyed the mob of reporters lined up on the walkway routinely used to escort prisoners in and out of court.

"I tailed Jessie last night. Think I got something."

"Are you deaf? Can't talk. I'm about to enter the courthouse."

"Boss, you okay?"

"Couldn't be better. I've just been indicted, that's all. Albert called last night with the news. Suborning perjury and conspiring to further the activities of a criminal enterprise. I bet you didn't know you were working for a drug lord lawyer, did you?"

"Jesus," Jake could barely hear Lenny's reaction over the shouts of the media circus.

"Kellerman saved my butt getting Mattson to agree to a personal bond. I should be in and out in a couple of hours." Jake rubbed his temple, hoping to God his kids weren't near a TV.

"Boss, what can I do?"

"Get to the office. I'm sure Isora has already heard the news. Have her calm the clients down when they call because I know they will. Gotta go." Jake snapped his phone shut.

Jake stayed right behind Kellerman as they moved closer to the courthouse. The shouts of reporters grew louder around him. One TV cameraman grabbed Jake's arm, trying to hold him for one last shot, before Jake was able to break free. "Hey Dalton, how long you been taking orders from the cartel?" hollered a TV newsman. Another yelled, "How do your kids feel about their dad being a paid mouthpiece for drug lords?"

Jake spun and squeezed his hand into a fist, seeking the asshole who made the last remark.

Following Kellerman's lead inside, Jake placed his personal effects on the conveyor belt, cleared the metal detector and then walked down the hall toward the marshal's lock-up. "Don't let the vultures pick at your bones, son. Answer every question with a smile. You have reason to, considering Judge Stern has been assigned to your case."

Jake's eyes opened wide. "Really? I hadn't heard. Finally, a judge who knows the meaning of a fair trial."

An hour later, Jake used a paper towel to wipe the ink from his hands after being fingerprinted and photographed. He and Kellerman then followed a deputy marshal into the basement elevator for the ride up to the sixth floor for Jake's arraignment. As the doors opened to their floor, they were instantly mobbed by more reporters, three of whom seemed to know Kellerman well as he made short work of a granola bar.

"Hey, Albert," a woman called, "does this mean you're off the links and back into the fray? Are you concerned about getting paid with drug profits?"

Kellerman waved her off, the tip of his cane clacking as he lumbered with Jake down the marble corridor while reporters still continued to pepper Kellerman with questions.

"What made you decide to come out of retirement and take this case? Care to comment on the twenty-two-page indictment? The U.S. Attorney seems really confident of a conviction."

The last word sent a chill through Jake. Kellerman stopped, and with a broad smile turned to the young reporter who made the last remark.

"Now, young man, has there ever been a time when the prosecution wasn't confident of a conviction, even hours after the jury returned a verdict of not guilty?"

Everyone roared with laughter.

"Mark my words," Kellerman added. "My client is innocent, and we expect you to provide the same kind of coverage when he is absolved of all wrongdoing. Promise me that."

"One last question," a veteran reporter shouted out as she squeezed through the crowd. "Aren't you feeling pretty good about your chances now that Judge Stern is on the case? Wasn't he a student of yours when you taught constitutional law at Harvard?"

Kellerman's face opened into a wide grin. "Judge Stern is one of the brightest, ablest jurists ever to sit on the federal bench. It'll be an honor to try this or any other case before him." He grabbed Jake's arm. "Time to go, son. After all these years, I don't dare be held in contempt my first day back."

Jake pushed open the double doors of Courtroom 6-2 and froze. Richter. The federal prosecutor stood by his counsel table, conferring with Special Agent Nettles. What was he doing here? Certainly, Richter didn't intend on testifying and prosecuting the case, too.

As Jake and Kellerman continued inside, U.S. Attorney Adrian Mattson stood hunched over the prosecution table, reading the Miami Herald's front-page headlines of Jake's indictment. He pointed Richter to something in the newspaper and the two of them shared a laugh. A stark study of contrasts: Mattson, in his sixties, chubby with thinning gray hair and drooping jowls on a small head, and Richter, appearing ten years younger, marine-like with a chiseled face, broad shoulders and short hair. Although dressed in a pin-stripe suit and crimson tie, Richter seemed better suited to battle fatigues.

U.S. Magistrate Takahashi entered and took her seat behind the raised bench. From her perch in the tall leather chair, she motioned the attorneys to take their places. Her gaze shifted to the defense table.

"Mr. Kellerman," she called deferentially, "after so many years, it's a pleasure to welcome you back to my courtroom." She smiled at the renowned lawyer, who distinguished himself from other counsel by his deep tan and polka-dotted bow tie. "It appears time away from the rigors of trial has agreed with you, sir. I take it you'll be representing the defendant."

Jake stiffened at hearing his new title, defendant.

Kellerman stood. "Yes, Your Honor. And it is *I* who am honored to appear before you today." He placed his hands by each side and bent his head and shoulders slightly forward, as though familiar with the Japanese custom. "For the record, we waive reading of the indictment and enter a plea of not guilty to all counts. With the court's permission, the government and I have already stipulated to the release of my client on a personal recognizance bond."

"That's correct, Your Honor," Mattson said, rising from his chair. "We do not view the defendant as a flight risk."

"Will you be trying the case, Mr. Mattson?" the magistrate asked, looking down at the U.S. Attorney. Her soft eyes and smooth complexion made her appear to be in her thirties, though Jake knew her to be considerably older.

"Yes, Your Honor, along with Special Assistant, Crawford Richter. I might add that Mr. Richter will also be a witness for the prosecution."

Richter stood and nodded his greeting.

The magistrate smiled. "Classic movie, but I don't believe I've ever seen it play out in my courtroom before." She glanced at Kellerman. "Does the defense have any objection?"

"Not at this time. I would add that if the U.S. Attorney wishes to sabotage his case by putting on obviously biased testimony, who am I to object?"

The magistrate struggled to suppress a smile.

"I should also note," Kellerman added, "that my client will be trying the case with me."

"Alright." She peered at Jake. "Certainly not unheard of. I take it, Mr. Dalton you're aware of the adage of having a fool for a client?"

Jake rose. "I am, Your Honor. But under the circumstances I'm just grateful to have someone with Mr. Kellerman's experience and prestige by my side." He swiftly took his seat.

The judge nodded her agreement. "Gentlemen, I have an announcement to make. As you may know, Judge Stern had been initially assigned to preside over this case. Regrettably, I must inform you that he has been recently diagnosed with a serious illness and has elected to take leave to attend to his health. Accordingly, the clerk has reassigned this matter to Judge Henry."

Jake slumped in his chair. "What the fuck," he moaned softly. From his seat, he caught Richter smiling. Jake could now kiss goodbye any chance of a fair trial. He envisioned Henry chortling from the bench as the guilty verdict was announced to a packed courtroom.

Kellerman leaned close to him. "Tough break, son."

"Isn't there any way to knock him off the case," Jake whispered back to Kellerman. "I might as well plead guilty now and save everyone the trouble of a trial."

Kellerman shook his head. "Let's see how it plays out."

The magistrate continued, "I have consulted with Judge Henry. He has set the trial to commence on Monday, November 15, 2010. Please note your calendars, accordingly. As you know, Judge Henry does not favor continuances."

"Is that okay?" Kellerman asked Jake. "Speak up now if there's a problem."

"Problem?" At a loss for words, Jake could only shake his head a what lay ahead.

PART 3

Chapter Forty

From the defense table inside Judge Henry's courtroom, Jake watched as newspaper reporters jockeyed for their seats in anticipation for the start of U.S. vs Dalton. The promise of a drug lawyer on trial guaranteed extraordinary coverage. Articles all but convicting him of aiding and abetting Mexican drug lords, even exposing Jake's troubled marriage and Drew's repeated hospitalizations, had been splashed across Miami's newspapers on a daily basis.

Jake fingered his dad's pocket watch, thankful he wasn't alive to see this sorry spectacle, then glanced at Kellerman and Lenny, bookends on either side of him, appearing relaxed and confident.

Kellerman leaned close to Jake and teased with a smile. "You certainly know how to attract a crowd, young man."

Jake tried to smile back but couldn't.

U.S. Attorney Mattson, Richter and Nettles marched single file into the courtroom, all wearing dark suits and lugging heavy briefcases. Ignoring Jake, they took their seats at the prosecution table.

At the sound of a loud rap, the courtroom turned silent. Jake rose with the gallery. He muffled a cough to clear the tightness in his chest.

A deputy marshal bellowed, "All rise. Here ye, Here ye...All those having business before this court..."

Jake tuned out the ritual greeting as Judge Henry settled into his tall chair behind the carved wooden bench, adjusting the sleeves of his black robe. He paused long enough to nod at those at counsel table, then studied a list of potential jurors in front of him.

"Madam Clerk," the judge called, "bring in the first thirty from the jury pool. I intend to swear in a panel by lunch."

"Yeah, let's give the defendant a fair trial before we hang him," Jake muttered to no one in particular.

Throughout the morning, Judge Henry questioned potential jurors over possible bias. His questions were superficial and robotic, nowhere near the depth Jake would have liked. But this was federal court where the judge has near total discretion on how to conduct voir dire.

At twenty minutes past noon, a jury of six men, six women, and two alternates were sworn. Mattson rose for his opening statement. He, not Richter, would be taking the lead role.

"Ladies and gentlemen of the jury," Mattson began, "the government will prove beyond a reasonable doubt that for the past several years the defendant has been living a double life. At day, he played the role of a devoted family man, a lawyer struggling to make ends meet. But at night, the real Jake Dalton did his sordid legal work as a crucial player inside the Mexican Santolisma cartel, an organization identified by both U.S. and Mexican law enforcement as one of the most notorious and violent criminal enterprises in the southern hemisphere. We will show that the defendant conspired with another corrupt Miami attorney to launder millions in illicit drug money, and further conspired with his former client Thomas Tifton, a convicted drug trafficker, as well as Tifton's wife, Jessie, and brother, Dave, to suborn perjured testimony and subvert the administration of justice."

The jury sat back, hanging on to Mattson's every word.

"The defendant," the U.S. Attorney continued, "has violated the most sacred oath a lawyer can make: that is, to represent his clients ethically and within the bounds of the law. And why you may ask did the defendant commit these crimes? For the love of money, of course. Indeed, when the defendant's criminal activities came to light, his wife of seven years took their children and fled in abject fear for her family's safety. The evidence will also show that the defendant admitted, months before his client went to trial, that he knew him to be guilty. Nonetheless, the defendant helped concoct a fabricated alibi in Tifton's defense, thus obstructing justice. The defendant's admission of his client's guilt was made to none other than my top assistant, Crawford Richter, who will so testify."

Jake caught Richter nodding his agreement and turned to Kellerman. "He can't do that. I'm pulling Richter's plug."

Jake shot out of his chair. "Your Honor, at this time, the defense invokes Rule 615 of the Federal Rules of Evidence. It is my understanding that AUSA Richter not only intends to be present and assist in the prosecution of this case, but also testify as a government witness. This, he cannot do. Sequestration requires that he be excluded from the proceedings. The language of the rule is clear, leaving the court with no discretion."

Mattson nervously pulled on his tie. "Your Honor, may we take this up at side bar?"

"No, you may not. You know I resent side bars. Lawyers abuse them and they end up being a glorified waste of time."

The entire panel laughed. Jake sensed a chink in the prosecution's armor.

Mattson's shoulders sagged. "But Mr. Richter's presence is critical to the prosecution."

"Judge," Jake answered back, "we have no objection to Mr. Richter's presence as long as he forgoes his right to testify. He can't have his cake and eat it, too. If the government withdraws Mr. Richter as a witness, the problem is solved. But if they insist on having him testify, then he must be excluded from the proceedings. The federal rule, Your Honor, could not be any clearer."

"Mr. Mattson, I believe the defendant, uh, Mr. Dalton, has a point. Which will it be?"

Mattson, Richter and Nettles huddled together. Mattson heatedly waved his arms at the two while the jury looked on with amused interest. The U.S. Attorney finally raised his head.

"Your Honor, the government elects to proceed with Mr. Richter at counsel table and thereby withdraws his name as a witness. He will not be testifying for the government."

"Satisfied, Mr. Dalton?" asked the judge.

"Yes, Your Honor." Jake sat back down. He knew Richter's testimony, though untrue, would have been crippling. But now he had to watch out for Agent Nettles since he was at the meeting when Jake went to inspect the plane.

Mattson continued to outline the rest of his case to the jury and concluded by saying, "At the end of the day the government will show that the defendant was paid handsomely with drug profits by drug lords who seek to destroy the very fabric of our way of life. The defendant is the worst of his kind and gives all who seek truth a bad name. Therefore, I am confident that after considering the evidence you will return a verdict of guilty on both counts of the indictment. Thank you very much."

The judge looked at Kellerman. "Anything from the defense?"

"Yes, Your Honor." Kellerman buttoned his suit jacket and moved to the lectern.

"Ladies and Gentleman. The matter before you represents a classic example of government overreach, a case that given the facts never should have filed, much less brought to trial. Witness after witness that the prosecution intends to call are nothing more than a sleazy, pitiful group of individuals who would gladly sell their souls to avoid punishment for their crimes. They include a lawyer convicted of laundering millions for the cartel, as well as a string of drug smugglers, family and friends. Contrast that with witnesses who will testify for my client—distinguished members of the Florida Bar and retired judges. Mr. Dalton will also take the stand and explain why he decided to represent Tifton in his first and only drug case. In defending Tifton, my young client, a good man, an honest man, made a rookie mistake—he believed, hook, line and sinker in the innocence of his client. That's his only crime."

The veteran lawyer steadied himself against the lectern, clearly tiring. "When all is said and done, you will see that Jake Dalton has been falsely accused, and that all twelve of you will speak the truth and find him not guilty of these spurious charges." He thanked the jury and returned to sit beside Jake.

Jake leaned over to Kellerman. "I couldn't have asked for more."

Kellerman squeezed Jake's arm. "Let's hope so."

Without waiting any further, Mattson stood and faced the rear of the courtroom. "The government calls Jessie Tifton."

Chapter Forty-One

Jake twisted his head around as the rear door swung open and twenty-two-year-old Jessie, head held high, strode down the narrow aisle between rows of curious spectators. Deep auburn hair brushed her tan shoulders as she stepped through the low swinging doors toward the witness stand, clearly relishing her moment of fame.

In an attractive navy dress and matching high heels, she looked considerably more mature than when Jake first met her a year and a half before. She adjusted the small silver cross around her neck and took the oath. Jake braced himself for what was next.

Mattson threw out his first question. "Mrs. Tifton, you are the wife of Thomas Tifton?"

"I am."

"Do you have any children?"

"The Lord blessed us with a son, Mathew five months ago."

"And is it true your husband was convicted last year of trafficking in cocaine and is presently serving a thirty-year sentence for his crime?"

Jessie quietly nodded.

"Mrs. Tifton," Mattson said. "You have to speak out loud so the court reporter can take down your testimony."

Jessie again nodded.

The jurors laughed.

"Oh, sorry. Yes, I'll do my best."

"And is it true that in the past you have assisted your husband in his criminal activities?"

"I'm afraid so." Jessie shifted in the witness chair. "I'm very sorry I got mixed up in that."

"But you have never been arrested or charged for what you did, is that also true?"

"Uh, huh."

"And you're here today to testify pursuant to an agreement you made and a grant of immunity given to you by the United States government?"

"That's right. I agreed to testify against Jake…uh, Mr. Dalton."

"And you understand the agreement you made is conditioned upon you testifying truthfully and putting all criminal activity behind you?"

"That's true." Jessie reached over and poured herself a glass of water.

"Mrs. Tifton, let me take you back to June of last year. Do you remember the night when your husband returned home after flying through a tropical storm?"

"Oh Lord, that's a night I'll never forget, watching TV all night, looking for any news about Tommy, just crazy with worry. I didn't know if he was dead or alive."

"Where had he traveled to that night? Some sort of business trip?" Mattson asked, seemingly amused with himself.

Jessie blushed. "Well, kinda. His business then was runnin' drugs. He and Butch took off for Colombia two nights before. I begged him not to go, but he wouldn't listen. We got into a big fight over that. We hadn't been married all that long and I wanted him home with me."

Several jurors smiled.

"But he went to Colombia anyway, over your protests?"

"Uh, huh. Tommy promised it'd be his last, his biggest trip yet, almost a thousand keys of coke. Said it was too much money to pass up, and he couldn't let Butch go it alone."

"When you say keys of coke, that's drug lingo for kilos of cocaine, right?"

"Sorry. Yes, that's right." Jessie's smile was smooth.

"What happened when your husband returned from Colombia that night?"

She took another sip of water. "He called from the airport, told me Customs stopped him and searched his plane, but didn't find no drugs, so they had to let him go. I never heard Tommy like that before, carrying on how he'd thought he'd crash in that storm and be burned alive, like what happened to his buddies in the Gulf war."

"Go on."

"He got home shaking somethin' awful. Said while they was trying to find a place to land, he saw a plane chasing 'em, so he had to ditch the coke or go to jail. When he got home, he made me leave and go to his brother's. He was sure the Mexicans would come and kill us." Jesse stroked her hair. "I was scared out of my freakin' mind."

"What happened next?"

"I pleaded with Tommy for us to get like Butch did." But that did him no good neither, got caught just like Tommy."

"Once your husband was arrested, did he hire a lawyer?"

"Yes sir." She gestured toward Jake. "Tommy knew this lawyer Pendleton, who he used in the past to buy land. He told us about Jake."

"Let the record show that the witness has identified the defendant."

"So noted," the judge said. "Please continue, Mrs. Tifton."

"Me, Tommy, and Dave," she said, rotating in her chair toward the jury, "that's Tommy's big brother. We went to see Jake in that fancy office of his, right in the heart of downtown, real high up. You should see what a nice a view he's got of the water, with all those pretty—"

"Mrs. Tifton," Mattson interrupted, "please stick to the facts. Otherwise, this trial will drag on and the judge will be mad at us all."

"Sage advice, counsel." The judge looked down at Jessie. "Young lady. Answer the question that's asked. No more, no less. Can you do that for me?"

"I'm doing the best I can."

Jake grabbed Kellerman's arm. "Don't be fooled, it's all an act. Jessie's as shrewd as they come."

Mattson continued. "Mrs. Tifton, when you met with the defendant for the very first time, did your husband make it clear to him that he was running drugs?"

"You bet."

Jake stiffened in his chair, stunned how easily Jessie could lie.

"And did your husband tell the defendant that on the night he was stopped by Customs he had tried to import a thousand kilos of cocaine?"

"Absolutely. Jake was cool with it. That's why we went to him. Attorney Pendleton said Jake would do right by us." Jessie smiled at the jury.

"So after your husband was arrested and made bail, you, your husband and his brother, Dave, met with the defendant to discuss how he would defend your husband?"

"Jake asked if we knew anyone willing to give Tommy an alibi, and if we didn't, he'd find someone. I thought Mr. Dalton was real clever to think of that."

Jake clenched his teeth. Jessie was making a convincing witness.

"And did you find such a person?"

"Actually, two. A Mr. and Mrs. Mendoza. He's a big shot with the Cozumel Board of Tourism. We decided to use them after Jake gave us the ok."

"And where are the Mendozas now?"

Jessie shrugged. "Got me. They just vanished into thin air, never heard from again."

Murmuring grew loud in the gallery.

Mattson leaned against the lectern. "Mrs. Tifton, is it your testimony under oath that you, your husband and your brother-in-law, along with the defendant, conspired to put forward a fabricated alibi at your husband's trial?"

Kellerman grasped Jake's sleeve as he was about to leave his feet. "Leave it, son. It might be objectionable, but let it go."

"That's exactly what I'm saying. Jake came right out and said he wanted to win Tommy's case in the worst way so he could score points with the Mexicans. Said he'd been hurtin' for more business and talked about needing money for his sick boy."

At the mention of Drew, Jake shot up, then quickly sat back down, resigned that his son's name would be dragged through the trial.

Mattson nodded in agreement. "And when you testified at your husband's trial that he was *not* running drugs the night Customs stopped him, you were lying, weren't you?"

"I'm real sorry about that. I just didn't want my Tommy to go to jail."

"And the defendant knew you were lying?"

"Oh, he knew."

Mattson smiled. "That's all, Your Honor."

"All right," said the judge, glancing at the wall clock. "It's been a long day. We're in recess until tomorrow morning at nine o'clock." He taped his gavel and left the bench.

The jury filed out.

"Take a deep breath, son," Kellerman said. "I know you feel like a hot poker's been shoved down your throat, but you'll have your chance tomorrow. Go home and get some rest."

"I can't wait to see the look on that twit's face when you show her the photos," Lenny chimed in. "She's up to her eyeballs running drugs."

Still shaken by Jessie's testimony. Jake could only nod.

"And notice how Red's name never came up, not once, and how she practically stammered when asked about Pendleton?" Lenny added. "She's scared of getting killed." He pulled a thick manila envelope from his briefcase and handed it to Jake. "It's everything you'll need, and more. Break her into tiny pieces and the tide will turn. Promise me, Boss, no more mister nice guy."

Jake quietly placed the photos in his briefcase, knowing he would not sleep a wink that night. He looked back at Lenny. "I stopped being a nice guy a long time ago."

Chapter Forty-Two

The moment court was called to order Jake fired off his first question standing behind the lectern. "Mrs. Tifton, when did you first meet representatives of the federal government to discuss the possibility of becoming their witness?"

"March of this year."

"And as part of your deal with the government you agreed not only to testify against me but to persuade your husband to do so as well."

"Yeah, I got Tommy to talk."

Surprised by her candor, Jake pressed, "And that took some doing didn't it?"

"I'll say."

"Because he was tired of lying, tired of being used and abused by his own government?"

"That's not true. *I'm* the one who's tired, tired of him protecting you for no good reason." She looked down. "He's got this thing about honor and loyalty."

"Honor and loyalty," Jake repeated, scribbling a note to himself to use later.

"I just wanted him out of that jail," she volunteered. "If you were me, wouldn't you do the same?"

"Not if it meant convicting an innocent man," Jake snapped back.

"Counsel, you're out of line," the judge barked before Mattson could object.

"And your husband," Jake continued, ignoring the judge's stare, "had no way of cutting his thirty-year sentence unless he cooperated with the government. Isn't that true?"

"You'd better ask him."

Jake knew he'd hit a wall and changed his line of attack. "Mrs. Tifton, for all the times you've helped your husband traffic in drugs, you've never once been charged with a crime. Right?"

"Yep."

"And you knew that if you wanted to keep your baby, you'd better tell the government what they wanted to hear. Correct?"

"What's wrong with that?"

Several jurors exchanged looks.

"As long as I told the truth," she quickly added.

"You and your husband made quite a bit of money dealing in drugs, didn't you?"

"But it's all gone now."

"Then what are you living on?"

"Friends help out."

"Friends like Red Armstrong, a major player in the cartel?"

Jessie looked away.

"Mrs. Tifton, I can't hear you. Perhaps you should move close to the microphone."

She picked at her fingernails, avoiding Jake's gaze. "I'm not sure."

"Yes, you are. This Red is still giving you money to live on. Isn't that a fact?"

Jessie's face grew tight. "He's got nothing to do with this. As far as I know, he's living somewhere in Mexico. And stop trying to change the subject, that's what you lawyers always do. You knew Tommy was running drugs the minute we stepped foot in your office. You're one of those smooth-talking lawyers always twisting things around, making it sound different than it really is." She stabbed her finger at him. "That's what your kind does. But I'm here to tell ya the truth, so help me God."

Jake's mouth turned dry. Jessie's tirade was effective, her performance better than feared.

"Your Honor," Jake said, regaining his composure, "I move to strike as unresponsive and ask the court to admonish the witness to answer only the question that's asked."

The judge glared down at Jessie. "Motion granted. The jury will disregard the last response. Young lady, I won't say it again. You are to answer only the question that is asked of you, nothing more. Do I make myself clear?"

Jessie sheepishly nodded, but she knew what she had done. Her last diatribe clearly stung and there was nothing the judge could say or do to erase it from the jurors' minds. All Jake could do was move on.

"I'll ask again. Has Red Armstrong given you any money in the past year?"

Jessie paused for several moments. "It ain't much." She cleared her throat and looked up at the judge. "Can I have some more water?" A deputy marshal brought a fresh pitcher to the stand and poured her a glass. She offered a faint smile and took a sip. "What were you sayin'?"

"And in exchange for your testimony today the government has given you complete immunity from prosecution. Isn't that true?"

"They promised I wouldn't be charged and I'd get to keep Mathew."

"You knew if you ever violated your agreement to stay clear of drugs you'd go to prison and lose your son?"

"But I haven't."

"You sure about that?"

Jessie scoffed. "Of course, I'm sure. I'd know if I was doing drugs. I'm not stupid."

Several jurors laughed. Time for Jake to set his trap.

"When was the last time you had any dealings with Red?"

"Right before Tommy got arrested, about a year and a half ago."

"You expect the jury to believe that?"

She shot a look at the jurors. "They should 'cause it's the truth."

Jake pulled out photos that Lenny had taken of Jessie. "Your Honor, I'd like to have these eight photographs marked for identification as defendant's composite exhibit A1 through A8. There're being offered for impeachment." Jake handed a set to Mattson and a set to the clerk, who put her stamp on them before handing them up to the judge.

"May I approach the witness?" Jake asked, having already moved toward Jessie. He spread the eight 5 x 7 photos on the edge of the stand.

"You may," the judge answered, leaning toward the witness stand. "I assume these will be offered into evidence, counsel?"

"Yes, Your Honor." Jake stepped closer to Jessie. "Mrs. Tifton, do you see yourself in each of these photographs?"

Jessie's eyes popped open. "Where'd you get these?"

"That's not my question."

Her hand shook as she lifted and studied each photograph.

"I'll ask again," Jake said, his voice growing stronger. "Is that *you* in each of the photos?"

Jessie nodded. "It was just before Mathew was born."

"On the back of each photograph there's a date. Please tell the jury what that is."

"June 16, 2010."

"That's three months *after* you met with Agent Nettles and AUSA Richter and agreed to be a government witness. True?"

"I guess so."

Jake pointed to the photos. "Tell us what you were doing the night of June 16th as depicted in these eight photographs."

"I don't wanna talk about it."

"I'm afraid you have to," Jake shot back.

The judge leaned toward Jessie. "Answer the question or I'll hold you in contempt."

She gave a deep sigh. "Uh…Dave called, real upset. Told me to come right over, said he didn't trust the phones. I was in such a panic I forgot my cell. Said I had to go right away to meet Red and pick up a couple of suitcases."

"Just so we're clear, Dave Tifton has also pleaded guilty to drug trafficking and as a part of his deal has agreed to testify against me?"

"Why you asking me this if you already know?"

Jake turned to the jury. "I was just wondering if the government's war on drugs meant ridding the streets of smugglers by bringing them to court to testify."

The room shook with laughter.

Jake waited for the noise to subside. He glanced back at the gallery, wishing Elena were here. He needed so badly for her to see the truth, that he was being framed.

"Pray tell," Jake said, feeling his confidence surging. "Why in the world would you agree to meet Red that night? Was it a social call?" He sensed Jessie was close to cracking.

She pushed the photographs away and twisted in her seat toward the judge. "Do I have to talk about this? That's not what I agreed to do."

The judge frowned. "You'll answer the questions put to you young lady unless and until I say otherwise. Are we clear on that?"

Jessie looked at Jake, the fear in her eyes palpable. "I went—met Red at this airfield." She pointed to one of the photographs. "Outside

Marco Aviation. He sometimes uses it to refuel. The second he landed he came running at me with the two suitcases and threw them into the back of my truck, said I had to take them to an associate of his."

"Let me direct your attention to defendant's exhibits A1 through A5. Is that Red Armstrong, the broad-shouldered guy with short hair, shaking you by the shoulders and threatening to hit you?"

Several jurors recoiled in their seats.

"You've no right to make me talk about this. You got no idea what it means."

Jake moved even closer, his face inches from hers. "If you want to keep your deal with the government and not be forced to give up your child, you'll answer my question."

Jessie stayed silent for several seconds, then spoke. "God knows I didn't want to be there but I had no choice."

"Mrs. Tifton, please tell the jury what was in the suitcases?"

Jessie looked away. "I'm not sure. I honestly don't remember."

"Which is it? Not sure or don't remember. I remind you, you're under oath."

Jessie's eyes never left Jake while she sipped more water. Then she blurted out, "Red said it was a million dollars."

"So, with suitcases stuffed with a million dollars in cold cash, where did you then go after leaving the airfield?"

Jessie gripped the edge of the witness stand. "Why you asking me these things? I swear it's got nothin' to do with you."

Mattson stood as if taking his cue. "Your Honor, the government objects. This entire line of questioning is irrelevant and immaterial. It has no bearing on the charges in this case."

Jake gave Mattson a look of disbelief, then turned to the judge. "How would he know? Besides, the question bears directly on the credibility of the witness who has sworn in open court that she has been completely faithful to her plea agreement in that she has not been involved in any drug activity whatsoever."

Judge Henry rocked back in his chair. "I'm inclined to allow it."

Jessie looked up at the judge. "What does that mean?"

"It means answer the question."

"Mrs. Tifton," Jake persisted, "we're waiting for an answer. Where'd you go with the suitcases full of cash?"

"To the Taco Bell near my home, to meet this associate of Red's."

"Does this associate have a name? And how'd you know what he would look like?"

"All Red told me was that he's a tall, dark-skin Cuban, and that he wouldn't be hard to miss." Jessie took her index finger and rubbed it across her upper lip. "Said he got a nasty scar from a knife fight."

"Is this you and the Cuban meeting that night in the Taco Bell parking lot as depicted in defendant's A6 through A8?"

Jessie pushed the photos away. "Please don't make me talk about this. I've already said too much. Tommy warned me to stay clear of that man."

"Why was that?"

"I'm not saying."

Mattson rose from his chair. "Objection, Your Honor. The question calls for hearsay." Jake's response was immediate. "Judge, it's not offered for the truth of the matter but to determine the witness's state of mind at the time. I'm surprised the government doesn't want to know *why* Mrs. Tifton did the things she did if they were, as she describes, entirely innocent."

"Overruled." The judge stared down at Jessie. "Answer the question."

"Tommy warned me about that man, said he'd slit the throat of a government snitch."

A loud murmur swept the courtroom.

Jake waited for the room to quiet down, and continued. "What's the name of this murdered informant?"

Jessie shook her head. "Dunno. All Tommy said was that the boy used to help off-load coke before he got busted."

"Then tell me the name of this Cuban who you met at Taco Bell?"

"Don't know and don't want to. Tommy's warning was enough. I didn't want them finding me floating in the Miami River like that boy."

An alarm exploded inside Jake's head. Was this Carmen's kid brother?

"I gave the man his money," Jessie continued, "and got out of there as fast I could."

"Did you tell the government about Red's money and your meeting with the Cuban?"

Jessie nodded. "Right after it happened."

Jake turned toward the prosecution table. "You told the U.S. Attorney about meeting this Red, a known drug smuggler, and handing over his million dollars to this mysterious Cuban in the middle of the night?"

Jessie pointed to the prosecution table. "Not him, Richter."

Judge Henry's brows shot up. He glanced over at the federal prosecutor, who sat staring at his lap, motionless.

"And what was Mr. Richter's response?"

"Just to keep it between us, that he'd look into it."

"He asked you to keep it a secret?" Jake was beside himself. "He didn't ask you where to find Red or this Cuban or about the government informant who was murdered?"

Jessie shook her head. "I can't tell ya what was on his mind."

Jake half-turned and saw Kellerman gesturing to him to move on.

"Mrs. Tifton, isn't it true that as recently as last June, a year after your husband had been arrested and charged with drug trafficking, you continue to help Red Armstrong in his drug operations?"

"No fricking way," Jessie shot back.

"Come on, Mrs. Tifton, you just testified that only a few months ago you received a million dollars cash from Red after he landed his plane at a remote airfield in the dead of night, and then you brought this cash to a mysterious Cuban at a Taco Bell miles across town. Yes?"

"Uh, huh."

"And, in spite of this, you expect the jury to believe that you're not involved in running drugs?"

Jessie fidgeted in her chair. "Are you deaf? I already said that this is got nothin' to do with you. Besides, I would never do such a thing and risk losing my boy."

"You still haven't answered my question. Given everything you did that night, how do you expect anyone to believe that you weren't doing something illegal? It's simply not credible. Once and for all, it's high time you told us the truth."

She rocked forward, shaking her head. "'Cause Red said the man was CIA."

The courtroom erupted into pandemonium.

Chapter Forty-Three

"Your Honor, I object!" Mattson said, shouting over the uproar. "That's outrageous and blatant hearsay, it should be stricken from the record."

Judge Henry banged his gavel. "Quiet! Quiet in the courtroom." Slowly, the commotion died down. The judge glared at Jake as though he had planned it.

"Your Honor," Jake argued, "the testimony of Mrs. Tifton, a government witness, that she conspired with a CIA operative, demonstrates the total hypocrisy in bringing these charges against me. They should be dismissed."

Mattson raised his arms in protest.

"Objection sustained. The jury will disregard any reference to the CIA." He leaned forward over the bench. "Counsel, any more theatrics like that and I'll hold you in contempt. Are there any more questions of this witness?"

Jake looked at Kellerman, who shook his head. "No, Your Honor." Jake had gotten more than he could have hoped for. He promptly had the photos admitted into evidence and sat down.

"Does the government have any redirect?"

"No, Your Honor. The witness is excused."

Jessie grabbed her purse and scurried from the courtroom.

That's right Jessie, Jake thought, run like you've never run before. Go tell Red how you avoided jail by exposing his dealings with the CIA. Jake was convinced that but for Tommy's special bond with Red, Jessie wouldn't be long for this world.

Jake grasped Lenny's arm. "One helluva job, buddy. Those photos saved my ass big time. I won't ever forget it."

Lenny grinned. "Tis what I do."

"One more thing. I need you to check out a hunch."

Lenny's eyes shot open. "What'd you got?"

"Get ahold of that detective friend of yours in narcotics and find out the ID of that dead informant. And do it now, we don't have much time."

Lenny grabbed his briefcase and left.

The government next called a seasoned female DEA agent, with a long face and short blonde hair, who Jake recognized as being present during the search of his home. She recited in excruciating detail the events leading up to the discovery of fifty thousand dollars in a locked safe in his den.

Mattson had a deputy marshal wheel a dolly loaded with a large cardboard box into the courtroom and place it in front of the witness stand.

"Special Agent, kindly stand down, open this box and describe to the jury the contents of government exhibit 14?"

The agent stepped off the stand, lifted a pocket knife and effortlessly sliced through the masking tape that sealed the container. After studying the contents for dramatic effect, she looked up. Jake braced for what was next.

"Yes, sir. I marked each stack of bills with my initials." She turned to the jury. "See? This is the identical United States currency we found in the defendant's home, all in denominations of twenty- and fifty-dollar bills, amounting to $50,000."

Mattson then moved the box and its contents into evidence. "And during this search, did the defendant say anything in your presence?"

The agent sat erect as if she'd waited her entire career for this moment. "The defendant denied the money was his and said he had no idea how it got there."

Jake cringed as several jurors chuckled at the apparent absurdity of such a statement.

"That's all," Mattson announced and swaggered back to his seat.

Jake's swallowed hard. The agent's testimony was devastating. He loosened his tie and fought the impulse to crow out his innocence. Instead, he rose and did the only thing possible. "No questions, Your Honor."

After the judge adjourned for the day, Jake turned to Kellerman. "She stuck it in pretty deep, didn't she?"

"Put it behind you, son. We still have Pendleton and Tifton to deal with." Kellerman rose from the table, pressing down on his cane.

"Go grab a bite downstairs, son. Mattson asked me to stop by his office. I shouldn't be more than an hour."

Jake sucked in his breath. "What's going on?"

"You got me," Kellerman answered and left.

Jake again checked his watch as he sat alone in the near-empty canteen waiting for Kellerman to arrive. Six P.M., the shop was about to close. What did Mattson want with him? Growing impatient, Jake paid his bill and hurried down the corridor to an open elevator. To his surprise he found Kellerman inside, about to get off. He greeted Jake with a wide smile.

"So, is Mattson ready to drop the case?" Jake asked, stepping inside. He immediately pressed the button to close the doors before anyone else could enter.

"Not quite, but we did have a most interesting chat."

"About what?"

"Let's get some fresh air. The U.S. Attorney just offered you a deal."

Jake stumbled back. "A deal? What kind of deal?"

"Plead guilty to accessory after the fact, reduced down to a misdemeanor, six months', max, most likely a halfway house." Kellerman's eyes softened. "I was more than a little surprised by the offer. Mattson must think his case is crumbling."

"Or desperate to bury the government's involvement in running drugs," Jake bristled. "Such bullshit." He leaned against the wall, listening to the tired sounds of the elevator as it carried them to the ground floor.

"Could be, son. Or maybe Mattson's having second thoughts about your guilt. I saw his reaction when Jessie testified about the million dolars. Mattson didn't know."

"Then tell him to toss the case entirely, he can do that. All the time and money spent going after me for what. They had to know I had nothing to do with those people." Tommy's words suddenly came back to him—that his prosecution never should have been brought. At the time, he thought Tommy was simply ranting about getting caught, but now Jake knew better. Was Tifton in on the government's dirty secret and indicted so he wouldn't be believed if one day he decided to talk?

"I admit it's peculiar," Kellerman agreed. "But Mattson won't dismiss the case. That'd be political suicide and he knows it."

"So now it about politics."

The elevator doors opened. Kellerman put his arm around Jake's shoulder as they walked toward the shops at Bayside. The sun cast a reddish glow as it set in the horizon.

"Let me buy you a cup of java," Kellerman offered, as they approached the marketplace alongside the bay. "Son, I know this is a bitter pill to swallow, but frankly I've never had a client offered a misdemeanor before. By the way, you'll get to keep your license."

"Great. Remind me to send Mattson a Hallmark card."

Kellerman laughed. "I wish I could tell you what to do. Just promise you won't let pride stand in the way."

Jake pressed his face against the autumn breeze and watched as seagulls took flight over the Venetian Causeway, stoking fond memories of his very first job as a paper boy. Life was so much simpler then.

As they continued to walk, the smell of barbecued ribs from street vendors wafted through the air. They stopped to let a group of camera-toting tourists pass so he and Kellerman could continue their talk in private.

"I know if I reject the deal and I'm found guilty, I'm looking at eight to ten years, and that's assuming the judge doesn't deviate from the guidelines and slap me with more. But how could I ever look my kids in the eye and explain that their dad admitted he was guilty when he wasn't? There are no grays in their world. You're either one of the good guys or you're not. And it would only confirm to Elena that I was bought and paid for. She'd never believe I did it to cut my losses, to keep my family together. Hell, I'd never get her back, and that's far worse than going to prison."

Chapter Forty-Four

Thirty minutes after calling Lenny to meet him, Jake pulled into the Tobacco Road parking lot and squeezed into a spot next to a row of motorcycles. He pulled off his tie and breathed deep, massaging the stiffness at the back of his neck. The trial was taking its toll.

As he entered, Jake nodded at the two guys on either side of the front door, their flexed pecs stretching the word security on their T-shirts. Inside, at the far end of the long rectangular bar, a Stevie Ray Vaughan wannabe belted out delta blues on an electric guitar. Through thick smoke, Jake searched the crowded bar for Lenny.

As he was about to step out to the patio, Jake heard a familiar deep voice call out, "Hey counselor, can I buy you a beer?" Jake turned and immediately waved at the same friendly biker he'd met the year before in the flower shop while trying to buy Elena roses. He remembered how humiliated he had been when his credit card was rejected by the snippety saleslady, and Diesel was there to bail him out.

Diesel slid off his stool and stuck out his massive hand. Jake shook it and gestured at several of his biker buddies standing alongside the bar. "Man, I been watching you get trashed in the papers on a daily basis so I figure you could use one."

"And all this time I thought lawyers were the most popular," Jake said, reaching into his pants pocket and pulling out a twenty. "This one's on me. You single-handedly restored my faith in the human race when I needed it most."

Diesel chuckled. He half-turned and raised two fingers at the bartender. "Couple of Buds."

After paying for the beers, Jake led Diesel out to the patio to an empty table where they sat facing each other. "At least, out here you can breathe."

Diesel removed his leather jacket and threw it on a nearby chair. "Fresh air never killed anyone."

Jake took a swig from his bottle, savoring the cold brew as it ran down his throat. "Boy, I'd forgotten how good this feels. Simple pleasures, that's what it's all about." He flashed back to the time, before Drew and Nicole arrived on the scene, when he and Elena would meet here after work, kick back with a few cold beers and share their love of the blues. "Hopefully, I can do it again when it's all over."

"I'm betting on it." Diesel raised his bottle in salute. He then reached for his wallet and pulled out the business card Jake had given him. "Counselor, I wouldn't have kept this sucker if I didn't think you were the real deal."

"Sonofabitch, you still got it," Jake said, looking at the worn card. "If you're free tomorrow, I could use you on my jury."

Diesel laughed.

Jake downed the rest of his beer and bobbed his head to the music. "For the past year, I've got this crazy-ass prosecutor coming after me like there's no tomorrow and no matter how hard I twist and turn, the fucker just won't let go." After a long pause, he added. "And to this day I don't have a clue why."

Diesel chugged down his beer, then let out a belch. "Maybe you got it wrong. Maybe it's the other way around. Maybe he sees *you* as the threat. You play chess?"

Jake nodded. "Some."

"Don't waste all your time and energy dissecting the other guy's last move, keep your eye on the entire board. What's his game plan? Where's he coming from? Where's he going? Things seldom seem as they appear. I learned that the hard way in Afghanistan. Took one in the back, lucky to be alive. Could be this prosecutor's sly as a fox. At least, that's how I'd look at it if it were my nuts in a vise."

Jack spotted Lenny trying to make his way through the crowd and waved him over. He looked back at Diesel. "I'll definitely chew on your words. I only hope there's enough time to figure it all out."

Chapter Forty-Five

The loud knock on the door caused Mattson to look up from reading Sam Pendleton's grand jury testimony. "Come in."

Richter entered the office of the US Attorney. "You wanted to see me?"

Mattson gestured to one of the three upholstered chairs lined in front of his desk. "Take a seat." He opened the top drawer groping for a cigarette. "I was wondering why I haven't heard from you after that bomb went off yesterday in court. Nearly knocked me out of my chair. Red Armstrong and some CIA operative running drugs. What the hell is that about?"

Richter shrugged. "News to me."

"Horseshit. It's me you're talking to Crawford, not some ignoramus. For too long I've given you free rein around here on who to indict and what deals to make. But when shit like this goes down, I expect to be informed the moment it happens. Do I make myself clear?"

Richter nodded.

"How in God's name do I explain this? The Herald's going to have a fucking field day." Mattson slammed his desk drawer shut and reached for the pack of Camels sticking out among the files on his desk, then decided against it. His doctor had warned him that at sixty-two he'd better quit, lose thirty pounds or find himself dead within a year from a coronary.

"Simple," Richter answered with a smile. "Deny, deny, deny. Works with my wife every time."

"Is this some kind of game to you?"

Richter stiffened in his seat. "Jessie doesn't know what she's talking about. Besides, who's going to believe the wife of a convicted coke smuggler? It won't go anywhere."

Mattson stood from behind his desk. "That's not the fucking point. I get the feeling you think you're in charge around here. Be very careful, Crawford. The last thing you want is to piss me off."

Richter remained still.

"Yesterday," Mattson continued, "as soon as court adjourned, I had Kellerman come to my office and offered Dalton a deal. Plead to a one-count misdemeanor, do a little time and we call it a day. I expect he'll take it."

Richter sat up in his chair. "You can't be serious. The guy's up to his neck with the cartel. You can't just let him skate with a few months in a halfway house. Where's the justice in that?"

"You heard Jessie, nothing short of explosive. It's time we put a lid on it, and fast. I can't have the average guy think we're in business with drug lords. That would ruin me politically. I won't take that chance."

"But Dalton's guilty as all hell. At least wait until you hear from Pendleton and Tifton. They'll nail his ass but good. He's as dirty as they are, maybe more so. All this talk of the CIA is nothing but a smokescreen, trying to get the jury to take their eye off the ball. In all the years you've known me, have I ever steered you wrong?"

Mattson shook his head in agreement. "No, that's true. Your record's been pretty remarkable, I'll give you that."

"And what about the fifty grand we found in Dalton's home? Have you forgotten? Money he says he knows nothing about. Gimme a fucking break. Who's going to believe it? That cash matches to the penny what Pendleton will testify he gave him. It couldn't be any clearer. Trust me, the sonofabitch is guilty, and I'll prove it."

Mattson checked his watch, not wanting to be late for court. "All right. Just make damn sure their testimony is as convincing as you say it is or we'll both be looking for a job."

Once the judge climbed the bench, Richter stood and announced, "The government calls Samuel Pendleton III."

From his seat at the defense table, Jake watched as Sam ambled down the aisle toward the well of the courtroom, his gaze fixed straight ahead. He hadn't the guts to look Jake in the face. Sam was dressed in a royal blue Armani suit, French-cuffed shirt and red silk tie; he looked the part of someone on his way to the dais to accept an award. More than a year had passed since Jake last saw or spoke to him.

Richter opened his direct examination with the usual questions—name, background, family ties and professional life. He probed Sam's relationship with Jake, then set out Pendleton's deal with the government: plead to a one conspiracy count, testify against Jake, and in exchange receive a maximum sentence of eighteen months and a $500,000 fine.

"Five hundred thousand," Jake mumbled under his breath. Sam most likely laundered that in a week. Pendleton Sr. evidently knew where to pull the strings.

Wasting little time, Richter honed in on the point of his direct. "Mr. Pendleton, why did you refer Tifton to the defendant?"

"At the time, Jake was in dire straits for money, I felt bad for him. He almost lost his boy and was having a rough time of it, complained he wasn't getting enough business from the cartel, wanted a bigger piece of the action."

"What kind of action?"

"The usual. Locate investments to funnel drug profits, represent those subpoenaed before the grand jury, and handle trials, when necessary. Since Mr. Dalton was a very capable trial lawyer and experiencing a financial slump of sorts, I urged the Tiftons to retain him."

"They evidently followed your recommendation?"

"Of course. It was also a plus that he wasn't known for doing drug work. Mr. Dalton could remain under the radar, so to speak. Tifton felt that getting a known drug lawyer to defend him would be like erecting a billboard on I-95 advertising what he did."

Several jurors chuckled.

Sam continued to avoid Jake's stare.

"And Tifton's alibi, whose idea was that?"

"Dalton's. When I sent him the case, I made it clear that the client was willing to pay whatever it took to stay out of jail. He thought fabricating an alibi would not only win the case but earn him a sizable bonus as well."

Jake could only shake his head at the lie.

Richter shifted his eyes to the jury. "And did it?"

"Yes and no. He was paid a hundred grand for trying the case and would have received an additional hundred if he'd won. That's not counting the other cash I gave him."

Jake leaned over and whispered to Kellerman. "What other cash?"

"For representing Tifton, was the defendant paid by check?"

"The first fifty thousand, yes. After that, he insisted on cash so he could avoid paying taxes on the entire fee."

A buzz spread through the courtroom.

"Mr. Pendleton, we've established that you have laundered a great deal of money for the Santolisma cartel. Was the defendant similarly involved?"

Sam nodded. "We began working together off and on since '06. So, I'd say the better part of three years."

"And during this time how much had you paid to the defendant?"

Sam pivoted toward the jury as if coached to do so. "Personally, give or take two hundred thousand dollars, always in increments of fifty thousand, usually in twenties and fifties."

The jurors' attention was fixed on Sam. They were swallowing his crap.

"And this is in addition to the hundred thousand he received representing Tifton?"

"Correct."

"Did the defendant ever confide in you where he planned to hide all this cash?"

Sam sat back in his seat, appearing to enjoy all the attention. "Well, since he knew the money was from drugs, he couldn't very well put it in a bank where it would be flagged and reported to the IRS. He told me he'd stashed it in his home, that no one would be the wiser, not even his wife."

A smile spread across Richter's face. He turned to Kellerman. "Your witness."

Jake started to rise but Kellerman grabbed his arm. "I'll handle this, son. You're wound much too tight."

Jake saw Lenny nodding his agreement and eased back down. Kellerman was right. He wanted to rip Sam's heart out.

Kellerman threw out his first question. "How much have *you* made laundering drug profits for the cartel?"

"I'm not really sure."

"Really? Come on, Mr. Pendleton, take a stab at it, one million, ten million, hundred million?"

"You'd have to ask my accountant. But I would say in the millions. I can't be more specific than that."

"My, my," Kellerman said, his tone scathing. "You can't tell us poor folk whether you've made five million or ten million laundering drug profits? You think the IRS might want to help you figure that problem out?"

The jurors laughed. Kellerman was beginning to connect.

Pendleton's face drew tight. He looked down and mumbled something.

"I can't hear you, sir," Kellerman said, cupping his ear. "Perhaps it's my age."

More laughs, especially from the retirees on the jury.

Sam pursed his thick lips. "My deal covers any and all tax issues. So whatever the number, it doesn't matter one iota. I'm immune from prosecution. So laugh all you want."

Circling back, Kellerman snatched a document off the defense table and studied Sam's plea agreement. "Well, it appears you may be right," he said, shaking his head in disbelief. "So correct me if I'm wrong, the government struck a deal where you would serve at most eighteen months and pay a fine, and for that you get away with laundering millions for the cartel and get to flub your nose at the IRS?"

Sam folded his arms across his chest and smiled. "That's my deal."

"Did Mr. Richter, when he made this sugar-coated deal, ever press for more details as to how much money you laundered to determine whether your imminent sentence was fair and just?"

"He accepted my proffer."

"You mean your word."

"That's right."

"So, we know for a fact," Kellerman continued and extended an index finger from his raised hand, "that you've grossly misrepresented your income on your tax returns. Yes?"

"I admit that."

"And even though you've led a life of fraud and deceit, you've yet to spend a single minute in prison, right?" Kellerman extended a second finger from the same hand.

"I'm out on bond, waiting to be sentenced."

"And," Kellerman extended a third finger, "when you testified that in addition to his fee for handling Tifton's trial, Mr. Dalton made approximately two hundred thousand from the cartel, we have only your lying word that it actually happened. Correct?" Kellerman lowered his arm and faced the jury, looking to gauge their response.

Sam sat up in his chair, his face contorted with rage. "I don't have written proof, if that's what you driving at. But look, your client's smart, Ivy League smart. He may come across as this sorry-ass, destitute lawyer, but believe me, he's anything but. He made plenty from the cartel and now wants to blame me for his troubles. Well, good luck with that. But we both know that's not the way it went down."

For the next hour, Kellerman continued pounding Pendleton about his numerous trips to the Caribbean, his lavish lifestyle, and with the exception of Tifton, never once referred Jake a case in the six years he'd known him. But Jake could see that his lawyer had made little headway in breaking Sam. In fact, Pendleton seem to grow more confident as the day wore on, and Kellerman, to the contrary, was clearly tiring.

"And finally, Mr. Pendleton," Kellerman pressed, "stamps on your U.S. passport indicate that beginning in 2005 you've traveled on eleven different occasions to Mexico. Were you there for business, pleasure?"

"A little of both."

"Did the business portion of your trips include money laundering? I remind you, sir, you're under oath."

"Some."

"Kindly identify those individuals in Mexico you've helped launder money."

"I can't answer that. They're clients of mine. I invoke the attorney-client privilege."

Kellerman smiled. "Nice try. You know, of course, that you can't hide behind the privilege to conceal the identities of co-conspirators. Or maybe you skipped that class in law school."

The gallery shook with laughter.

Pendleton turned to the judge for help.

"Counsel's correct," answer the question."

Sam threw back his shoulders. "Then I take the fifth."

"Apparently, that's another class you missed," Kellerman said, with the judge nodding his agreement. "As you so aptly stated, 'I've been given complete immunity from prosecution.'"

"I-I can't reveal that information, Your Honor," Sam stammered.

The judge leaned toward Pendleton. "Sir, I'm directing you to answer the question."

Sam paused for several moments, then sighed. "Mr. and Mrs. Mendoza. The same couple who agreed to give Tifton an alibi."

"Who else?"

"That's all. If there were others, the Mendozas made sure I didn't know who they were."

Kellerman moved a step closer to the witness. "Aren't you forgetting about Red Armstrong?"

"He was one of my many real estate clients but I never laundered money for him."

"You sure about that? Remember, sir, you're under oath. You're plea agreement doesn't protect you from a charge of perjury."

Sam maintained a straight face. "Yes, I'm sure."

Kellerman could only shake his head, he had no way of showing that Sam was lying. "No more questions, Your Honor." He returned to his seat, dejected.

The judge looked over at Richter, who indicated he had no redirect. "We're in recess until two o'clock." He banged his gavel and left the bench while the jury filed out.

Kellerman put his arm on Jake's shoulder. "Sorry, son. Guess I'm losing my mojo. Plan on taking whatever witnesses Mattson's got left. I can't go on."

"Aw, you did fine," Lenny chipped in, but his tone suggested otherwise.

Jake's heart pounded out of control. Pendleton's testimony had been toxic, worse than he'd imagined. Now he was thrust into going it alone, without Kellerman. Jake tried to put on a brave face, but deep down he was scared to his core like never before.

Chapter Forty-Six

Once the judge returned from the lunch recess and settled on the bench, Mattson stood and announced: "The government calls Special Agent Edwin Nettles."

Nettles left his seat at the prosecution table and took the stand. The agent adjusted his wire-rimmed glasses, then signaled to Mattson that he was ready.

"Agent Nettles, you were the DEA agent in charge of the investigation of Thomas Tifton?"

"Correct."

"And in that capacity you were present in June of last year when Tifton's then attorney Dalton inspected a Cessna at the Homestead Air Force Base?"

"I was."

"Were you also present at the base when the defendant and AUSA Richter discussed the possibility of Tifton changing his plea before trial to guilty?"

"Correct"

"Then please tell us what AUSA Richter and defendant discussed."

"Certainly. The defendant initiated the conversation and inquired if the U.S. Attorney's Office was amenable to Tifton pleading guilty for a reduced sentence."

"And Mr. Richter's response?"

"Negative. AUSA Richter remained adamant that Tifton plead guilty to all counts and receive the maximum sentence under the law. If, after pleading guilty, Tifton were to provide substantial assistance by testifying against higher-ups, Special Assistant Richter would then and only then recommend at the time of sentencing that Tifton be shown leniency."

"And the defendant's reply?"

"He asked AUSA Richter to reconsider. Said on the night in question his client was on his final trip smuggling cocaine because he wanted to settle down and start a family."

"That's crazy," Jake whispered to Lenny. From his seat, he saw Richter nodding at Nettles.

"The defendant went on to say that his client was remorseful and wanted to make amends for his past criminal behavior," Nettles added.

A hum swept through the courtroom.

Jake grabbed Kellerman's arm. "It never happened."

"What was your reaction to the defendant's admission?" asked Mattson.

"I was shocked. As a special agent, I've never had an attorney come right out and admit his client's guilt."

"No more questions." Mattson gathered his notes and returned to his seat.

The judge looked at Kellerman. "How long do you think you'll need with this witness?"

Jake yanked on Kellerman's sleeve as he started to rise. "Tell him fifteen minutes. That's all I'll need to clean this guy's clock."

Kellerman looked at the judge. "Thirty minutes at most. And with the Court's permission, My client will conduct the cross."

"All right, be quick. We need to complete the trial by the end of the week."

Pumped with adrenalin, Jake marched to the lectern. "Agent Nettles, you say you were shocked when I so readily admitted my client's guilt before trial. Is that your sworn testimony?"

"It is."

"Is it possible you could be mistaken?"

Nettles emphatically shook his head. "No sir."

"And in your long and illustrious career as a DEA agent you say my alleged admission was a first in your career?"

"Yes sir, but it wasn't alleged. It happened."

"'Shocking.' That's the word you used? Not surprising, or intriguing, but 'shocking?'"

Nettles refused to back down. "That's what I said."

"And on that 'shocking' day, did you take notes of what was discussed between me and prosecutor Richter?"

"I normally do."

"Well, if you did, then your notes would certainly be in your briefcase, would they not?"

"Most likely."

Jake followed Nettles' gaze to the prosecution table. "Sir, isn't that your black briefcase under the prosecution table?"

"It is."

"Why don't you take a look and see if by chance your notes are in there?" Jake asked, a bit wary that Nettles was making this all too easy.

Nettles glanced at Judge Henry who signaled his consent for the agent to retrieve his briefcase. Nettles complied and quickly regained the stand.

"Please," Jake urged, "look inside," motioning to the briefcase Nettles held in his lap.

Nettles unlocked his briefcase and pulled out a large spiral notepad.

"Now sir, please take a moment and confirm that those are your notes taken of that day we met at the Air Force base and that they are in their original condition. That is, they haven't been supplemented or altered at some later time."

A half-minute passed while Nettles examined his notepad. He finally looked up. "These are my notes, taken contemporaneously, in their original condition, never modified."

"Do you mind if I look at them?" Jake asked and turned to the judge. "May I approach the witness, Your Honor?"

"You may."

Nettles handed Jake his notes as he reached the stand. Jake studied them to make sure there wasn't any type of alteration, such as fresh ink marks. Nothing seemed out of order.

Satisfied they appeared to be in their original condition, Jake returned Nettles his notes, then looked up at the judge. "We'd like a copy, Your Honor. After all, they should have been provided before the start of trial."

Mattson rose. "I accept full responsibility, Judge. There must have been an oversight."

The judge pulled off his reading glasses. "Mr. Mattson. If such an oversight crops up again in this trial, sir, I'll consider sanctions. Make a copy for Mr. Dalton at the next recess."

Mattson nodded and sat back down.

Jake studied the judge. Was the old goat coming around?

"Agent Nettles," Jake continued, standing by the agent's side at the witness stand, "I assume you would consider your notes more reliable than your memory of what occurred on that fateful day, a year and a half ago, because memories can fade. True?"

"True." Nettles agreed, too readily.

"Then please read from your notes my *exact* words, words you found so *shocking*."

Nettles flipped through several pages of his notepad, then glanced up, pointing to a paragraph on the bottom of the second page. "Here it is. Exactly as I recalled."

Jake snatched the notepad from Nettles' hand and stared in disbelief. The words were there, just as the agent had said. "When did you write this?" He had trouble coming to grips that a federal agent would flat-out lie under oath. "Long after our meeting at the Air Force base wasn't it?"

Nettles gleamed in triumph. "No sir. On that very day, all at the same time."

Jake felt the gaze of the jury burn right through him. There wasn't a chance in hell they would doubt the word of a battle-tested DEA agent. Nonetheless, Jake had to press forward, hoping somehow he could put a dent in Nettles' testimony.

"Are you saying *under oath* that your notes have never been altered, supplemented or modified in any way?"

"Never. I'm extremely careful about the notes taken during the course of an official investigation. At the time, I was shocked that you had made such an admission, and as you can see for yourself, I made a point of writing it down."

Time seemed to stand still. Jake was at a loss at what to do next. He should have known better than to walk into Nettles' trap. Too naïve, Jake never imagined that an agent would reconstruct his notes and then perjure himself, with no way to prove otherwise. And, of course, Nettles knew that. In fact, he had probably baited Jake to ask for his notes. Jake considered calling a handwriting expert to determine whether the writing had been made with the same pen and at the same time, but he was sure Nettles was much too clever not to have already thought of that. He and Richter had planned this long ago.

"No further questions, Judge," was all he could manage to say.

"Redirect, Mr. Mattson?" the judge asked.

"No, Your Honor."

After court was adjourned, Jake angrily threw his files into his briefcase. He was still shaking from Nettles' testimony. Nothing short of an unmitigated disaster. By far, his worst day yet. Jake was completely drained. Somehow, he had to collect himself, put the debacle behind him and concentrate on who was next: Thomas Tifton, the most important link in the government's case against him. Jake knew that the following twenty-four hours would determine whether he'd get to leave this courtroom a free man.

Chapter Forty-Seven

The blood-red glow of the early morning sun painted the eastern sky with an array of colors as Red rolled his Chevy van to a stop next to a wooden area, a half-mile from the gated community of Palmetto Estates. He watched with mild curiosity as a yellow-throated warbler fluttered its wings moments before taking flight. Leaning against the hood of his van, he felt invigorated by the crisp autumn air. This was, after all, his favorite time of year, when typically he would travel upstate to duck hunt on the St. Johns River. Perhaps, after finishing what he came to do, he'd still have time.

After twenty minutes, Red spotted a solitary jogger coming toward him. He waved casually as Sam stopped in his tracks, looking confused.

"Hey, it's me," Red called.

Sam slowed his pace, wary. "Jesus, Red, I didn't recognize you with the short hair. I couldn't for the life of me figure out who it was."

"Sorry to startle you. I remember you telling me this was your favorite place for a morning run." He casually stepped closer to Sam. "I thought better than to call ahead. You know me and phones."

Sam put his hands into his pants pockets to keep them warm. "Yeah, you never know who might be listening."

"Exactly, that's what I wanted to talk to you about. How much have you told feds about me?"

Sam shuddered. "Not a word, I swear. You know me better than that. I would never say a thing. But Jessie, that's a whole different ballgame."

"Yeah," Red said, shaking his head. "I still haven't decided what to do with her."

"Well, you never have to worry about me. If you could have been in court, you woulda seen for yourself. I only dumped on Dalton, like I said I would. You know that, don't you, Red?

"Of course."

Sam glanced around, as though hoping someone would pass by.

"Expecting somebody?" Red asked, smiling.

"No, nobody. What else did you want to see me about?"

"To say we can no longer do business. I'm sure you understand, given that you'll be going away for a while."

Sam removed his hands from his pockets and rubbed them together. "Pretty cold for Miami, don't you think?"

Red continued to stare at him.

"Probably not more than a year," Sam added. "I'm waiting to be sentenced, and when I get out I see no reason why we can't pick up where we left off, just like old times." He smiled nervously. "I'd like that."

Red spat on the ground between them. "I always thought you had shit for brains. You're kryptonite, man. Don't you get it? And a major fuck up. First, you put Tommy's name all over those goddamn papers for the whole world to see, then you make things worse by getting your poker buddy involved. Now, I've got heat like never before. On account of *you,* I've got to haul my ass to Colombia for a good long while. So tell me, why the fuck would I want to continue doing business with *you*?"

Sam raised his hands as if to apologize. "I had no idea it would turn out that way. And I'm sorry it did. Tell you what. Let me know what it cost and I'll make good, I swear." His eyes darted back and forth.

"Money's not the issue."

Sam stumbled backward. "I would never cause you a problem. Come on, Red, you believe me, don't you?"

"This will guarantee it." He pulled out his semi-automatic and fired three rounds into Sam's chest.

"They killed him!" Marilyn screamed into her phone the moment Elena answered.

"Marilyn? Is that you? Killed who?"

"Sam. They found him…shot…blocks from here," she stammered through sobs. Marilyn pressed the cell against her ear and grabbed the bottle of valium from her medicine cabinet. "The police…they just left. I got worried when he didn't come home from his run. What am I going to tell my boys?"

"Oh, dear God…oh, Marilyn, That's horrible. I'll be right over. Let me first take Drew to the doctor's. He's overdue for his blood work."

"You're in town?" Marilyn's cries softened as she regained her voice. "When you get in?" She washed down two valiums with OJ and walked out to her patio, still in a daze.

"Late last night. God, Marilyn, is there anything I can do? I don't know what to say. I'm so, so sorry."

"I still can't believe it. I'm so lost. Sam's gone. I had a bad feeling something like this would happen, ever since that goddamn government forced him to testify. He didn't want to. And last night, he wasn't himself. Told me he'd said things about Jake—"

"Oh my God!" Elena shouted through the phone. "Jake could be next. Does he know about Sam?"

"I've no idea. All I know is that Sam felt awful about the mess he caused Jake, practically told me things he said in court weren't true."

"What do you mean?"

"He wasn't specific. Sam never is…was." Marilyn began to cry again.

"I've got to warn Jake before it's too late. I'm sorry I can't be with you right now. But you've gotta stay strong, for your boys. I'll come over as soon as I can. Gotta go. Love you."

Chapter Forty-Eight

As Jake began his climb up the steps of the federal courthouse, he spotted Lenny running toward him.

"Hey, Boss, wait up. Glad I caught you. I just left my detective friend." Lenny paused, trying to catch his breath.

"Any luck?"

"You were dead right." Lenny waved his hands as if to apologize. "Sorry, bad choice of words. The guy they fished out of the Miami River six years ago was none other than Gustavo Moreno, Carmen's kid brother. I'd have gotten back to you sooner but the case was in cold files. In fact, it never went anywhere."

"What'd you mean?"

"She says pressure from the feds was intense, basically ordered the locals to back off, claimed that since the kid was a federal witness under their protection, they had sole jurisdiction."

"I should be so protected."

"My thoughts exactly. Gustavo got snatched from a DEA safe house hours before he was to testify to a federal grand jury concerning, you'll love this, the CIA's part in drug trafficking. Naturally, the grand jury never got to hear from him."

Jake flashed back to that time in court when Carmen insisted on settling the case immediately. "No wonder she freaked out. Carmen thought she could be next." He took Lenny's arm and led him up the steps. "Come on, Tifton goes on in fifteen minutes. Where's Carmen now?"

"I asked my contact the same thing. Nobody knows. Word is that she fled with her kids back to Guatemala."

Jake tried to digest what Lenny just told him. Even if the feds were behind Gustavo's murder, how does that help him? "On second thought, go back to that detective, find out if there's anything else connecting me to Gustavo other than Carmen. There's got to be another link we're not seeing. And do it now. In forty-eight hours, it won't matter, by then I'll have already been convicted."

The U.S. Attorney rose and gestured to the courtroom's side door. "The United States calls Thomas Tifton."

Escorted by two marshals, Tifton shuffled past the jury in a loosely fitted suit and stopped in front of the clerk. With shoulders slumped, he waited for the reading of the oath to be completed, then mumbled, "I do."

That's his first lie, Jake thought.

Tifton settled in the witness stand and with vacant eyes stared back at Mattson.

Seated at the defense table, Jake leaned over to Kellerman, "My God, Tifton looks like he's just escaped a Nazi death camp."

From his bench, Judge Henry nodded to the U.S. Attorney. "You may proceed."

For the first two hours, Mattson questioned Tifton about his past war service, his treatment for PTSD and bouts of depression. Tifton explained his decision to traffic in drugs, as a result of his perceived mistreatment by the government after his return from Operation Desert Storm. Tifton further testified to dropping the appeal of his conviction, and in exchange for his cooperation the U.S. Attorney had agreed to seek a substantial reduction of his sentence.

"Mr. Tifton, pursuant to your plea agreement you have sworn to tell the complete truth in these proceedings?"

Tifton hesitated. "Yes."

"With the court's permission, defense counsel and I have agreed to bend the rules slightly and permit the witness to narrate the events which led to his arrest and hiring of the defendant."

"So stipulated, Judge," Kellerman said, half-rising from his chair. "And for the record Mr. Dalton will be conducting cross-examination."

Mattson continued, "Mr. Tifton, let me draw your attention to your final trip to import cocaine into this country. Describe what took place."

Tifton bent closer to the microphone and cleared his throat. "Butch was at the wheel that night, I didn't wanna go. Jessie was on my case about leaving the business and starting a family, but Butch convinced me that with the extra fuel bladder we could fly nonstop, piece of cake. I swore to Jessie it'd be my last time."

"Where did you pick up the cocaine and how much did you attempt to smuggle into the U.S.?"

"In a jungle near El Retiro, about an hour outside Medellin. It was our biggest load yet, just under a thousand kilos of coke."

"What happened next?"

"After the product was on board, a dozen or so Colombians carrying AK-47s circled the Cessna, taking their sweet time counting the five million we'd given as a down payment. The runts wouldn't let us take off till they were satisfied it was all there. Butch kept the turboprop running, smoking a cigar in the cockpit, cool as a cucumber. I was on the dirt strip, swatting mosquitoes bigger than a Ram truck, fingering my Beretta, in case we had a problem. Weather reports had us on edge, knew we'd better haul butt to beat a tropical storm bearing down on the Keys. Finally, right before dark, we got the green light to go."

Tifton sipped water from his glass and blinked incessantly.

Jake could only shake his head at hearing this for the first time.

"Where did you intend to land?"

"Key Largo. There's an airstrip near my brother's, but the storm knocked us off course. About fifty miles northwest of Cuba the turbulence got insane, lightning all around. We were flying low to avoid radar, then out of nowhere two fighter jets were on our butt. They kept circling, like they were toying with us. Suddenly, Butch banked hard, that's when I smashed my nose against the side window." Tifton pressed his finger to the bridge of his nose. "I realized then the whole world knew we were there." He lowered his voice. "Those boys could have blown us out of the sky, but then for no good reason they peeled off and left."

"Speak up, Mr. Tifton," Mattson urged, "I want the jury to hear every word."

Tifton nodded. "I wanted to turn back, but Butch said there wasn't enough fuel."

"What happened once the fighter jets withdrew?"

"I lined the duffels against the door figuring Customs would be next. The storm got real bad, rain pelting us at forty-five degrees. A bolt of lightning just missed the wing. I thought for sure I would never see Jessie again." Tifton stop talking and stared straight ahead as if in a trance.

"These duffel bags, were they filled with cocaine?"

No answer.

"Mr. Tifton, I asked about the duffel bags. Were they filled with cocaine?"

Tifton's eyes darted, then seemed to focus. He sighed. "Yeah, about fifty million worth."

"What happened to the cocaine?"

"I somehow made my way to the rear and heaved the bags against the cabin wall, then I froze. Knew if we ditched the coke, the Mexicans would kill us for sure."

Chatter filled the courtroom.

"Butch started hollering he wasn't going to jail and that the feds couldn't touch us without the coke."

"Did you eventually ditch the cocaine?"

"Butch said we were over water, that the coke would never be found, so I kicked open the passenger door, held on for dear life, and tossed the duffels into the storm. I then crawled on all fours and combed the cockpit for any remnants of coke or anything that might link us to drugs, and airmailed everything I could lay my hands on."

Jake flicked a glance at the jury. They sat mesmerized, their eyes never leaving Tifton.

"After landing at the airport, you and Butch were searched, detained for questioning and released, then a few days later you were arrested and charged. Shortly thereafter you retained the defendant to represent you. Is all of that true?"

"Yeah. I hired Jake on Pendleton's word that he knew what he was doing. In my mind, as long as the lawyer was sharp and could be trusted, I was okay with it." Tifton's gaze danced around the courtroom, never landing on Jake.

"Whose idea was it to concoct the alibi?"

"Mine. I knew it was the only way to beat the case. To me, Mexico was the obvious choice 'cause that's the one place nobody'd think we'd admit to coming from."

"How much did you pay the defendant?"

"Fifty thousand by check and a second fifty in cash. If we'd won, he would have gotten another hundred."

"At your trial," Mattson said, his voice growing louder, "when you took the stand and lied about being in Cozumel for a fishing tournament, did the defendant know then you were committing perjury?"

Tifton leaned back and blew out a deep breath. "He knew."

"One final question. Why did you retain the defendant who had never handled a drug case before? How'd you know he could be trusted with the intimate knowledge of your operations?"

"I balked at first, knew he hadn't much experience and I'd never heard of him before. But Pendleton said the man would be completely loyal, that he wouldn't cut corners. What sealed it for me was when Pendleton said he'd be monitoring my case and promised I'd be in good hands, that the two of them had already worked together for the cartel."

Mattson turned to Jake. "Your witness."

"Before you begin counsel," Judge Henry said, glancing at the wall clock. "I suggest this would be a good time to adjourn for lunch. We'll stand in recess until two o'clock."

After returning from a lengthy recess, Jake approached the lectern. "Mr. Tifton, earlier you testified that you shared with me, a total stranger, the most intimate details of your elaborate network of drug traffickers? Did I get that straight?"

Tifton looked down, refusing to make eye contact with Jake. "Pendleton said you could be trusted, so I did."

"How'd you know I wasn't a government informant looking to infiltrate your organization?"

For the first time Tifton looked at him. "I'm a pretty decent judge of people."

A damn lot better than me, Jake thought. "So you risked your entire operation, your life and the lives of your family on the word of Sam Pendleton?"

"Affirmative." Tifton resorted to military speak.

"And during your entire lifetime you've met Pendleton a total of one, maybe two times?"

"Once before. A real estate deal he handled for my brother." Tommy lifted the pitcher from the stand and poured himself a glass of water. "But Dave also vouched for you, said you could be trusted,"

Tifton quickly added. "I wasn't about to hire you without making sure you were a part of the team."

"And now you're serving a thirty-year sentence with a promise of getting out in one or two years," Jake asked, altering his line of attack.

"If everything goes as planned." Tommy looked up at the bench. "But it's eventually up to the judge."

"Goes as planned means if I'm convicted. So your testimony needs to be awfully convincing for you to have any chance of seeing your wife and son anytime soon. Pretty strong motivation, wouldn't you agree?"

"I won't deny I'd like to be out of jail, and be with my wife and boy. Who wouldn't? I made my deal with the government and agreed to tell them what I know. For that, I get what I want."

"Is that what you'll be telling your boy one day, that you had no choice but to lie and destroy another man's family to be reunited with your own?"

"I'm here with a heavy heart. I bear you no ill will."

Jake sensed a crack in Tifton's veneer. Did Tommy have a conscience after all? "Thirty years of new-found freedom to be with your son, a son you've always wanted. Who could blame you?"

Tifton started to speak.

"Objection," Mattson shouted as he rose from his chair. "Argumentative."

"Sustained," the judge snapped, without waiting for Jake's response.

Jake turned toward Tifton, ignoring the judge's stare. "You say you bear me no ill will, yet how do we know you're not lying right now, like you did at your own trial?"

"You don't," he then quickly added, "but I'm not."

"But if you were—"

"I'd have to live with that."

Emboldened by Tifton's admission, Jake continued his attack, feeling a slight shift in the tide. "So you admit—" He turned to the commotion at the rear. Elena stood facing the packed courtroom, her entire body gripped with fear. Jake had never seen her like this before. She let the door close behind her and beckoned him. Elena wouldn't be here unless something was horribly wrong with Drew or even Nikki. Jake pivoted to the judge and struggled to find words.

"Your Honor," he said, his voice cracking, "I know this is highly unusual, but I respectfully request a brief recess—ten minutes, at most." He stood numb, waiting for a response.

Kellerman instantly rose, seeing Jake's distress. "Judge, I join in the request. And since it is already late in the day, may I suggest an adjournment until tomorrow morning?"

The judge looked at Mattson, who nodded his agreement.

"All right, we'll be adjourned until tomorrow at nine o'clock."

Without waiting for the judge to leave the bench, Kellerman called to Jake, as he started for Elena. "Son."

Jake half-turned. "What?"

"Mattson's about to rest. I need an answer to his offer before we put on our defense."

The room closed in on Jake. Everything was happening at once. "I can't think about that now. I've got to see what's wrong with Elena."

"Jake! Give me a minute."

"Al, not now. Please." He waved to Elena that he was coming.

Kellerman grabbed Jake's arm, ignoring his protest. "You need to give serious thought to Mattson's offer. I don't want to see you waste half your life in prison."

Jake froze. He pulled himself from his attorney's grasp, trying to digest what he just heard. Kellerman all but said he was going down, that a guilty verdict was imminent. "I'll deal with it later. I've got to see Elena."

Jake lengthened his stride to the back of the courtroom. He feared the worse. Drew, Nikki, were they hurt? God help him if they were. Taking her arm, he led her out into the crowded hallway.

"Are the kids okay?"

She shook her head. "They're fine, but I came to warn you."

"Warn me? About what?" Jake followed her eyes to someone or something behind him. Richter was just leaving the courtroom with Nettles at his side, sharing a laugh.

Elena pointed to Richter. "Who's that man? And why is he looking at you like that?"

Jake caught Richter sneering at him and thought back to Diesel's words at the blues bar. And then it hit him. That's it, that's the link between him and Gustavo. Of course, it made perfect sense. Why hadn't he seen it before? Years back, in one of his cases Richter had persuaded Gustavo to flip and become a government informant.

Gustavo agreed but somehow learned of the government's complicity in running drugs. Things must have gotten messy. Gustavo had now become a liability, had to be silenced. Richter must have known of the contract on Gustavo's life and did nothing to stop it. That explains his fixation on Jake. Richter was convinced that Carmen must have told Jake about Gustavo and why he was killed, and if left unchecked Jake could expose the government's liaison with drug lords. What better way to marginalize Jake than to indict and convict him? As a disgraced lawyer, who would believe his wild and unproven accusations that the government was in the business of helping the cartel run drugs.

He grasped Elena's hand and quickly moved down the hall. "Let's get out of here."

"Jake, what's wrong You're scaring me." She gripped his arm and stopped. "Would you for once tell me what's going on?"

His mind was careening out of control. "It's too much to explain right now. I just figured out why I'm here." All the pent-up rage he had been keeping inside was about to erupt. "The corruption, the fucking corruption, it's unbelievable. But I don't know if I can do a thing about it." He breathed deep, fighting his emotions, and rubbed the small of her back. "You're here, nothing else matters."

Elena's eyes welled up. "Oh, baby." She snuggled close and put her head against his chest. "I love you so much."

Instinctively, he wrapped his arms around her, unleashing a flood of tears. Jake's whole body softened. "All this time, when I looked for you in court and you weren't there, I imagined the worst, that you didn't care. That…that you gave up on me, like my mother."

Elena reached up and held his face in her hands as tears continued to stream down her cheeks. "I'm here because I love. Always have, always will. I can't believe I ever doubted you. But I'm frightened, I can't help it, not after Sam."

"Sam?"

"You don't know."

"Know what?"

"He's dead. This morning. Marilyn's convinced the cartel killed him."

"Dear, God," was all Jake could say. With his hand, he gently wiped the tears from her eyes.

"I can't bear the thought of losing you, too."

He shook his head. "They wouldn't. I'm no good to them dead. I'm Tifton's only ticket to freedom. Besides, by tomorrow this ordeal will be finally over."

"What do you mean?"

"The government offered me a deal. Plead guilty to a misdemeanor, a few months in prison and all charges will be dropped. I'd get to keep my license."

"But you're innocent. I know that now."

"It doesn't matter," Jake said, wearily. "It never has."

"It does to me. Don't compromise who you are. I married a fighter, didn't I?"

"I don't know if I have anything left," he said, stroking her hair. "Look at it this way. If I roll the dice and lose, I could be locked up for years. Where does that leave you and the kids? I'd be crazy to take that risk."

"Then nobody will ever know the truth. You can't let that happen. Come on. You've never shied away from a good bet before. My money's on you. Even if, God forbid, the worst should happen, I'm not going anywhere. I would never leave you behind. Never."

"What'd you say?"

"That I'll be there for you, no matter what."

"Baby, I gotta find Lenny." He hugged her tight and kissed her passionately on the lips. "I'll call you later. You've just given me an unbelievable idea."

Jake ran from the courthouse, his mind filled with thoughts of Elena. He'd never seen her like that before, so emotionally raw and honest, so vulnerable. She really did love him. He slid behind the wheel of his Saab and punched the speed dial to Lenny's cell. He spoke the second Lenny answered. "Where are you?"

"Grabbing a pizza, then back to the office. I was just about to call."

Jake peeled out of his parking garage. "Whatcha got?"

"The missing piece of the puzzle."

"Richter, I know. I just figured it out, too. The bastard's dirty. He couldn't take the chance I might learn about his part in Gustavo's murder. Richter was convinced that in all my years representing Carmen she must have told me about her brother, why he died, and--"

"That's not all," Lenny interrupted. "Can you believe the sick sonofabitch was running the grand jury when Gustavo was killed?

The kid was Richter's witness. He had to know the location of the safe house where Gustavo was hiding."

"Okay. Now what? The case is almost over."

"Dunno." Lenny paused. "You called me, Boss."

"Yeah," Jake said, trying to refocus. "Stop what you're doing and spend all night if you have to and dig up the names and rank of everyone in Tifton's squad during Desert Storm. Especially, his buddies who died."

"Stuff might be confidential."

"Just do it. Check the notes of my meetings with Jessie. She carried on about Tommy and how to this day he feels guilty about those killed when his chopper went down."

"Where you going with this?"

"I'm not sure, but it's all I got."

Chapter Forty-Nine

The courtroom was teeming with reporters when Jake took his customary seat between Lenny and Kellerman at the defense table. From her seat in the back row, Elena waved her encouragement.

"Any more thoughts on Richter?" Jake asked Lenny and Kellerman, continuing the conversation he had with them the previous evening. "It undoubtedly shows his motive in prosecuting the case. Even if we can't convince the judge to dismiss, we should at least get a mistrial."

Kellerman shook his head. "I sympathize with what you're saying but without more we can't prove a thing. Making such an explosive accusation would only alienate the judge more than he already is. Leave it alone, focus on Tifton. He's key."

Lenny nodded his agreement.

Jake sighed. They were right, of course. "I just want to nail Richter so bad it hurts. People like him have to be crushed."

Within moments, the judge took the bench. As if on cue, Tifton shuffled through the side door, a blank expression on his face.

Jake nudged Kellerman. "Tell Mattson to take that misdemeanor offer and shove it."

"You sure?"

"I'm not pleading guilty to something I didn't do."

The look on the U.S. Attorney's face told Jake the message had been received loud and clear. There would be no deal, the case would be fought to the bitter end.

"Counsel," the judge called, "you may continue with your cross-examination."

Jake stepped to the lectern, trying to make eye contact with Tifton, to no avail. "Yesterday, sir," Jake began, "you testified that you didn't bear me any ill will, that you were here with a heavy heart. You remember saying that?"

"It's true."

"Your heart is heavy because you want very much to be with your wife and son. Yet, you know the price you must pay for that to happen."

"I won't deny that I want to be with my family. Who wouldn't?"

"But the problem you face, your moral dilemma so to speak, is that the only way you can accomplish that is to lie. Lie and ruin the life of an innocent man, a man who fought for you like no other since your return from Operation Desert Storm. Isn't that true?"

"You did your best, I'll give you that. But that's what you got paid to do."

"But betrayal wasn't a part of our bargain was it?"

Mattson jumped out of his chair. "Judge, that's argumentative. We object."

The judge leaned over his bench. "Counsel, up to now I've been more than willing to give you a wide berth given your former relationship with the witness. But let's not stray too far out to sea. Objection sustained."

Jake looked down at his notes, his stomach was tied in knots, he needed to stay focused. "That night, flying with Butch through the tropical storm, not knowing if you'd live or die, you relived horrific memories of the war, didn't you?"

"Uh, huh." Tifton's response was barely audible.

"And in that cramped cockpit with the turbulence knocking your aircraft around like a toy, you smashed your nose against the side window, and to use your words 'started gushing blood like a stuck pig.'"

Tifton looked at Jake for the first time. "Sounds like something I'd say."

"And while gushing blood you recalled that time in Iraq with your buddies, on fire and spiraling out of control in the Apache helicopter. Right?"

"You've got a good memory."

Jake waved the notes he held in his hand. "I had some help. And when those horrific memories of the war returned to haunt you, you decided then and there you were not going to be burned alive, even if it meant taking your own life."

A loud gasp swept the gallery.

Mattson stood. "Your Honor, again we object. Irrelevant and immaterial."

"Judge," Jake responded, "the mental state of the government's most important witness is indeed relevant here. I ask for some latitude."

"And you will have it. Overruled."

Tommy placed his hands on the edge of the stand and leaned toward Jake. "Ever hear the screams of men on fire, smell the stench of burning flesh, wishing to God you could do something but knowing you can't."

Jake shook his head.

Tommy slumped back in his seat. "I didn't think so. Well I have, and it's somethin' I'll never ever get out of my head. Never."

"That's because your buddies and the country they died for meant so much to you."

"You're damn right."

"But to this day you're still haunted by the tragic deaths of Staff Sergeant Patrick Donnelly and Corporal Roberto Gomez, who pushed you to safety and saved your life moments before the chopper crashed into flames. Isn't that true?"

Tommy let out a low groan. "I tried to take Robby with me but he wouldn't budge, stubborn sonofabitch. I don't know why…he just wouldn't. With every fiber of my being I tried to pull 'em out, but they were already dead. I would never dishonor what they did for me...for our country. I would never leave them behind. I'd rather die than do that."

Mattson stood. "Your Honor, while I admit this is all quite moving, we must, nonetheless, object to the relevancy of this line of questioning."

Jake took a step toward the bench. "Judge, if you would allow me, I promise to tie it up, momentarily."

"Overruled." The judge peered at Jake. "Make it quick, counselor. I'm fast losing my patience."

Jake steadied his nerves. It was now or never. "And so we've come full circle."

"Huh?"

"You say you would never dishonor the bravery of those men or betray their service to your country, but isn't that exactly what you're doing now, in this courtroom?"

Tifton emphatically shook his head. "No. No, I wouldn't do that."

"Do you think for a second that your buddies, who paid the ultimate sacrifice, would be proud of what you're doing today, to see you betraying the trust of an innocent man? Even worse, what would they say about a government that would ask you do to that? Ask you to lie? Is that what they died for?"

"Objection!" Mattson shouted. "That's contemptible. There's no basis for that whatsoever."

"Sustained. Watch it, counselor."

Jake ignored the warning and pressed on. "What would your buddies think of what you're doing today? If they could, wouldn't they remind you that *I'm* not the enemy?"

Richter jumped from his seat. "Your Honor, this has gone on long enough. It's highly inflammatory and a total waste of everybody's time."

"That man," Jake said, pointing to Richter, "has no standing to make an objection. It's not his witness. Moreover, this line of questioning is anything but a waste of the Court's time and I intend to show just why."

"Mr. Richter, stay seated," the judge snapped. "You're out of order. The objection, if there was one, is overruled." He turned to Jake. "Get to the point, counsel."

Jake could feel the wind at his back. "What would Robby and the Sergeant say if they were sitting in the gallery watching our government treat you like this?" Jake did a complete one eighty and pointed toward the rear. "Would they stand and applaud what you're doing?"

"They'd be sickened."

"Wouldn't they say enough is enough? Wouldn't they say, 'come on Corporal, we all know who the enemy is.' Aren't you tired of all the lies, the deceit, the shady deals? Aren't you fed up with being pushed around by a government that could care less about the courageous service given by you to your country? A country you deeply love. Not even a thank you. What kind of government would ask you to betray your own *code of honor*?"

Tommy cupped his head in the palms of his hands. "It's wrong. It's all wrong. I can't do it anymore."

"What's wrong?" Jake fought to keep from shouting. He glanced back at the defense counsel table and caught Lenny pumping his fist.

"Everything. This trial. Our government. It's one big lie. I can't, I won't live with it any longer."

Richter bolted from his chair. "Judge, again I must object. Obviously, the witness is a mental case, and doesn't know what he's saying."

"Counsel, I warned you not to leave your seat," the judge barked.

"He's the one who's delusional," Tommy shouted, pointing his finger at Richter. "He's the one who told me to lie. Told me what to say, how to say it. Said I'd be outta prison in no time, promised my family would be taken care of."

"Judge, that's preposterous," Richter screamed.

Mattson rose from his chair. "Judge, I request an immediate recess so the witness can gather himself, try to come to his senses."

Tommy sat erect in his chair, his eyes gleaming with renewed strength. "I've never felt better in my life. It's about time I set things right. I should have long ago. Jake didn't do what they're accusing him of doing. He didn't know I was running drugs or that the alibi was a lie. He certainly never got any money from Pendleton." Tommy glared at Richter. "You knew the fifty thousand was planted in Jake's home, but didn't care, truth be damned. All you cared about was getting Jake. All it's ever been was getting Jake, keeping the truth from getting out, that the CIA was running drugs with your full knowledge. In fact, I wouldn't be surprised if you had something to do with that boy getting murdered. Did he know too much, tried to tell the world who you really are?"

"Judge," Richter yelled, veins bulging in his neck. "These accusations are scandalous and should be stricken. The man is deranged. He's making stuff up."

"I know exactly what I'm saying, and it's the truth, so help me God." Tommy shot back, half out of his seat. "The station chief warned you not to bring charges against me, but you wouldn't listen. Now it's your time to pay."

Mattson stared wide-eyed at Richter and grabbed his arm. "What the hell is going on?" He turned to Nettles, as though asking him the question. Nettles shook his head, trying to distance himself from what was happening.

Judge Henry slammed down his gavel, then pointed it at Richter. "One more word from you, sir, and I'll hold you in contempt." He then signaled Mattson, Kellerman and Jake to approach the bench. Richter started to follow.

"You," the judge shouted, continuing to point his gavel at Richter, "stay put."

"Judge," Richter shouted back, "the man's testimony is a stain on my reputation. He simply sits there and lies and you don't do a damn thing to stop it. What the hell kind of courtroom are you running here? It's a disgrace, a damn disgrace!"

The judge's eyes flared. He looked down at one of the marshals standing close by and gestured toward Richter. "Take that man and remove him from my courtroom, at once. Use force, if you have to."

Immediately, the deputy marshal descended on Richter and grabbed him by the arm. Before Richter could be led out, Jake rushed up and looked him in the eye. "You corrupt sonofabitch. If it's the last thing I do, I'll see to it that you're old and gray before you ever see the light of day."

Richter straightened his shoulders but said nothing. The marshal pulled him away.

The judge shifted his gaze to the U.S. Attorney. "Mr. Mattson, the ball appears to be in your court. I think, at a minimum, a mistrial would be in order, given what has just transpired."

"Yes, Your Honor."

"And," the judge added, "seeing that your main witness has recanted his entire testimony, and even insinuated the existence within your office of serious prosecutorial misconduct, if not more, I believe only one course of action remains."

"I understand, Your Honor."

"Sir," the judge said, in a raised voice, "do you have an announcement to make at this time?"

The courtroom became deathly quiet.

Jake couldn't breathe. Every fiber in his body was on fire.

The eyes of every juror were locked on Mattson. Even sporadic coughing in the gallery stopped when the U.S. Attorney began to speak. "With the Court's permission, in view of testimony elicited in open court, the government, in the case of United States versus Jake Dalton, moves that all charges against the defendant be dismissed."

The courtroom erupted.

Jake wheeled toward Elena, jumping out of her seat. Lenny wrapped his arms around Jake and lifted him into the air. It took some doing but

Jake was able to finally break free. He tousled Lenny's hair. "LB, I owe you everything. I mean everything."

"Does that mean I get a raise?"

Jake and Lenny hugged and laughed together, sharing a bond to cherish.

Jake then found Kellerman and hugged him, his lawyer who had become his friend.

"Al, you were amazing. I'm free! Can you believe it? This hell I've been living in is finally over. Thank you, thank you. I don't know how to thank you."

Kellerman grinned. "Nobody deserves it more than you, son."

The judge banged his gavel several times to quiet the room, but nobody seemed to care. He half-rose from behind the bench and hollered, "Quiet. We need quiet in the courtroom."

Jake glanced at Tommy still seated on the witness stand as a deputy marshal approached to take him back to his cell. Tommy's face had softened. He appeared at peace with himself. As he was about to be led out, Jake half-waved and nodded his thanks, satisfied that in two years he will have served the remainder of his reduced sentence and be reunited with his family.

Tommy smiled back, giving Jake a thumbs up.

The judge continued. "Mr. Dalton, in view of the government's motion, I am dismissing all charges and discharging your bond forthwith. Sir, with the Court's sincerest, and I mean sincerest apologies for what you have been through, you are free to go." He thanked the jury for their service and left the bench.

Nettles approached Jake with his hand extended.

Jake waved him off. "You've got to be kidding. I haven't forgotten the crap you pulled on the stand with your trumped-up notes. And when the special grand jury is convened, I'll see to it that they investigate your actions and particularly the cold-blooded killing of Dr. Cunningham. So get yourself a damn good lawyer, you're going to need it."

Nettles stiffened. "I-I don't know what you're talking—"

"Stuff it. I've heard enough of your lies."

Jake moved away and quickly found Elena. He pulled her into the well of the courtroom, hugging her with a fierceness he hadn't felt before. He fervently kissed away her tears, tears of joy.

"Can you believe it, baby? It's over, it's finally over. God, I love you." He held Elena tight, swearing never to let her go. He glanced to his side and saw Kellerman beaming. "Baby," Jake said, keeping his arm firmly around her waist, "I want you to meet one of the nicest guys and the greatest lawyer I've ever known."

"Not a bad golfer either," Lenny quipped.

Kellerman continued to smile at Elena. "Now I totally understand what drove this young man out of his mind."

Elena laughed. She reached over and gave Kellerman a kiss on the cheek. "Nice to meet you, Mr.—"

"Al, please." He looked at Jake. "When word gets out what you've done, son, you'll be so busy…I think I'll come work for you." Kellerman laughed. "You took on that corrupt sonofabitch," he winked at Elena, "please excuse my language, and kicked his ass. Let me be the first to say that you've got one bright future ahead of you, my boy, and nobody deserves it more." But before Jake could answer, Kellerman lowered his face close to Elena's. "I promise, no drug cases."

"And gambling," she added.

Jake laughed. "And gambling." He swept her into his arms. "Should we go for it?"

Elena caressed his cheek. "Whatever makes you happy?"

He looked into her eyes. "I already have what makes me happy. What do *you* want? I'm not doing a thing unless you're on board one hundred percent." Jake hesitated. "Or maybe we should wait, count our blessings, not rush in to it. Maybe I'll look into teaching law for a while. I don't know, everything's moving so fast. You decide. All I know is that I love you from the depth of my soul and never want to put you through anything like that again."

"Me? What about you?"

"Wait, wait, I've got an idea," Kellerman interrupted, putting one arm around Elena and the other around Jake. "Why don't the four of us discuss it over dinner and a bottle of the finest champagne. I'm buying."

Elena, Jake and Lenny couldn't stop smiling at one another and in one voice shouted, "Count us in!"

About the Author

After graduating law school, Mr. Rachlin embarked on his over thirty-year career as a board-certified civil trial attorney by serving as a law clerk to U.S. District Judge, Wm. McRae, Jr., President John F. Kennedy's first appointment to the federal bench.

From there Mr. Rachlin served as an Assistant Florida Attorney General. One of his first cases was to file suit in Washington D.C. and obtain a permanent injunction against then President Nixon and his administration, compelling them to release funds previously designated to Florida for the cleanup of neighboring waters.

Early in private practice, Mr. Rachlin assisted in the criminal defense of John Ehrlichman, Assistant to President Nixon, for his role in the infamous Watergate break-in. Throughout his career Mr. Rachlin has represented clients accused of having ties to foreign espionage, racketeering, and bank fraud. One such case led to the making of the motion picture, *Donnie Brasco*.

During his career in law, Mr. Rachlin, as an Adjunct Professor, has taught at universities in both Florida and California.

Born and raised in Miami, Florida, which serves as the setting of *Conspiracy of Lies*, Mr. Rachlin currently lives in Idaho.